DEADLY GREETING

Walker saw the smoke of the fires of the Osage town before he could see any houses, so he knew that he was almost there. He hurried ahead. The ground was rolling hills and patches of pine forest and oak groves, and as he moved along the trail where rocky, tree-covered hills rose on either side, suddenly four young Osage men were barring his path. He stopped still, and he held his hands out away from his weapons.

One of the young men spoke, but Walker could not understand a word of the language. Slowly he raised his right hand in a sign of peace, hoping that it was as universal a sign as he had been told. He'd never tried to use it on an Osage before.

"I come in peace," he said in English. "Do any of you speak the white man's language?"

Apparently none of them did. He wondered if he should try his own language, but as he was considering the idea, one of the young Osages fitted an arrow to his bow and drew back the string. The point of the arrow was aimed just about at Walker's sternum.

Other *Leisure* books by Robert J. Conley:
BACK TO MALACHI

INCIDENT AT BUFFALO CROSSING

ROBERT J. CONLEY

LEISURE BOOKS   NEW YORK CITY

A LEISURE BOOK®

June 1998

Published by

Dorchester Publishing Co., Inc.
276 Fifth Avenue
New York, NY 10001

ISBN 0-8439-4396-3

Printed in the United States of America.

INCIDENT AT BUFFALO CROSSING

One

His name was Uwas' Edoh'. At least that's what he called himself at home among his own people. The whites he met, and some other Indians, the ones he had to speak with in English because they didn't speak his Cherokee language and he didn't speak their tongues, all called him *Walker*. He decided that would do just fine. It was, after all, much simpler than trying to explain the full meaning of his real Cherokee name to someone who didn't understand the Cherokee language.

The first part of his name was not at all difficult: *Uwas'*, short for *Uwassa*, meaning *alone*. It was the second word that gave people trouble. *Edoh'*, or *Edohi*, might mean *walking*, or rather, *he is walking*. Or it might mean *he is standing*, but whichever interpretation a speaker might intend, the word also carried with it the additional implication that the subject referred to was *off over there somewhere*.

So Uwas' Edoh' carried with him a complex name: *He is off over there standing alone*, perhaps, or maybe, *He is over there walking along by himself.* Either way, it would never do for a name in English, of course. They would almost certainly shorten it and call him *Stands Alone*, or *Lone Walker*, or some such thing that sounded "Indian" to a white man's ears, but Walker thought that *Walker* would do just fine.

For there were white men who carried that same Walker name, of course, and, of course, they thought nothing about it. White men's names don't mean anything anyway. They're just names. So going by the name of Walker, Walker would not likely be questioned about the strangeness of his name or about its meaning. His name would not become a subject of conversation, nor would it be laughed at, because it was just like the name of some white men.

On the other hand, Walker was not an inappropriate name for Walker, for Walker had indeed walked. He had walked a great deal for a good long while, and he was still walking and would be walking yet for a good while to come. His home was the Cherokee country, now more and more being occupied by white intruders who were claiming the land under the names of North Carolina, South Carolina, Kentucky, Alabama, Georgia, Tennessee. These white "settlers" were crowding ever closer, and the Cherokee land holdings were shrinking steadily, treaty by treaty.

There had been the Treaty of Hopewell in 1785, the Treaty of Holston in 1791, the second Treaty of Holston in 1794, the Treaty of Tellico Garrison in 1804, a second Treaty of Tellico Garrison in 1805, a third Treaty of Tellico Garrison, only two days later than the previous one, in 1805, the Treaty of Washington in 1806, the Treaty of Chickasaw Old Fields in 1807, the second Treaty of Washington in 1816, the Treaty of Cherokee Agency in 1817, and, he had heard while on his travels, yet a third Treaty of Washington in this year of 1819.

Each of these remarkable documents had taken land away from the Cherokees, and each had promised that it would be in force "forever." The longest forever Walker could find between the treaties was a period of ten years.

So the Cherokees had their problems with their white neighbors, but Walker had a special mission, for Walker had died. He had died, and while he was dead, he had been given a task to accomplish. He had seen a hill as in a vision, and then he had heard the voices, and they had told him to find the hill. It was a Sacred Hill, and once he had found the hill, they said, he was to bring peace to a troubled land. And this hill and this troubled land and therefore his mission were all somewhere to the west.

And then Walker had come back from the dead, and he had known at once that he had been given this extra time on this earth in order to accomplish the special mission the spirits had assigned him. And so he had started walking, walking west. He was looking for the Sacred Hill he had seen in his vision, the hill the spirits had shown him while he was dead.

Walker was not an imposing figure. He was a man of medium stature, perhaps five feet seven inches tall, and he weighed no more than one hundred and forty pounds. His age was difficult to guess, but he was not a young man. His dark skin was leathery and lined, and he probably retained a somewhat youthful appearance because of his still coal-black hair, which he wore cropped off at his shoulders.

He wore moccasins, leggings, and breechcloth of deerskin, fringed and decorated with colorfully dyed porcupine quills. From the waist up, however, his dress showed ample evidence of the trade with whites that his people had been engaged in for some years. He wore a white shirt with ruffled cuffs and collar, a hunting jacket made from a colorful blanket, in style much like that of a southern plantation owner's smoking jacket, and on his head he wore a turban, a long strip of colorful cloth wrapped round and round. A few pheasant feathers had been added to it to give it some flair.

Each of his cheeks bore a large *X* tattoo, one line running from about the top of the ear down to the chin, and the other, which crossed it, running from the back of the lower jaw almost to the eye. The projection on the front of his throat, called by the whites an Adam's apple, was covered by a tattoo of a cross patee. There were other tattoos on his arms and legs and chest, but they were almost always covered by his clothing.

A bandolier bag, elaborately decorated with porcupine quills, rested on his right hip, supported by a wide sash-like shoulder strap which was slung over his left shoulder. The designs on the bag and the strap were stylized floral designs, typical of both his own people and other eastern woodland Indians.

He carried a knife in a leather scabbard at his waist. Slung across his back was a deerskin quiver of river cane arrows, a bois d'arc bow, and a river cane blowgun with honey locust, thistledown-tufted darts. He carried no other weapons.

A blanket roll pack containing a few extra items of clothing was also slung on his back. He traveled light, carrying but little trail food: some jerked meat and a modest supply of parched corn, which he called *gahawista*. He hunted, fished, and gathered wild plant foods along his way. He also carried with him, for emergencies when he might need to buy something from whites, a small bag of gold nuggets, each carefully wrapped in clay, so that it appeared to be a bag of clay beads. He traveled light, for, most of the time, he walked.

He had left his old home at Noonday Creek in that part of the Cherokee Nation the whites were now calling Georgia, and he had not looked back. He might see it again, and he might not. That was of no immediate concern to Walker. He had been given extra time on earth after his death, and he had also been given a special mission to accomplish with that time. That was his only concern.

He was walking on the south bank of a wide river, a river which ran red because of the red clay of its bed and banks, and he was approaching a settlement, a white man's settlement by its looks. All along the long way of his journey, Walker had talked to people he met, and so he had a pretty good idea of where he was and what the settlement was. The last people he had stopped with just a few days earlier had been Coushatta people, originally from near his own homeland. These had moved west because of pressures from the encroaching white population back east.

Walker was moving along beside what the whites were calling the Red River, and, as he was on the south bank, he should be in the land they called Texas, land claimed by the Spanish. Just across the river was land the United States was calling Missouri Territory. They claimed to have purchased it from France, although Walker did not believe that France had ever owned it. France had supposedly acquired it from Spain, but Walker was also skeptical about Spain's claim to ownership.

As he drew close enough to the settlement to make out individual forms, he could see a number of white men and women and children. He also saw a Native man wrapped in a blanket, and he saw soldiers. Walker had seen soldiers before. He had fought with U.S. soldiers, in both senses of that ambiguous English phrase. He had fought against them alongside the great Cherokee war leader Dragging Canoe back in the eighties, and more recently he had fought with them, that is alongside them, against the Creeks under the command of Andrew Jackson at the Battle of Horseshoe Bend.

As he moved even closer, though, he noticed that these soldiers did not quite look like the soldiers he had seen before, and that made good sense to Walker, for these would be Spanish soldiers. He hoped that he would not have any problem with them, but then, he couldn't think of any reason he should.

11

He walked closer to the settlement and dogs began to bark. He could see that most of the people there were looking in his direction, curious to see who was approaching from the east. He walked on. Ahead in the small settlement, a soldier mounted a horse and rode hard toward Walker. He slowed his steed as he came close to the man on foot, then halted it just a few feet in front of Walker.

"Buenas dias, Señor," he said.

Walker gave the man a faint smile and raised a hand.

"Hello," he said.

"Oh," said the soldier, shifting to English, "so you do not speak Spanish."

"I regret that I do not," Walker said.

"Luckily I speak English," said the soldier. "I am Capitan Rey del Monte, at your service."

"I'm called Walker," said the pedestrian. "Have I arrived at the place called Jonesboro?"

"You have indeed," said del Monte, swinging a leg over his horse's back to dismount. "Come. I'll walk in with you."

They walked along in silence for a few paces, del Monte leading his mount. Then, "You have come a long ways, Señor?" del Monte asked.

"Yes," Walker said. "It's been a long journey. The longest I have ever made. I come from the Cherokee country. The white men are calling it Georgia now."

"Ah, yes," del Monte said. "I know Georgia. We were there not too many years ago. We—the Spanish."

"Yes, I know," said Walker.

"You must know also then," del Monte said, "that some of your own people are not far from here."

"Yes," said Walker. "In Arkansas. I stopped to see them along the way."

Del Monte shot Walker a curious glance. "On your way—to where?" he asked. "If I may be so bold."

"Oh," Walker said. "That's all right. I don't mind the question. I just don't know the answer."

"Oh, a wanderer," del Monte said with a smile. "A wanderer with no certain place to go. It must be an interesting life."

They reached the few scattered hovels that were known as Jonesboro, and the first person they encountered was the Indian man with the blanket over his shoulders. Del Monte approached him.

"Cut Hand," he said, still speaking English, "this traveler is from the Cherokee country in Georgia. He calls himself Walker." Then he turned to Walker. "Cut Hand is a Delaware," he said. "I think he's as far away from his home as you are from yours. Cut Hand, I leave this guest in your charge."

As del Monte walked away, the two Indians glanced one another over.

"You speak my language?" Cut Hand asked in English.

"No," Walker said. "Do you speak mine?"

"No," said Cut Hand. "I guess we'll have to talk in this ugly white man's talk."

"I suppose we must," Walker agreed.

"Are you hungry?"

"Yes. I am."

"Come with me," said Cut Hand, and he turned and started walking. Walker followed Cut Hand through the middle of the small settlement: a cluster of hastily constructed cabins, an inn, a store. They finally stopped at a lean-to on the far edge of the village where a fire was burning beneath a black kettle. Cut Hand found two bowls and spoons, and with a ladle which was there by the fire, he dipped out two bowls full of venison stew and handed one to Walker. They sat across the fire from one another and ate in silence. Then Walker produced a clay pipe with a river cane stem and a bag of tobacco from out of his bandolier bag. He filled the pipe bowl and lit it with

13

a small fagot from the fire. After he had taken a few puffs to make sure he had it going well, he offered it to Cut Hand. Cut Hand puffed awhile and returned it to Walker.

"I'm looking for a certain hill," said Walker, "or mountain. I'm not sure which word to use. I've seen it, but I've never been there. I started walking west from the Cherokee country, looking for it. All I know is that it's west."

"Can you tell me what this hill or mountain looks like?" Cut Hand asked.

"Yes," said Walker. "I think so. I don't think the English-speaking whites have any name for the kind of hill it is, so I think they use the Spanish name. I think they call it a mesa. It's near a river, and I believe that it may be this Red River. I think that the mesa I'm looking for has steep sides, covered with green trees and bushes. It would be very difficult to climb, but there are caves in its sides, I think, and one of them might provide a way to the top. And I think that it stands alone. There are no other hills around it."

Cut Hand took the pipe from Walker once again and puffed four more times. Then he handed it back to its owner. He stared off into the distance in profound silence for a long moment.

"I think that I've seen this hill or mountain you speak about," he said. "This—mesa. I think it's just down that way." He gestured casually over his shoulder toward the west. "Not far from here," he said.

Walker breathed a sigh of relief. If Cut Hand was right, then his journey was just about over. On the other hand, he considered, if the journey was indeed over, that meant that the trouble he was to prevent was just about upon him, and he had no idea what form it would take. He had no idea what to expect or what was expected of him.

Two

Captain Mat Donald stood leaning on the rail at the bow of the steamer *John Hart* as it chugged its way west through the murky waters of the Red River. Donald, only twenty-four years old, was proud to be in command of the fifteen soldiers aboard the steamer. It was a small command, true, but he was young, and he could see a bright military future ahead of himself. He had already distinguished himself in action during Andrew Jackson's campaign against the Seminoles in Florida and again during the Battle of New Orleans against the British. And though his new command was small, it had an important assignment, and if he was successful with it, as he knew he would be, he knew also that it would lead to bigger and better things.

To his left, looking south, was Spanish Texas, and to his right the almost unknown reaches of the recently acquired Missouri Territory, a part of the Louisiana Purchase. Donald imagined future military missions for himself somewhere in that vast region, perhaps dealing with people he had never even heard of before. There were dozens, perhaps hundreds of Indian tribes in that mostly unexplored territory. And there were hundreds, perhaps thousands, of adventures to be had there. But there was already more than enough to occupy young Donald's mind for the present without dreaming of future exploits. He recalled the words of warning included in the description of his orders.

General Andrew Jackson himself had come aboard the *John Hart* there at Natchitoches, Louisiana, where the army was headquartered, and he had called the entire command together at the deck table and called for whiskey all around.

"The situation out there is damned volatile, men," the general had said. "There's the Spanish military presence to the south, and in addition to the tribes of Indians native to the area, bands of several different eastern tribes have moved in because of pressures on them back home. Pressures that in many cases we ourselves applied. Remember?"

He grinned, and his eyes twinkled, and the men laughed. Jackson allowed the laughter to subside before he continued.

"These savages don't always get along even with one another," he said, "nor do they have any respect for international boundaries. They may commit depredations on one side of the river and then cross that river to avoid retaliation. In order to prevent their getting away with that, we must establish a good working relationship with the Spanish military in the area. That will be your first job, Mat."

"Yes sir," Donald said. "Is it true that Capitan Rey del Monte is in charge of the Spanish troops in that region?"

Jackson glanced at some papers lying there before him on the table.

"Yes," he said. "That's the name I have here. You know him?"

"Yes sir," said Donald. "Casually. We met socially once in New Orleans."

"Good," said Jackson. "By God, that should help considerably."

"Yes sir," said Donald. "I think that it will. We got along well enough."

"Good," Jackson said again, and he slurped some whiskey from his cup. "The next thing then will be doing everything you can, in cooperation with the Spanish, of course, to maintain the peace. Once Indians get to fighting among themselves, they're liable to turn on anyone. So we don't want the different tribes warring with one another. It's in the best interests of our country to keep the situation peaceful—if possible. At least for the time being."

Jackson gave another of his looks and caused another round of laughter.

"The biggest problem, of course," he continued, "is the feelings of the native tribes toward the damned newcomers. They see them, naturally, as interlopers and intruders. You'll want to develop a relationship with each of the different tribal groups in the area."

"Yes sir," Donald said. "I'll do my best. It certainly does sound like a volatile situation."

"Oh?" said Jackson. "You think so, do you? Just wait. You haven't yet heard it all. You know Zeno Bond?"

"Not personally," Donald said. "But I certainly know of him. A hero of the revolution."

"Yes indeed," the general said. "A hero indeed. Well, this hero has recently gone out to Jonesboro. Jonesboro is, as you know, an American settlement on the Red River. However, it's on the Spanish side of the river, beyond our jurisdiction. From what I've heard, Mr. Bond is not planning to stay in Jonesboro. He obtained a land grant from the government in Washington, and he's taken a group of settlers with him. The grant is for land on the American side of the river. We don't know how the Indian tribes will react to this newest intrusion into their territory."

"I see," Donald said.

17

"And on top of all that," Jackson continued, "every move you make will be closely watched, I'm afraid. Senator Reddels is going out there to join Bond for a time. His self-appointed mission is to take back to Washington reports on the Arkansas and Missouri Territories. You're going into a hot spot, Donald, with only a fifteen-man command, a tough assignment, and with a nosy goddamned politician watching over your shoulder."

"I'll remember that, sir," said Donald.

And there was a further complication, but Donald had not bothered giving voice to it in front of the general. He had thought it best, at least for the time being, to keep it to himself that back east, he had been more than casually acquainted with the lovely Eva Reddels, the senator's very marriageable daughter. It would be, to say the least, interesting to have Reddels, his possible future father-in-law, watching over him on this assignment.

When General Jackson had left the *John Hart*, Captain Donald immediately ordered more wood to the furnace and full steam in the boiler. The *John Hart* headed upriver, paddle wheels kicking water, making rainbows in sunlight, startling alligators and river birds. Donald stood on deck, his face to the wind, exulting in the wild, free feeling he had every time he headed into the wild country.

The river had calmed, lowered by summer drought. Still Donald would have to take the steamer through the narrow, twisting channels ahead. Paddle wheels splashed water, turned by the one-cylinder Watts and Boulton engine, and the boat chugged along the river.

It wasn't long before the heat had become unbearable, and Captain Donald, at the urging of Sergeant Scot, had allowed the men to strip to their waists. Then he had done the same thing. The hot sun scalded their bare backs, and mosquitoes swarmed and stabbed viciously and sucked human blood when the steamer neared the tree-laden banks of the river. The men rubbed their skins with oils and sulphur and other nostrums. They put their shirts back on. Still the insects stung them.

Then they came to the Great Raft, a mass of fallen trees that had tangled together for a thousand years, clotting the Red River and extending more than a thousand miles. They nosed carefully into bayous and chutes and lakes, finding their way upstream, past jungles of alligators and snakes and rotting trees.

They hung up on sawyers they couldn't see, back-paddled, sashayed, came clear and kept going in the drought-lowered current. Navigation was made difficult, to say the least, by the sluggish water with no telltale swirls.

After two more days of fighting clumps of logs, the *John Hart* skirted past jungle as the river became more open, and they at last came to the end of the Great Raft. The men on board cheered loudly and waved their hats in triumph, as the boat swung into the strong current in the middle of the Red River. River birds, alarmed by the shouts and the clatter of the boat, screeched, flew in fright, and settled down again.

Captain Donald stood on deck with Sergeant Scot, Corporal Burns, and the scout, Krevs, and watched as Caddo Prairie stretched out west for miles ahead of them.

"Well, we made it, sir," said Krevs. "I'm always surprised to survive it."

"What's it like ahead?" Donald asked.

"Smooth sailing," said the scout. "We've come through the worst of it. There's a Coushatta village just ahead. Let's stop and visit and buy some peaches."

"Peaches?" Donald said

"Yes sir," Krevs said. "They have an orchard there."

"Indians raise peaches?" Donald asked.

"They got them from the Spaniards three hundred years ago," said Krevs, "or so I heard tell. They have fine orchards, and the orchards at Jonesboro and Pecan Point are too young for fruit. And the Coushattas are friendly."

"Then by all means," Donald said, "let's stop and buy some peaches."

So, in spite of the words of warning from Jackson and the rough beginning of the trip, Captain Mat Donald was headed for Spanish Texas and the far west still eager. He was young and bold and full of ambition, and he had accepted the assignment readily, even enthusiastically. The more difficult the assignment, the more praise and glory is bestowed on the commander who is ultimately successful with it, he had thought.

There on the deck of the *John Hart*, Donald stared ahead, studying the dark red waters of the river and the landscape on either side. It had changed considerably since their departure from Natchitoches on the rickety and noisy old steamer. Staring at this far western landscape, the farthest west he had ever been, Donald thought that Natchitoches seemed a lifetime away. Anything smacking of real civilization seemed a lifetime away.

He contemplated his assignment. It was a strange one. A command of only fifteen men. Not counting the boatmen, of course. And then there was the boat. Soldiers on a riverboat. It was a strange command. At times Donald thought that had he wanted to be on a boat, he'd have joined the navy instead of the army.

On the other hand, he admitted, the boat was not really a bad way to travel. The *John Hart* was not a new boat, but Donald wondered whether it had ever been in much better shape than it was at present. He was not a boatman, but it seemed to him that the thing was flimsily constructed to begin with.

A Mississippi side-wheeler, the *John Hart* drew six feet of water as it chugged along at what seemed a snail's pace, vibrating so that at times Donald feared that it would fly to pieces. He had almost gotten used to the constant racket made by the powerful engines, the boilers, and the sloshing of the huge paddles. The clatter of the vibrations was something, though, that he felt he would never get used to.

And the accommodations left much to be desired. The *John Hart* was a three-tiered steamer, with the deck level mostly open. The engines and boilers were located there, and wood was stacked just in front of them. Some closed cabin space was provided toward the stern. On the port side, just ahead of the wheel, was a small galley where a cook and his helper struggled to prepare three decent meals a day. The second tier was mostly cabins and a dining room with balcony-like decks at each end, and the third tier consisted mostly of deck. A small cabin was perched almost in its center to house the crew of the boat, and on top of that an even smaller pilothouse.

The fifteen soldiers were billeted in the lower cabins toward the stern. Between them and the engines, supplies were stacked and horses and mules were stabled. Donald had a stateroom on the second level.

The weather was warm, and for that Donald was thankful. He could not believe that the flimsily built steamer could do much in the way of keeping out the cold. All in all, Donald would be glad when they reached the Jonesboro settlement. In the meantime he had little to do but muse. He had Sergeant Scot, a very competent man, to keep the men in line.

So Donald's mind wandered from thoughts of the future to thoughts of the past. Standing at the bow of the *John Hart* in his tailored dress blue uniform, the brass buttons shining, he sometimes recalled his experiences during the War of 1812, and often, though he tried to put it out of his mind, he thought of the man who had whipped him and had killed his only brother. The gashes on his back had healed into scars that would be with him for the rest of his life, but the deeper wound, the one caused by the loss of his brother, would never heal—at least not until that senseless death had been avenged.

21

He knew the man's name and he knew his face. He even carried with him a sketch of the man for something to show around any time he found himself in a new area. "Have you seen this man?" he would ask. Donald himself had not seen the man nor heard of him for four long years.

It had been 1814, a year before the end of the war, a time in which Murkens had been involved in the kidnapping of young men for impressment into service on British ships. Donald and his younger brother had fought Murkens and his gang, but they had been overcome. Donald had been knocked senseless, and when he had regained consciousness, he found himself tied to a pole, his shirt stripped from his back. He had been lashed mercilessly with a cat-o'-nine-tails, and shortly thereafter he discovered that his brother had been killed in the fight. He had later managed to escape and rejoin his unit in time for the Battle of New Orleans, but Murkens was still at large.

Donald had his orders, and he was a good soldier. The mission always came first. Even so, he had with him the sketch of Murkens, and he carried with him always in his heart a burning desire to run across the man. Perhaps it would even happen on this trip. The area he was headed into seemed to be drawing just about everyone in for some reason or other. Perhaps.

And, of course, he had thoughts of Eva Reddels, the senator's daughter. She was a lovely thing, and a marriage to her could do wonders for his career. He had met her at a ball in Washington City, and they had danced almost every dance together. The other young officers present had been terribly jealous of Donald. It had showed. Still, Eva had given him almost all of her attention.

He had called on her at the senator's house after that, and they had walked in the garden together. After that, he had often been invited to dine at the senator's home, and eventually, on one of their garden walks, Donald had actually kissed Eva, a brief, tender kiss, and they had even talked of marriage.

Then came the night that she had showed her true colors. She had invited Donald into her room at night. He'd climbed the ivy on the outside wall of the house, and she had let him in a window, and then he had discovered that she was not a virgin, and that she enjoyed a lively romp in bed. And still they had talked of marriage.

But Captain Mat Donald wasn't quite ready for marriage. He had only recently achieved his rank of captain, and he felt like he needed a firmer grip on his career. Perhaps the successful completion of this peacekeeping western mission would accomplish that purpose. If so, a marriage to the senator's daughter might not be far away.

The sky to the west grew suddenly dark with ominous clouds, and Donald felt a slight chill come into the air, and the wind in his face grew stronger. There was a storm ahead, and it was moving east. They would run headlong into it. He wondered how soon, and he wondered how far they were from Jonesboro. The storm looked big and ferocious, and the idea of weathering it aboard the *John Hart* was not appealing to Donald.

He wobbled his way up to the pilothouse and found the pilot, an old sea dog named Bolt, at the wheel. "Big norther a-coming," Bolt said.

"Yes," Donald said. "I've seen it. How soon will it be on us?"

"An hour, maybe two," said Bolt. "Hell, maybe even less. Who knows? It seems to be moving in on us pretty fast."

"And when do we reach Jonesboro?"

"Not sooner than two more days."

"Great," Donald muttered. Then out loud he said, "Thank you," and he turned to head back down below.

"Prepare yourself for a damn good soaking," the old river rat said with a laugh. Donald hesitated, then went on

23

down. He found Sergeant Scot and told him to prepare the men and supplies as best he could.

"Try to keep the weapons and the powder dry," he said. "And set someone to watch the livestock. We might be in for some rough sailing."

"Yes sir," Scot said.

Donald went up to his own room on the second tier and looked around. He tried to spy out where in the walls and the ceiling water might come through, but it looked to him as if it might come through anywhere and everywhere. He gave a shrug and left the room, returning to his earlier spot at the bow of the boat.

The sky was darker than before. The clouds were closer. A bolt of lightning flashed suddenly across the sky, slicing the dark clouds from left to right. A low rumble of thunder followed. Then Donald felt the first heavy drops of rain.

Behind him the engines clanged and the boilers roared. The stacks above belched smoke and cinders. Donald walked around behind the engines to the area where the livestock was kept. The horses stamped and blew and reared, and Krevs's mule brayed and kicked, all clearly troubled by the approaching storm. Two soldiers were standing by. They were young and appeared to be nervous. Then Scot came walking up to Donald.

"Everything's under control here, sir," he said.

"Very good, Sergeant," said Donald. "If you need me, I'll be in my room."

And then it was upon them, and the rain came down in torrents.

Three

The wind howled out of the west, and the rain slashed sideways, knocking the *John Hart* viciously from side to side. Donald was certain that the flimsy boat would be blown to pieces. His mind made desperate plans for rescuing men, horses, the mule, and equipment from the choppy waters in the midst of the raging storm. He was afraid that the plans were not very good and much would be lost if it actually came to that. Human lives, of course, would be the first priority.

And unfortunately, he had been right about his stateroom. Water dripped from the ceiling and blew in through the walls. But there was nothing more he could do there to protect his personal belongings, so he pulled his rain slicker tight around him, snugged down his cap, ducked his head, and started out again to see how things were going on the main deck.

The blast of wet wind which met him as he opened the door slashed at his face and almost blew him back into the room. He pushed his way out against it and pulled the door shut behind himself. Clutching tightly to the rail, he made his way down the stairs to the bottom deck. He still had to cling to something to keep from falling, for the boat was rocking violently and the deck was wet and slick. Footing was treacherous at best.

In the stables he found a chaotic situation with the soldiers on duty there busy in a seemingly futile attempt to keep the frightened animals under control. Horses stomped and nickered. Donald's own favorite mount, a gelding called Prince Charlie, tossed his silver mane and screamed as he fought the ropes which held him. Other horses neighed and stamped as well. Krevs's red mule brayed and kicked and hee-hawed. Donald pitched in and did what he could to help the harried soldiers hold down the stock.

At last, at the more than welcome suggestion of the pilot, Bolt, they pulled the *John Hart* to the edge of the wild water and tied her up to a large oak tree to wait out the storm. "It's blowing up a perfect damned hurricano," the old salt declared.

Donald thought seriously about disembarking, but at last he decided against it. Getting the frightened animals off the boat in the middle of the storm might prove to be a near impossible feat. Better to keep everyone on board and try to control the situation right there as much as possible. And so they waited it out there on the wildly rocking boat for the rest of the day and for most of the following night. The next morning all was amazingly calm, and the sky was bright and clear.

"Well," Krevs said, "at least we won't have to worry about no low water for a spell, I reckon."

It was a hot Sunday afternoon, the Fourth of July in the year 1819, when the *John Hart* at last arrived at the small settlement of Jonesboro, with steam up and whistle blowing and the American flag flying proudly from the mast at her bow. White and Indian men, women and children came running from the tiny settlement toward the banks of the river, excitedly waving and cheering. They helped tie up the boat to giant cottonwood trees there on the Spanish side of the river.

Captain Mat Donald made a point of giving the little settlement a quick study. A number of small log buildings were spread out in a seemingly random fashion in a clearing which had been hacked out of the piney woods that grew thick along the banks of the river. Most of the rude structures appeared to Donald to be single family dwellings. A few appeared to be commercial: an inn, a store, perhaps, a smithy. Donald noticed too that across the river on the American side, the land had also been cleared and a lone brush arbor stood there.

Not fifty feet from the American flag flying on the *John Hart*, Royal Spanish colors flew from a post in front of Capitan Rey del Monte's tent. Other Spanish military tents were there in neat rows in a camp just beside Jonesboro. The Capitan stood near the flag smiling, and he waved a welcome to the American soldiers. Donald saw him and returned both smile and wave.

"Sergeant Scot," said Donald.

"Yes sir."

"It's Independence Day," Donald said. "Take Corporal Alan with you and go ashore. Invite everyone aboard for a celebration."

"Everyone, sir?"

"Everyone," Donald repeated. "And have the men set up deck tables and prepare for the feast."

As Scot and Alan disembarked, Capitan del Monte came aboard. Donald met him enthusiastically and greeted him with a warm handshake.

"Welcome aboard, Rey," he said. "It's good to see you again, my friend."

27

Robert J. Conley

"Welcome to Texas, Mat," said del Monte. "What is it that brings you out here to this wild land?"

"I've been ordered out to patrol the river," said Donald. "To make friends with everyone and to maintain the peace. Nothing more."

Del Monte shrugged. "You should have an easy job," he said. "Things have been very quiet out here of late."

"That's just fine with me," Donald said, and both captains chuckled. "Rey," Donald went on, "we're inviting everyone aboard for an American Independence Day celebration. You'll join us, I hope."

"Today?" del Monte asked.

"Yes," said Donald. "Today, the Fourth of July, is American Independence Day. I hope you'll come."

"I'd be delighted," del Monte said.

Soldiers were busy carrying long planks out on the deck to be used in setting up tables, and the two captains stepped back to get out of the way.

"You'll find me in a more presentable shape for the celebration," Donald said, referring to the unkempt condition of his uniform. He felt a little self-conscious, for del Monte looked as if he was ready to stand inspection. The Spanish captain chuckled. "It's been damned hot on that river," Donald added by way of explanation. "And we just came through a hellacious storm. Well, but of course you must have had it here too."

"Oh yes," said del Monte. "It gave us a thorough drenching before moving on east to interfere with your travel. I suspect it bounced you around quite a bit on the river."

"Yes," Donald said. "It certainly did that. We finally had to tie up and wait it out. I'm surprised that this damned fragile boat survived the wicked lashing it took out there."

The conversation continued informal, and the meeting was cordial. More than that. It was genuinely friendly. Each captain sincerely liked the other. Yet both of them knew

28

that it was only a matter of time before the land south of the Red River would become a battleground. Texas was already becoming a terrible temptation for land-hungry Americans and entrepreneurs with dreams of empire building. The very existence of Jonesboro and Pecan Point was evidence of that.

And with Zeno Bond and others of his ilk planning settlements just across the river, there would be white American settlements on both sides. They would have everything in common with one another and no real loyalty to Spain. The likelihood that they would eventually form some sort of alliance was strong, and it would certainly be an alliance against Spain.

That, of course, was a large part of the reason for Donald's peacekeeping mission. Both men knew that, and both men knew as well that the young U.S. government's desire for peace in the region was at best temporary. The U.S. had just been through two wars with Great Britain, not to mention a few costly wars with Indian tribes. It was far from ready for another war just yet. But even in its youth, and under its current peaceful stance, the U.S. was already clearly expansionist-minded. It was only a matter of time before it would look toward Texas.

In the meantime, however, the two young men could be friends. They liked each other, and they had much in common. Their missions too were much alike. Keep the white settlers within the boundaries of their respective land grants, and keep the peace.

On this particular Fourth of July, it seemed as if that task would not be a difficult one to accomplish. With the American flag and the Spanish flag flying so close to one another, and the American and Spanish captains engaged in friendly conversation there on the deck of the *John Hart*, the plans having been made for the celebration, with the excitement of the Jonesboro settlers at the arrival of the riverboat, everything seemed right with the world.

Robert J. Conley

The soldiers having set up the tables, they began bringing out whiskey and peaches and cakes and coffee. And the odor of meat cooking in the cookhouse wafted in the breeze. Capitan del Monte excused himself and vowed that he would return for the celebration. Then del Monte left the boat, and Donald went to his stateroom to change his clothes.

When Captain Donald returned to the deck in fresh white trousers, shiny black boots, and a formal blue blouse, he noticed a gathering on the north side of the river under and around the brush arbor. It seemed to be mostly Indians, and they seemed to be dividing into two groups. He called Krevs to his side.

"What's going on over there?" he asked.

Krevs squinted his eyes as he looked toward the gathering.

"Looks like a couple of prayer meetings about to happen," he said. "Yeah. Yeah. Over yonder's the Reverend Stevenson with his congregation—mostly displaced Choctaws, I think. That other bunch there, well, it's the same bunch of Indians, but they've got a Baptist preacher, a Kickapoo woman named Sings Loud. She's been doing everything she can to pull the reverend's flock away from him."

"Why are they gathering over there across the river from Jonesboro?" Donald asked.

Krevs shrugged. "It's as good a place as any, I reckon," he said.

The sun set in a blaze of glory. Darkness came, and with it a west wind that blew away mosquitoes and cooled the air. Stars lit the sky. The moon rose, owls hooted, and wolves called from forests on both sides of the river. Small fires were built for the two separate prayer meetings to the north, and from the south the people of Jonesboro and of the Spanish military camp began to board the *John Hart*.

Four

Sergeant Scot stepped up beside Captain Donald as the people of Jonesboro began to approach the planks that would lead them on board the boat.

"That's Zeno Bond coming there, sir," he said.

Donald studied the man Scot had indicated. So that was the famous "boy hero" of the American War for Independence, he thought. An old man now with white hair, Bond still stood straight, but he was a much smaller man than Donald had expected to see, and he certainly didn't look at all formidable.

"I don't see any sign of Reddels," Donald said quietly to Scot.

"Oh," said the sergeant, "you don't have to worry about him for tonight, sir. He's somewhere back on the trail between here and Pecan Point with the bulk of Bond's settlers."

"Fine," said Donald. "That's fine."

"Cut Hand, a Delaware Indian who hangs around Jonesboro, is coming," Scot said, "and he's bringing along a newcomer, a Cherokee who wandered in alone recently. He calls himself Walker. He's crazy, I think."

"Walker?" Donald asked.

"Yes sir," said Scot. "Walker. He's crazy. Claims to have died back in Georgia and then come back to life with a mission to fulfill that was given to him by the spirits while he was dead. He's walked all the way out here just to do his duty. Claims that the trip took him a whole damned year."

"He sounds crazy, all right," said Donald.

"You did tell me to invite everyone, sir," Scot said defensively.

"Yes," said Donald. "I did say that."

Capitan del Monte came aboard and joined Donald and Scot, and a moment later Krevs walked over to stand with them. He looked toward the Christian gatherings on the American side of the river. The sounds of hymn singing were in the air.

"I hope that damned Kickapoo preacher woman stays over there," Krevs said. "The last time she came aboard, she dumped my whiskey in the river. I don't care for any more of her damned Baptist bullshit messages."

Capitan del Monte laughed out loud. "If you see her coming, amigo," he said, "send her right away to my tent. She can deliver her message to me anytime—in my bed. She is a fine-looking damned Kickapoo preacher woman. I'll make her welcome, and your whiskey will be safe."

Then Zeno Bond, wearing an old-fashioned three-cornered hat, was on deck and walking toward Donald's group. Just behind him came two more men and two women. They shook hands all around and introduced themselves. By far the tallest of the group was Claiborne Wright, a six foot ten inch red-haired giant. He and the other man, Henry Stout, had been laughing and talking together as they were approaching. The two women with them were their wives.

Mrs. Wright took Donald by the arm and gestured toward a man and woman standing alone and looking slightly ill at ease. "Captain," she said, "allow me to introduce you to our most recent arrivals, a delightful young couple, fresh from the Eastern Seaboard."

She walked the few steps with Donald to confront the couple.

"Welcome aboard. I'm Captain Mat Donald," Donald said, extending his hand.

"Tom Booker, sir," said the other, taking Donald's hand and giving it a vigorous shake. "This is, uh, my wife, Bethie."

Donald thought that Booker seemed like a clerk or a teacher or something, certainly out of place in this setting. He also seemed to have been just a bit hesitant at pronouncing the word *wife*. A little embarrassed maybe. Well, perhaps they were newlyweds, and Booker was not yet used to his new situation.

But Bethie, well, Donald thought that she looked like an angel, a very small, young, and perfectly formed angel of delight. She couldn't have been more than seventeen years old, he thought. Her angelic face, framed by short, blond ringlets of honey gold, caught the light as it tilted up and looked at Donald and smiled. Her cheeks dimpled.

"Oh, Captain Donald," she said. "I've heard so much about you."

Donald thought that she stood just a little too close to him and held his hand a bit too long. He felt a little as if he were engaged in an intimate display in public, and he was embarrassed by it. She was lovely, but she was also a married woman.

Out of the corner of his eye he could see the soldiers passing out glasses of whiskey to the guests, and then over the head and shoulders of Bethie Booker, he saw two Indians coming aboard. That offered him the excuse he needed.

"Excuse me," he said. He went to meet the Indians, and Sergeant Scot joined him, a glass in each hand.

"Captain," said Scot, "may I present Cut Hand of the Delawares?"

Cut Hand played the stoic Indian as he shook Donald's hand and grunted. Scot handed him a glass of whiskey, and he grunted again.

"And this is Walker," said Scot. "A Cherokee."

Walker held out a limp hand for Donald to grasp, and said, "It's a pleasure to meet you, Captain." Scot handed the other glass to Walker. "Thank you," Walker said.

Donald thought, the man doesn't seem crazy, but he also thought that he appeared just a little humorous with his spectacles on his nose and that turban around his head.

A sudden howl ripped through the air, and Donald looked to the starboard to see dimly in the firelight the outline of someone in a wagon bed pounding on some sort of contraption. The howling began to resemble music somewhat, and it was soon joined by human voices.

"What the hell is that?" Donald said.

"I believe it's hymn-singing, sir," said Scot.

Krevs stepped up just then to greet Cut Hand, and he overheard both the question and the answer. "It's Sings Loud on her damned church organ," he said. And then the sounds from the Christian camp became chaotic, and Donald winced as in pain. "The Baptists are singing one song and the Methodists another," Krevs explained. "I reckon the two preachers are fighting each other for souls."

"Does this go on often?" Donald asked.

"Too often, I'd say," Krevs said. And it was all the answer Donald got.

At last Sergeant Scot managed to get everyone seated and dinner served. The guests were given their choice of coffee, whiskey, or wine to drink, and they all attacked the food on their plates with enthusiasm. A number of small conversations were taking place at the same time. Suddenly there was a lull in the Christian racket, and the voice of Zeno Bond rose up to fill it.

"I tell you, sir," he was expounding to someone, "this is the land of opportunity, the land where I shall build my castle and create a town bearing my name."

Donald looked up. He noticed a slight tensing of the muscles in the face of Rey del Monte. It wasn't surprising that the words of American would-be empire builders so close to Spanish Texas would raise the hackles of a Spanish soldier. Donald hoped that no trouble would arise that would force him to move against the Spanish captain.

"Mr. Bond," said Bethie Booker, "do you believe that the land holds the same opportunities for women as it holds for men? May I too hope for fame and fortune?"

Bond rose to his feet, his face was red with passion.

"Aye, lass," he said. "That you might. Riches are here. They're here for the taking. I tell you, sirs and ladies, this land is the alpha and the omega of the future."

The sounds of a Spanish guitar playing the strains of "Granada" rose up from the military tents beside Jonesboro, and at the same time both groups of Christians on the north side of the river began to sing again—different songs. Zeno Bond leaned forward, hands on the table.

"I had this dream of new lands back in the seventies and eighties," he said. "But I was young, and we were at war with England. I dreamed of far lands, but my dreams were divided. When the war ended at last, I dreamed again of far lands, but then I would lie awake at night longing for my Maribelle, and so instead of pushing west, I married."

The old man's eyes took on a faraway look, as if he had no idea where he was or who was with him. Looking at him in the light of the lanterns, Donald suddenly thought that if anyone in the company were crazy, it was not the wandering Cherokee, but this onetime hero, Zeno Bond. He heard the impassioned voice of Reverend Stevenson, exhorting Choctaw souls, and then he heard again the organ strains of Sings Loud.

"I loved my Maribelle," Bond continued, "with all my soul. But the bride loves hearth and home, and when she became great with child, I found myself chained. I could not wander to far western lands. I was chained tighter than Prometheus. Wild longings tore at my heart when geese flew overhead on still nights, and I silently tore against my chains, but love held me riveted."

Bethie Booker leaned her chin in her palm, her elbow on the table and stared at Bond with dream-like admiration, his romantic tale appealing to her sensitive young soul. Sergeant Scot leaned toward Captain Donald and whispered in his ear.

"That's just the reason I never married, sir," he said.

"Excuse me," Tom Booker said, and he got up from the table and walked alone to stand in the darkness at the bow of the boat.

"I loved my wife and children," Bond went on, snow-white hair framing his bony, colorless face, his eyes still glowing in the lantern light, "but now I'm widowed, and my children are grown and scattered. And now there's nothing left to hold me back, to keep me from my dreams of taming a wild land and building a town where my name will live in legend and song."

"There is the infirmity of age," Capitan del Monte said in a calm and quiet voice.

"Age be damned!" Bond roared. "While I can move, I seek my Camelot. I ride out tomorrow at the crack of dawn toward my grant of land, guided by a plainsman, and there I will hew out my town and await the rest of my settlers."

Sounds of the Spanish guitar on the Texas side of the river joined the rise and fall of the voice of Reverend Stevenson and the howling of Sings Loud's organ from the U.S. side. A fish splashed in the river below. A night bird called. Walker lifted his glass and drained it of whiskey. Then he stood.

"Captain Donald," he said. "Thank you for a delightful evening. I hope we'll meet again, but now, with moon and stars to guide me, I must travel west."

"Better wait for daylight," Krevs said. "In the dark, you'll step on a rattler or water moccasin—or fall in the river or something."

Walker smiled.

"I'll be all right," he said. "Good night."

He vanished in the darkness as he left the boat. Then Claiborne Wright stood, and his wife stood immediately after. "We should be going too," he said. "We thank you for your kind hospitality, Captain."

Others took the hint and began to say their good-nights and their thanks and head for the gangplank to disembark and go to their homes for the night. Donald was feeling a sense of relief. He would not have to go through these kinds of formalities again, and he was glad to have them almost behind him. He noticed that the camp meetings on the north side of the river were breaking up also, and he wondered if the preachers had called their flocks together for the sole purpose of annoying the celebration on the boat.

Then he heard a voice shout the name Krevs, and he watched as a crusty frontier type fought his way against the current of debarking bodies to come aboard. Krevs spotted the man, met him, and, following a brief conversation, took a paper from him. The man spoke a few more words and left, and the old scout walked over to Donald.

"That old boy brought you a message here from the senator, Captain," he said, and he handed the paper to Donald. Donald straightened the paper and moved closer to the light of a lantern. It was a brief, formal letter from Washington, explaining that Senator Reddels and his party had been delegated to inspect the territory and asking that they be accorded every assistance and courtesy. This was nothing new.

Donald had heard all that from Jackson. Donald looked at Krevs.

"This came from Reddels?" he asked.

"Yep."

"He just wants to make sure that I understand his status out here," Donald muttered. "Well. Are they far behind?"

"The scout says it'll yet be several days before they get here," Krevs said.

"Good," Donald said. "I was planning a brief run up-river tomorrow. I still have time then. I'll be back here in three days, in time to wait for the senator's arrival."

"There's something else you might be interested in knowing about," Krevs said.

"Well, what is it?" Donald asked.

"My man tells me that the senator's got a young woman with his party," said the old scout.

"What? A young woman? Well, why the hell would—"

"It's his daughter, my man said. Anything else, Captain?"

"No," said Donald. "No. That's all."

Krevs walked off, and Donald turned to walk to the edge of the boat. He leaned on the rail and stared into the dark, murky waters below. What the hell was Eva doing out here, he wondered. She must know that he was here in command of the troops on the *John Hart*. Surely the senator knew, and just as surely he had told her. Had she come to see him? With thoughts of marriage? He hoped not. He wasn't ready for that.

Five

Walker began to feel as if he had been on this trail before. He knew, of course, that he had not, at least, not while he had been alive. But it seemed like a very familiar trail to him, and he knew that it was the trail to the Sacred Hill and that the spirits had taken him down the trail to show him the hill.

Cut Hand had given him a good deal of information back at Jonesboro. He knew now that he was just about another day's walk from his goal. He knew that the hill was recognized as sacred by the tribes of Indians living in its vicinity. Located near a place called Buffalo Crossing, the Sacred Hill was on neutral ground. No one tribe claimed it as its own, and all tribes made use of it. Even the Osage Iron Head and the Comanche Katay respected the neutrality of the Sacred Hill, according to Cut Hand.

And Cut Hand's own description of the hill, and Walker's description of the hill that he had seen in his vision (or while he had been dead) matched exactly. A large hill with steep, tree-covered sides and a flat top, a plateau, also tree-covered, it had, about halfway up on one side, an entrance to a cave which lead into the hill and came out at the other end on top. The Indians around the area all knew about the cave. The whites did not.

Walker moved along at a brisk pace. He was anxious to reach the Sacred Hill, and he was getting very close. Then he had a sudden sense that there were men coming up behind him, not yet too close, but riding in his trail. He sought out the highest vantage point he could find and got himself behind some brush. Reaching into the bandolier bag at his side, he produced a spyglass and extended it. He looked back down his trail.

A beefy giant with colorless eyes and dirty pale hair rode into a clearing. Walker had not seen the man before, but he recognized him from Cut Hand's description. This was the American albino called Cotton Rotison, a frontier renegade and bully. Cut Hand had warned Walker to be on the lookout for this man.

Walker watched the trail a little longer, and he saw that other men followed Rotison. He could see that they were heavily armed, riding good horses, and leading pack mules. They were partly obscured by trees and knolls, and he could not tell how many were in the party.

He snapped his spyglass back short and returned it to the bag. He squinched his face for a moment in thought. The albino and his company were probably on a trading expedition to the Comanches farther west, he thought. He could think of no other reason for them to be leading pack mules west. Anyhow, that was of no real immediate concern to Walker. He had his own mission, and he was very near the Sacred Hill. He knew that. His main immediate concern, then, was to stay out of Rotison's way, and to not allow Rotison and his crew to interfere with his sacred mission. He hunkered low behind the brush and waited for them to pass.

As he waited, Walker recalled the words of Cut Hand. "When trees give way to open prairie, and riverbanks are no longer cliffs or quicksand, and solid rock slopes gently on both sides of the river, and the river widens and spills in shallow rapids, look then across the river. You'll see buffalo fattening on lush grass, and you'll see the top of the Sacred Hill rising above the slope. You'll know it when you see it."

It was noon the next day when Walker saw it. And Cut Hand been right. Walker knew it as soon as it came into his sight. He stood for a moment, in awe of the sacred site, thankful for the end of his long trek, a reverent calm settling over him, and then he walked into the red waters, and he found that the river was shallow, and he could walk across to the other side.

This was Buffalo Crossing. He came out on the other side, the American side according to the whites, and he looked down, and he could see that his moccasins and his leggings from the knees down had been stained red by the waters of the river. And he kept walking toward the Sacred Hill.

Just as Cut Hand had told him, he could see only the top of the Sacred Hill because of the slope of the ground between it and the river. And he could see no buffalo, but he could smell them and hear them, and he knew that they were just there, on the other side of the slope, grazing down there beneath the Sacred Hill. He walked on.

He reached a slight rise in the ground, topped it, and then he could see the entire hill, and he was overjoyed. He could also see the vast herd of buffalo. Only a few of them were actually between him and the hill, the bulk of the herd being around on the west side. He walked on.

At the base of the hill at last, he stood and looked up. A man could climb about halfway to the top. Then the hill became sheer cliff. An ant could climb it, but not a man. But there was the cave. Somewhere up there was the cave.

He stood there looking up toward the top, and it seemed as if a voice from somewhere spoke to him, and the voice told him to move forward, and he started to climb.

The climb was not difficult at first. It began as a gentle slope, but it soon became steeper, and the going was slower. There was plenty of brush, though, to hang onto and to pull oneself up by. He climbed on, for the voice, it seemed, kept calling to him. And at last he reached the end of the slope, and above him the rock rose straight up like the face of a cliff.

He reached up with both of his hands to touch the nearly smooth rock, and he stood there for a moment leaning against it. And the voice seemed to speak to him again, and he moved slightly to his right into the tangle of a juniper tree which grew twisted among rock, just there at the point where the hill became cliff, and deep in the tangled branches of the tree, he found the entrance to the cave.

A dank and musty smell came out of the cave to assail his nostrils, as he divested himself of all his belongings, save the bandolier bag at his side, and tied weapons and all on a branch of the juniper tree. Then he moved slowly into the dark cave. The smell was powerful, and he was almost overcome by its pungency. He knew it. He recognized it. It was a familiar odor, one he had encountered before, and he was ready for the ominous sound before he heard it.

Sudden rustlings, sharp buzzings of rattles on all sides filled the dark, musky, tight air around him. He was in a den of rattlesnakes. One hissed near his head as he crawled forward, muttering a prayer to the great spirit of all the rattlesnakes: "Ujonati. I mean you no harm. I'm just passing through."

He could not see where he was going, but he continued to creep forward in what seemed like a vacuum between life and eternity. And the rattles continued to sound, and the sound grew louder and more intense until it filled the foul-smelling musty air. And once as he reached out with his

42

right hand, crawling forward, he laid his hand, not on solid rock, but on live and writhing flesh, and he slowly removed it and uttered a small apology and felt for another place to put down his hand, and he moved on.

And then he saw dim light above, and he could tell that he was climbing again, and he continued forward, moving through the musty air, through the sounds of the rattles, and then at last he came to the end of the cave, and he crawled out of the bowels of the Sacred Hill and emerged on the plateau. He stood up straight and breathed deep of the fresh air and gave thanks to the spirit of Ujonati, the rattlesnake, and to all of the spirits who had guided him thus far.

He looked around and found that he had come out on the far west side of the Sacred Hill, and down below he could see the vast herd of buffalo stretching west and south and north for almost as far as he could see. He turned around, looking out in all directions, and it seemed as if he could see the whole world from his vantage point.

The sun was hot overhead, and squat and twisted oak trees grew there on the plateau. Walker looked around and found one with a reasonably comfortable-looking flat rock beneath it in its shade. He moved over there to sit on the rock in the shade of the small oak tree.

He gazed at the river before him, the place they called Buffalo Crossing, for it was the only place within miles, according to Cut Hand, where man or beast could safely cross the river. Deep water, quicksand, whirlpools, and other dangers lurked everywhere else along the way. The great shaggy buffalo knew this, and here they came to cross south into Texas in the fall of every year, and here the buffalo hunters came to gather meat.

At this time, in this sacred place, even among warring tribes, there would be a truce. There would be no fighting among themselves while hunters slew buffalo and women cut the meat into strips, smoked it, and preserved it for the coming winter. This was a time of peace, a time when meat sent by the Creator could be harvested, so that men, women, and children would not starve or shiver with cold when winter winds blew once again from the north and ice covered plain and forest. Just there, west of the Sacred Hill, even now in summer, thousands of buffalo already gathered to graze on the rolling prairie. The hunters would soon follow.

Down below at the near edge of the grazing herd, Walker saw a cow in heat. Two nearby bulls fought, their great hard heads bashing into one another. The cow stood placidly and patiently to one side, bracing her feet and lifting her tail in preparation for the victor.

Walker reached into the bandolier bag at his side and withdrew a brown bottle of whiskey. He twisted the cork from the neck of the bottle and tilted it for a gulp. "Ah," he breathed, feeling the brown liquid burn its way down to his stomach. It was a good feeling. Truly, he thought, this part of the universe was in harmony, at least for just this time. No child near here need cry for hunger this winter, or freeze because of lack of thick, furry robes. He tilted the bottle again.

The whiskey burned his throat, warmed his belly, and eased his body and mind. He sipped slowly, timing his drinking so that when night came and the night breezes began to dispel the July heat, when stars and moon began to fill the heavens, he would be relaxed. Then he would talk to the souls of long-dead relatives. He had not been able to do that since he had left Georgia.

Perhaps the ancestral spirits were all back there in the ancient homelands of the Cherokees, the lands that *yonegs* were now calling by their own names: Georgia, Carolina, Kentucky, Tennessee. Perhaps that was the reason he had not been successful. Perhaps the spirits were all clinging to that ancient land.

He wondered what they would do if the white man's government should be successful in its attempt to persuade all the Cherokees to move away to some place in the West. If such a thing were to happen, if all the Cherokees were to leave their homeland, would the spirits of the dead follow them to their new homes, or would they still cling to the ancient land? He did not know the answer to that question.

The sun inched lower on the western horizon, and Walker thought about the old Cherokee tales in which the sky was described as a great vault of rock, a gigantic rock dome sitting on top of the flat earth. Each morning, in the old stories, the Sky Vault would rotate slightly, and the Sun would crawl beneath its lip there in the east. Then she would begin to crawl along the underside of the great vault, and it would be daylight on the earth.

In the middle of the day, the Sun would pause briefly for a visit at the house of her daughter straight above in the middle of the Sky Vault. Then she would go on her way again, moving slowly down the other side, down toward the far western lip of the vault. When she reached it, the vault would rotate again, and she would crawl under to the other side, and it would be dark on earth. During the night, she would crawl along the topside, making her way back to the east, where she would begin another day.

Walker knew the white man's opinion of the old Cherokee and other Indian tales, and he wasn't really sure whether he believed them either. But they were good stories, and sitting there atop the Sacred Hill, he looked around as the Sun was getting closer to the lower western edge of the sky, and he thought that it was easy to imagine that the sky was indeed a great vault over all.

He sipped some more of the wonderful whiskey, and he leaned his head back against the oak behind him to relax and enjoy the symphony of the universe. Mockingbirds and orioles sang from overhead branches. A cicada locust buzzed out in a loud call for a female with which to breed. Below and from all points to the west came a lowing and bellowing of buffalo.

Gazing at the buffalo in the dimming light, Walker pictured children laughing and running in play, just as Cherokee children must have laughed and run and played before the *yonegs* had come to Georgia and other parts of the Cherokee Nation. *Ah well,* he thought, *the spirits have sent me here to this fine place.* He did not know, though, what they wanted him to do. Just bring peace. That was all. He took another sip of whiskey. He would take this problem one step at a time. He had only just located the Sacred Hill and the way to its top. That was enough for now.

Six

The sky turned dark, lit by millions of stars and a bright
sliver of moon. The night air cooled. Birds sang, bugs
whirred, and buffalo milled and lowed. Sometime during the
night, Walker slept. It was a deep, quiet, and peaceful sleep,
a sleep from which, had someone walked right up beside
him, he might not have been aroused. It should have been
a most satisfying sleep.

Yet upon awakening in the early morning, Walker was
disappointed that he had received no spiritual visitations in
the night, his first night alone on the Sacred Hill. He reminded himself, though, that the spirits did things in their
own time, not his, and his role was to remain patient and
open to whatever presented itself to him.

His stomach reminded him that it had been twenty-four
hours since he had eaten anything. Well, he told it, it would
be longer yet. He sat again on the rock beneath the oak tree
and waited, for just what, he wasn't sure, feeling the sun
begin to warm the day.

It was mid morning when he saw the riders begin to gather across the river in Texas. Curious, he reached into his bandolier bag for his spyglass and extended it to its full length. He raised the glass to his eye and studied the riders over there. There were five of them, and they were dismounting in the open space by the riverbank.

Walker did not recognize any of them, but he thought, as he studied them, that they were a sorry looking bunch. They built a fire and dipped water from the river to make coffee. Walker noticed that they kept looking back, as though they were waiting for someone else to arrive. He kept watching them, and soon sixteen more riders came into view. Walker focused his spyglass on the leader of this new group. It was Cotton Rotison, the renegade albino giant.

Walker stood up and moved slowly over to the edge of the tabletop of the Sacred Hill for a better vantage point. He studied the different men there with Rotison, so that he would be able to recognize any one of them should he see them again.

And then he saw yet another rider approaching from the east. He carefully focused his brass-mounted glass on that one, and he recognized immediately the old fanatic from the Fourth of July celebration aboard the *John Hart*. Zeno Bond.

''Ha!'' said Walker out loud.

He recalled Bond's impassioned and somewhat loony speech, and he remembered that the old man had said that he would ride out early the next morning toward his land grant. He had also said that he had hired a plainsman to guide him. Had the old fool actually hired the outlaw Cotton Rotison? Given the foolish nature of white men, Walker thought that was likely. And it was just as likely, he thought further, that the albino would murder the old man for his horse and what money he might have on him.

As Walker watched through his tube, Bond rode his horse up onto a slight knoll and removed his blue, three-cornered hat, allowing unruly, shaggy strands of white hair to fall around his parchment face and blow in the wind. He waved the hat over his head and shouted something. The men all gathered around him to listen, and Bond launched into some kind of oratory. Then, as if in response to a military command, four of the men mounted their horses, readied their rifles, and rode out away from the camp in different directions. Walker figured they were being posted as sentries. If he was right about that, then these men were certainly up to something, probably no good.

The rest of the men, including Bond and Rotison, remained in the camp. Some cooked, some cleaned weapons, others tended to the animals, feeding them or leading them over to the river to drink the red water.

Walker's curiosity tormented him unmercifully. He wanted to know what the gathering was all about. He wondered what they were saying. He felt like he needed to know, for he had, after all, been brought back to life and sent west by the spirits in order to keep the peace, or to stop trouble, or something like that. And Bond and Rotison, individually, meant trouble, as far as Walker was concerned. Together they could start a war that would devastate the whole area.

And there were twenty-two of them altogether down there in this Bond and Rotison gang. And each one looked like a tough and mean outlaw. Each had a good horse to ride, and each was more than just well armed. They were almost a small army. They were a large gang, and if they were up to no good, as Walker suspected they were, then they could be a serious threat to peace in the area. Walker decided that he knew his duty.

Backing away from the edge of the plateau, moving slowly, Walker went back to the place from which he had emerged on top of the Sacred Hill. It was the only way up, and, as far as Walker knew, it was the only way back down. He slipped back into the dark cavern of snakes. On his way in, he announced himself, and he talked to the snakes or to

49

the spirit of the snakes, all the way through the long, dark, musty tunnel. And the snakes talked back to him with their raspy rattles, but they let him pass unharmed, as before.

Reemerging at last there at the juniper tree, Walker breathed deeply for a moment, relaxing and getting fresh air into his lungs. Then he retrieved his weapons from the branch of the tree and started to descend the lower, brush-and tree-covered half of the Sacred Hill.

He figured that the gang on the other side of the river would soon move on, for he couldn't think of any reason for them to remain at their campsite. They hadn't even prepared much of a camp, just a couple of fires in a clearing there by the river's edge. A meeting place, he figured. Nothing more. Bond would be wanting to get on to his land grant.

Reaching the base of the hill, still hidden by thick brush, Walker looked toward the river, but now the land rose in a gradual swell between him and the river, and he could no longer see either river or camp on the opposite bank.

He came out of his hiding place there in the brush and walked toward the red waters. He walked across a nearly level field, and then he started up the north side of the slope. When he reached the top of the slope, he knew, he'd have to be careful. From that spot he would be able once again to see the men across the river, but then, they would be able to see him as well. Walker thought it best to keep his presence a secret from these men. He thought that he might live longer that way, perhaps even long enough to discover the exact nature of his mission and then to accomplish it.

About halfway up the slope, he bent in a low crouch and began to move more slowly. Within a couple of steps of the top of the rise, he dropped down to his hands and knees. He crawled on up to peer over the edge. He saw the men over there in Texas. No one was looking in his direction. But he was still much too far away to hear anything that they were saying. Maybe, he thought, he should try to get closer. There were willows on the beach southeast of the hill. If he could get that close, maybe he could hear something.

He scuttled toward the willows, and he made it over there without being seen. He waited there long enough to be sure he had not alarmed anyone. Then he peered out again. Everything in the camp seemed as before. The murmur from across the river was louder, but it still came to him as only a murmur. He decided that he would not be able to eavesdrop on the conversation without crossing the river, and there was no way he could cross the river without being seen. Perhaps, after all, he would just wait until they mounted up again and watch to see in which direction they would ride off.

There didn't seem to be anything really going on in the camp anyway. Bond was no longer orating, and the other men were sitting or milling around in small clusters. Walker could see one of the armed and mounted sentries riding along the riverbank not too far west of the camp. Two of them, he figured, had likely gone south, one southeast and the other southwest, perhaps, of the camp. The fourth one, well, he must be patrolling the river to the east, to Walker's left.

He waited longer, and the sun was directly overhead, "visiting at her daughter's house," Walker told himself with a silent chuckle. Across the river, the ruffians were eating their lunch. Perhaps they would make some kind of move when they had finished eating. He would wait. His stomach growled, reminding him that he had not eaten since the morning of the day before. He mentally shrugged away that thought.

Then he heard a rustling in the willows to his left. Someone or something seemed to be moving toward him. He sat still. Perhaps it would go around him, whatever it was. The rustling grew louder, the something was coming nearer. He turned his head to the left to see if he could tell what it was, if he could see anything over there. The rustling was louder. It was getting closer. It was not going around him. It was almost on him.

He panicked and jumped up and found himself face-to-face with a big black horse. He yelled out loud in his astonishment, and the horse neighed in surprised fright, and reared, kicking its forelegs in the air, and the rider on its back shouted as he lost his seat and tumbled back over the horse's rear.

"Ow! Goddamn!"

The shout was loud enough to be heard across the river, and the men in the camp all looked toward the now riderless horse. The man who had been on its back landed hard on his own back, and Walker turned and ran back toward the Sacred Hill as fast as his bandy legs would carry him. The man on the ground sucked hard to get air back into his lungs. He clutched his rifle and struggled to his feet. His horse, stamping about nervously, was still there where it had dumped him, and he grabbed for the reins. It took a moment, but he managed to get the animal under control, and then he climbed back into the saddle.

The horse danced around in a circle, the man fighting to hold it still while at the same time swiveling his own neck to catch sight of the fleeing Indian who had frightened his mount. Walker was running hard up the slope between them and the Sacred Hill. At last the horse stopped turning, and the man raised his rifle to his shoulder. He snapped off a shot that kicked up dirt just a few feet to Walker's left. Walker picked up speed and disappeared over the rise.

On the other side of the river, Zeno Bond ran to the side of Cotton Rotison.

"What the hell is that fool trying to do?" he said. "Start an Indian war?"

"Ranik!" Rotison shouted. "Ranik! Goddamn it! Get back over here. Now."

Ranik looked longingly in the direction Walker had gone.

He looked back across the river toward Cotton Rotison. "Shit," he said, and he kicked his horse in the sides and headed it into the red water to ride back across and into the camp.

Walker did not look back. He kept running. He knew that the man would have to reload before firing again, but he did not know how long that would take, or if the man would ride after him without waiting to reload. The man probably had at least a brace of pistols, and if he got close enough he would be able to use those. Walker ran.

He ran until he thought his lungs would burst, and then he ran some more, and at last he reached the brush at the base of the Sacred Hill. He dove headlong into it like a scared rabbit running from a fox. Only then, under cover of the thick brush, did he turn and look behind himself, and he was relieved to see no one coming after him. He heard no more shots. He heard no shouting, no angry voices. Panting, gasping for breath, he stayed still and watched longer to be sure.

Perhaps the man had decided that Walker wasn't worth chasing. Perhaps he hadn't really wanted to kill him at all. Perhaps he had only come upon him by accident and been frightened and fired a shot before thinking about it. Whatever. He wasn't coming. Walker relaxed a bit then, but he was still breathing heavily. And, damn it, he thought, he had let himself be seen.

Seven

Ranik, the shooter, rode huffing out of the river and back into the camp, and Cotton Rotison hurried over on foot to meet him.

"Ranik," he shouted as he ran. "You damned fool. Just what the hell were you trying to do over there anyhow? Start a goddamned Indian war?"

"The son of bitch surprised me," said Ranik. "What am I supposed to do when a damned redskin jumps right up in front of me like that?"

Rotison reached up, grabbing the still mounted Ranik by his coat lapel and pulled him down so he could speak close in his ear.

"Never mind," he whispered. "That old fool Bond is kind of finicky, that's all. All this is just show for his sake. Get it? We have to keep him happy for now. The only thing that almost really pisses me off is that you missed the son of a bitch."

He shoved Ranik away from him again, and Ranik sat

back straight in his saddle, his puzzled face evidence that he was trying to figure out what Rotison had been talking about.

"From now on," said Rotison in a loud voice, "think before you shoot."

"Yeah," said Ranik. "I will."

He started to swing down out of the saddle, but Rotison stopped him.

"You might as well stay mounted," he said. "We're moving out."

"Now?" Ranik asked.

At just that moment the other three outriders came pounding back into camp. They had heard the shot and were riding back in to investigate. Rotison looked over his shoulder to make sure of who was coming.

"Yeah. Right now," he said.

The men all mounted their horses and formed a tight group with Zeno Bond and Cotton Rotison side by side in the lead. Bond extended his right arm as if holding an imaginary sword.

"Forward," he shouted.

Then twenty-two men kicked their horses into a hard run, headed straight for the river. The hot noon sun glistened on metal and leather and sweaty horses and men as they hit the water of Buffalo Crossing, splashing silver spray. Shouting and whooping like a band of outlaws, they came ashore on the north side of the river and rode straight over the rise, almost in Walker's own footsteps, and toward the Sacred Hill. From his secluded spot in the thick underbrush, Walker watched them carefully as they approached.

They rode to within a few feet of where Walker was secreted before they hauled back on the reins for a quick stop. Horses' hooves kicked dirt and rocks as they responded to the abrupt command. Walker sat still and quiet. Some of the horsemen rode around, looking at the hill from different spots. Others dismounted and walked into the brush. Walker held his breath. One man said, "I seen a redskin atop this damn hill from our camp over yonder."

"Bullshit," said another. "How the hell would he have got up there?"

"I don't know that, but I seen him."

"It might have been that same one I shot at," Ranik said.

"I don't know," said the other man. "I don't think he could have got down and over to the river that fast."

"Better keep our eyes open."

"But if you see one," Ranik said, "don't shoot unless you ask Cotton first."

Bond and Rotison still sat quietly in their saddles. At last Rotison broke the silence.

"Well, Captain Bond," he said, "this here's the place I told you about."

"It really is a magnificent area, Mr. Rotison," Bond said.

"I told you it would be well worth taking a look at," said the albino giant, jerking at the reins to maintain control over his spirited horse. "This here is the only good river crossing within miles of here in either direction, and from up there," he pointed toward the top of the Sacred Hill, "you can see damn near forever."

"Yes," said Bond. "I see. I see. It's good to know about, Mr. Rotison, but right now, I think that we should be moving on to my own grant of land. I'd like to reach it before dark."

"Mr. Bond," said Rotison. "I don't know why in hell you'd want to go back to your claim. This land right here's ten times better."

Bond raised his three-cornered hat and wiped sweat from his brow with the back of his thin white hand. Guiding his black horse in slow motion, he studied the river crossing, the near edge of the lowing buffalo herd on the far side of the Sacred Hill, and the thick trees and brush at the bottom of the hill. He shook his hoary old head, a disappointed look on his face.

"It wouldn't be legal, Mr. Rotison," he said. "This is not the land that was given me."

"Legal, hell," said Rotison. "Out here, who cares? Besides, from what I heard, you was one of the heroes that made America free from the redcoats, Mr. Bond. Don't you think the government would give you the best piece of land available? Hell, they ain't seen it, have they? Goddamned government—"

"You will please not insult our government in my presence, Mr. Rotison," Bond snapped. "I fought and bled for that government. I saw men killed for it, watched them die horrible deaths. I love this country—this government— more than anything in the world next to the great God Almighty himself."

"I didn't mean no harm, Captain Bond," said Rotison. "It's just that I think so much of this here place that I guess I kind of got carried away. That's all."

"Your apology is accepted, Mr. Rotison," Bond said. He looked around once more, heaved a sigh, and shook his head. "Ah," he said, "you're right about the beauty of the place and the lay of the land. And it could be so easily defended too. A few good riflemen here could hold off a hundred soldiers trying to invade from Spanish Texas." He leaned back and stretched his neck, looking toward the top of the Sacred Hill. "From that point right up there," he continued, "those same riflemen could defend the central area from all prairie savages."

"That's right," said Rotison. "You're damned right. They could do that."

Bond looked back toward where the vast herd of buffalo still grazed contentedly.

"And just look at all that lush grass immediately to the west," he said. His eyes began to take on a wild look. "First, of course, the buffalo would have to be killed off or driven away, then—"

"Shit," said Rotison, laughing. "Ain't nobody ever going to do that. Hell, I seen them come past this crossing by the millions, snorting and snuffling, smell so bad and dust so thick you couldn't hardly breathe. Long thick line of buffler reaching far as you could see to the south, far as you could see to the north, still coming for days at a time. Ain't nobody ever going to be able to kill off them buffler. No sir.''

"They must be exterminated, Mr. Rotison," said Bond, "to make way for the advancement of civilization. God gave man dominion over the animals, and the wild buffalo must be replaced with domestic cattle. The savages of the prairies will be more quickly pacified also, once their main source of food and shelter is gone.''

Rotison laughed again and shook his head.

"It'll never happen," he said.

"Oh yes, it will, Mr. Rotison," said Bond, nodding his old head with a benign smile on his face. "Of course it will. It must. It's inevitable, you know. Oh, if I had this place, I could build my town here, a trading post, fortified, strategically located. I could . . . You're right about this place, Mr. Rotison. Why, it would be a veritable modern-day Corinth.''

"Yeah?" said Rotison. "Well, I never heard of that place, that—whatever you called it. But this here is perfect. That's for sure.''

"A Corinth, Mr. Rotison," said Bond. "A crossroads to the world. Trade routes would flow naturally here, north and south, east and west, from our beloved country in and out of Spanish Texas, from Arkansas to and from the Pacific.''

Rotison's eyes gleamed. He smiled a sly smile and leaned toward Bond greedily and conspiratorially. He thought he had him now.

"A few good men could take it, Captain Bond," he said suggestively. "We could take it. Now.''

Old Bond suddenly shook himself out of his deep revery and stiffened militarily in the saddle, a look of hard determination set on his brittle old face.

"Gather the men back into formation, Mr. Rotison," he said. "We must move along now to the land that is legally mine. Thank you though for showing me this place. I need to know about it."

Walker watched as Bond and Rotison led their rowdy riders away from the Sacred Hill, and he breathed a sigh of relief. But the relief was temporary, he knew. He had heard the things that both white men had said about the area, and he knew that both men longed for it. It would have been lost already had not old Bond been so fastidious over legalities. But with or without Bond, Walker knew, Rotison would be back. And then Bond—well, maybe Rotison would eventually convince even him of his point of view, or maybe the old revolutionary would go back to his government and ask for a change in his land grant.

It seemed to Walker then that the Sacred Hill and Buffalo Crossing and the surrounding land would not be left alone by the whites for much longer. Sadly, he reconciled himself to the thought that even this solemn and sacred place would be taken over by them eventually. It was probably as Bond had said—inevitable. But then, he wondered if part of the job the spirits had given him might not be to delay that rude and unpleasant takeover of this most special place for as long as possible. Why not? he asked himself. Why not?

The riders had disappeared, riding back east along the north bank of the river, and Walker saw in the distance the telltale smoke from the stacks of the *John Hart*. It could be no other. Emerging from his hiding place in the brush, he started walking again toward the river. He would meet the boat and visit with Captain Donald.

Eight

It was a little after noon when Captain Donald, from the
bow of the *John Hart*, chugging west on the Red River, saw
the twenty-two riders moving single file along the north
bank of the river. They were riding east. Donald recognized
Zeno Bond riding alongside another man at the head of the
file. It wasn't long after that when he saw the strange little
Cherokee, Walker, standing on the north bank waving at
him. Donald ordered the steamer stopped and tied up in
order to take Walker on, and Walker came aboard.

"Hello, my friend," said Donald. "Welcome aboard."

"Thank you, Captain," said Walker. "You're very
kind."

"Will you have a glass of whiskey with me?" Donald
asked.

"I will," Walker said.

Donald called for a bottle and two cups and sat down
with Walker at a small deck table. Sergeant Scot brought
the whiskey and cups, left them, and then moved off again.

Donald poured the drinks. Walker took a sip, and so did Donald.

"Ah," Walker said. "It's good. Thank you, Captain."

"You're quite a ways out from the settlement," Donald said.

Walker shrugged. "It's not so far," he said.

"Well," said Donald, "I suppose it's not after all. I heard that you've been walking for a year."

"More or less," Walker said. "As they say, 'it's a fur piece' from my home to here."

"Your home is in Georgia?"

"My home is the Cherokee Nation, Captain," Walker said. "White men have pressed in on it. They're calling it Georgia there where I live."

"Uh, yes," said Donald. "I understand you. May I ask you, if it's not being too personal, why you've undertaken this remarkable journey?"

Walker sipped his whiskey and thought for a moment before responding to Donald's question. He put the cup down on the table and looked Donald in the eyes. Among his own people, that act would have been considered at least rude, at most hostile, but Walker knew that the whites took it as an indication of seriousness and sincerity.

"I don't think you'd understand, Captain," he said. "I don't mean to be impertinent. I don't think any white man would understand it. Let me just say that I'm here to do what I can to stop trouble—to keep the peace."

"I see," said Donald, choosing his words carefully. "You know, I suppose, that my mission is exactly that—to keep the peace."

"I didn't know, but I'm glad to hear it," Walker said. "I saw something today that you should know about."

He took another sip of whiskey. Donald sat quietly, waiting for him continue.

"I was up on top of the S—"

61

Walker stopped himself. He had almost said "Sacred Hill." He started over.

"I was on top of the big hill there." He glanced over his shoulder. Donald looked and saw the top of the Sacred Hill to the north. "A bunch of white men gathered on the other side of the river. The Spanish side. When they were all together there, there were twenty-two of them. One of them was Mr. Bond."

"I saw them just before we came on you," Donald said. "But they were on the U.S. side of the river and riding east."

"Yes," Walker said. "They camped on the Spanish side long enough to talk and to eat their lunch. Then they mounted up and rode to the hill. I hid in the bushes and listened to them talk. Mr. Bond was talking to a border ruffian named Cotton Rotison. I think that the rest of the men are followers of Rotison. He's a big man, an albino."

Donald thought that the albino must have been the man he saw Bond riding beside at the head of the file of riders.

"Rotison, did you say?" he asked.

"Yes," said Walker. "When I first arrived at Jonesboro, I was warned to watch out for him. Today I heard Mr. Bond calling him by his name. So they rode over to the hill, and I was hidden close enough to watch them and to hear what they were saying. Mr. Bond wanted to ride on to his land grant, but Rotison was trying to talk him into moving his settlement to this place because of the crossing here and because of the hill. They talked about the ease with which riflemen could hold off invading armies from the south and Indians from all over from atop that . . . hill."

"But they rode on," Donald said.

"Yes, they did," said Walker, "but I don't think that Rotison has given up his idea so easily. And Mr. Bond was thinking about it very hard. He'd have stayed, I'm sure, but he seems to take the issue of legality very seriously."

"Yes," said Donald. "Whatever else the man may be, he's a true patriot."

"You may not think of them that way, Captain," Walker said, "but so are many Indians, and the tribes in this region think of this place as very special, and they agree between them that it is neutral ground. All of them hunt the buffalo here. They would not take kindly any attempt to establish a white settlement here, or to turn the hill into a strategic military site."

He thought a moment, decided that he had gone thus far and might as well tell Donald the rest.

"That hill is a Sacred Hill to the Indians," he said.

Donald rubbed his chin.

"I see," he said. "Well, for now, let's be thankful that Bond and this Rotison have ridden away. I'd like to get a closer look at the hill and the surrounding terrain, and I'll send out some scouts to make sure that this neutral ground stays peaceful and secure. But first, have you had your lunch?"

"No," said Walker, "I haven't." He didn't bother telling Donald how long it had been since he'd had anything to eat.

"Would you join me?" Donald said.

"Thank you," said Walker.

They had lunch aboard the *John Hart*, and then Donald sent out four mounted scouts. "I'll have two horses saddled and unloaded for you and me," he said to Walker.

"It's an easy walk over there, Captain," Walker said. "Thank you, but I don't need a horse. Besides, I mean to spend the night up there on top."

"Then I'll walk over with you," Donald said.

They left the boat and walked over the swell in the ground to the other side, then across the open prairie to the base of the Sacred Hill. Along the way, Donald remarked to Walker on the immense buffalo herd just to their west. Even at that distance, they could both smell them and hear them. Donald studied the hill. He walked back and forth along the base.

"I can see why Bond and Rotison are interested in this place," he said. "I can see as well why the Indians want to keep it. Can we get to the top?"

Walker thought by now that he had taken this white man so far into his confidence that he couldn't well hold back anything from him.

"Follow me," he said.

He led Donald through the brush and trees to the juniper tree at the halfway mark, where nothing but sheer rock rose above them.

"I don't see how we can climb that," Donald said, looking up the slick side of the hill.

"We can't," Walker said, "but we can go through here."

He pushed aside branches to reveal the entrance to the cave, and he moved inside. Donald started to follow him. He had his head inside the hole, and the stench filled his nostrils.

"Ugh!"

He held his nose and backed out again, just as he heard the rattles.

"It's a den of snakes," he said. "Get out of there."

"I'll be all right," Walker said.

"Well, if I go in there," Donald said, "I won't be all right. The *John Hart*'s staying put for the night, Walker. Have breakfast with me."

He heard Walker's answer come back to him as through a tunnel.

"Thank you," it said. "I'll see you then."

"If you survive," Donald said, but he didn't say it loudly enough for Walker to hear. He stood there a moment unbelieving. Then he made his way back down the hill. One of the scouts he had sent out rode up then, and Donald sent the man back to the boat to get him a horse. While he waited, he studied the hill and its surroundings some more. When the soldier returned with the horse, Donald mounted up and rode all the way around the Sacred Hill. On his way back to the boat, he turned in the saddle to look back at the hill, and from the plateau on top, he saw Walker wave at him. He waved back.

"Damn," he said, and he rode back to the boat. Turning his horse over to a private, he called Sergeant Scot to his side.

"Scot," he said, "what do you know of a man called Rotison?"

"I've heard of the man," said Scot, "but I've never met him. Shall I get Krevs?"

"Yes," said Donald. "Bring him around."

Donald went over to the rail and leaned on it, staring at the Sacred Hill. He fancied that he could still see Walker there close to the edge. In another moment Scot returned with Krevs.

"Sergeant Scot says you want to know about Rotison," Krevs said.

"That's right," said Donald.

"He's one of the worst kind," Krevs said. "He's a renegade, a thief, and a killer. He's rude and he's crude. He's a troublemaker everywhere he goes. What else can I say?"

"I think you've said enough," said Donald, "but if all that's true, why hasn't he been arrested?"

"Who's to arrest him?" Krevs said. "Just the army, I guess, and there's no proof against him of anything that would be a serious charge."

"I wonder just who told Zeno Bond that Rotison was a plainsman," Donald said.

"A plainsman?" said Krevs.

"Yes, Mr. Krevs," said Donald. "Our war hero turned entrepreneur has hired Cotton Rotison as his guide, and it looks as if Rotison comes complete with a small army."

"I'd say that's trouble," Krevs said.

"Yes," said Donald. "Tell me about Buffalo Crossing and the nearby hill."

65

"The hill with the flat top?"

"Yes. That one."

"Well, Captain," Krevs said, "Buffalo Crossing is the only safe and secure crossing on the river for several miles in either direction. It's named Buffalo Crossing because that's exactly where the big herds cross when they're migrating south—or back north. The Indians all respect the area as neutral ground, and they believe the hill you spoke of is a sacred place, a holy shrine of some kind. There don't seem to be no way to climb that hill, but the damned Indians sure as hell know a way up to the top. I've seen them up there. What else do you want to know?"

"If you were planning a military campaign in these parts," Donald said, "how would you look at that area?"

"I'd damn well want to hold it for my side," Krevs said. "If the enemy got hold of it, there'd be hell to pay. Especially if they found the way to the top. They'd control the crossing and they'd sure as hell have the high ground. But I wouldn't want to be the one to try to take it away from the Indians. Why hell, Comanches, Kiowas, Osages, Caddos, all kinds of redskins would be after you over that hill and that crossing."

"Thank you, Krevs," Donald said. He dismissed the scout and the sergeant and stood alone at the rail, staring at the hill and contemplating what he had learned that day. Krevs had confirmed everything that Walker had told him. Not only about the hill and crossing, but about Rotison as well.

What the hell, he asked himself, was Zeno Bond doing hooked up with a character like Rotison? And, even though Bond had apparently insisted on living by the law and going on to the land properly designated by his land grant, was Walker right when he said that Rotison, with or without Bond, would return to the hill to make a settlement there? And would that mean a major Indian war in the area?

Donald had to prevent that from happening. The United

States was not ready for a war with anyone that far west. And Donald's specific assignment had been to keep the peace. When he had first landed at Jonesboro, he had thought that his task would be a simple one. It was getting more and more complicated with every new bit of information.

Suddenly Donald wanted badly to talk with the lone Cherokee again. He didn't know if Walker would have any more information for him or not, but he felt like he had not finished his visit. He felt like Walker might actually be of some help, might have some valuable suggestions, might even—

Ah, well, he would see the man for breakfast.

Nine

Walker spent yet another night alone on top of the Sacred Hill. Again he drank whiskey and prayed and waited. And when he slept, he did indeed have a great vision, but it was not the kind of vision for which he had prayed. Instead it was a frightening series of images: Hundreds of outlaws were riding at top speed directly toward him, and in front of all these bad men rode Zeno Bond and Cotton Rotison. They screamed. They shouted obscenities. They fired their weapons. The pounding of their horses' hooves was loud and terrible.

Then he was looking at the great buffalo herd grazing peacefully in the tall prairie grass, and then there were gunshots, and buffalo began to drop, at first one at a time, then several at a time, then dozens, and soon the prairie was carpeted with the bodies of slaughtered buffalo, and only one remained alive and on its feet, standing far away and looking very forlorn.

And then the outlaws came again, and then there were

outlaws and Indians and settlers and soldiers, and everyone was fighting, but Walker was standing there in their midst, puzzled and confused and not able to tell even who was fighting whom. And then the albino face of Cotton Rotison was right in his face, and Rotison suddenly threw back his head and began to laugh, and his laugh was loud and horrible, and his white hair blew in the wind, and the sickly pale flesh of his face flickered in the light of destructive flames which surrounded him.

The night on top of the Sacred Hill had been another cool one, but even so, Walker awoke in a cold sweat. He sat still for a few minutes, recalling the terrible images of his dream—or vision. He uttered a prayer to the spirits of the four directions which was a plea for help and understanding. Then he sat longer, waiting for some sign, but no sign came.

At last he told himself that the ghastly and horrible images of his dream or vision had themselves been the sign. The sign he had been given was a warning. It told him of the coming danger, the thing he was to prevent, and it told him further who would be the instigators of the trouble to come. It told him who it was he would have to stop, clearly identifying both Bond and Rotison.

Of course, he reminded himself skeptically, he had really already known all that, and what he had experienced in the night might not have been a vision at all. It might have been a nightmare brought about purely and simply by his own fears. But he decided that it was better to think of it as a vision, a visitation from the spirits.

Perhaps they did not fully trust his intelligence. It might be that they were afraid his brain had been adversely affected by his death. Maybe they simply wanted to make absolutely sure that he had correctly diagnosed the situation and correctly identified the players. So he had not learned anything new from the spirits last night. So what? They had confirmed his own suspicions, had they not? This latest vision was the proof that he was on the right track, that the combination of Bond and Rotison was in fact a dangerous one that must be checked somehow.

Consoling himself with that interpretation of his night's experience, Walker went back down through the rattlesnake-infested tunnel and made his way back to the *John Hart*, which was still tied up near Buffalo Crossing. Captain Donald welcomed him aboard as before, and breakfast was served to them almost immediately. When they had finished their meal, Walker and Donald sat together over cups of hot coffee.

"I've been thinking about what we talked about yesterday," Donald said.

"So have I," Walker said.

"Yes," said Donald. "And I wonder . . . Do you really think it a serious possibility that Zeno Bond will go back to Washington and ask our government to change his land grant and give him the hill and the crossing?"

"I would expect him to do that," Walker said. "He wants it as badly as Rotison does, but he's not willing, as is Rotison, to simply seize it. At least, not yet."

"Damn," said Donald. "Well, for now at least, it's neutral ground. It's still Indian land. And I'll act accordingly until I receive different instructions from my superiors."

Both men sat in silence, sipping their coffee for a moment after that. Then Walker spoke again.

"You know, Captain," he said, "the old white man wouldn't even have to bother making a trip back to Washington to make his request."

"What do you mean?" Donald asked.

"If I understood things correctly at your Independence Day celebration," Walker said, "Washington is coming out here to him."

"Reddels?"

"Of course."

"Damn," said Donald again. "You're right, of course. Reddels."

70

"Bond could make his request to the senator," Walker said, "and ask him to carry it back to Washington with him. Couldn't he?"

"Yes," Donald said with a sigh. "Of course he could. And speaking of Reddels, I'm turning the *John Hart* around and heading back to Jonesboro. I have to be there for the arrival of Senator Reddels. Would you like to return to the settlement with us?"

"No thank you, Captain," Walker said, looking longingly toward the Sacred Hill. "I have no business back there just now."

A few minutes later, Walker left the steamboat, having thanked Donald again for his hospitality, and Donald watched as the Cherokee trudged over the slight rise and disappeared from sight on his way back to the Sacred Hill.

Sacred Hill, thought Donald. *I wonder. Could it really be?* Donald had been raised a Presbyterian, but he had learned at an early age to question anything and everything. And now that he had gotten to know Walker, had talked with him, had seen him go into the snake-infested cave and had seen him emerge unscathed to wave from the top of the hill, Donald wondered if maybe the man had indeed died and visited with spirits and come back to life. And now he found himself wondering if the hill was indeed a Sacred Hill.

He knew his mission, though, and that was to keep the peace, and he was thankful that his mission coincided with his feelings about Walker and about the hill. His main concern now was to discover the intentions of Bond and Rotison. Just what were they? It was clear from what Walker had said that Rotison wanted the hill and the surrounding area, and that he had no scruples about how to obtain it. It was equally clear that Bond, although he did have scruples, also wanted the hill. And Bond knew of ways to get what he wanted without breaking the law.

So would Bond go back to the Congress to get the land

71

he wanted? Or worse, as Walker had suggested, would he simply go to Reddels with his request? And whether or not Bond decided to do either of those things, would Rotison wait for such niceties before he decided to just take control of the place, if not for Zeno Bond, then for himself? Rotison's outlaw gang was a larger force than was Donald's small command of soldiers, and Donald did not think that he could count on any help from del Monte, not on the American side of the river.

Donald shook his head clear and called for the *John Hart* to be turned around and headed back toward Jonesboro. The engines clanged and the boilers hissed and the smokestacks spouted clouds of blue-gray smoke and spewed sparks and cinders. The paddle wheels began to turn and splash red water, and slowly the steamboat turned, and slowly it began the return trip to Jonesboro. Donald took his usual place at the bow, and he leaned on the rail.

He wondered if he would get back to Jonesboro before Reddels and his entourage arrived there, or if he would find them waiting for him there. He wondered what the senator was up to. Why would Reddels have determined to make this arduous journey to report on conditions in the recently acquired territory? What conditions? What could Reddels possibly report back to Congress that would be any different or any more valuable to those damned politicians than a letter from General Jackson, or from Captain Donald for that matter?

What could he say? There are two American settlements in Spanish Texas along the Red River. There are a number of bands of different Indian tribes from other parts of the country which have moved in here. Zeno Bond is in the area with his land grant, planning to develop a new settlement north of Red River. In spite of the presence of a band of the lowest type of white renegades led by a man named Cotton Rotison, the area so far remains peaceful. That was it. What more could the senator possibly learn to put in his report? So far as Donald could tell, the senator's trip was purely and simply a waste of government money.

And why in the name of God would he bring his daughter along? First of all, she was an added expense. Second, she was a lady, meaning that she was worth absolutely nothing in this western setting. She didn't know how to do anything, and had she known, she wouldn't have bothered. She wouldn't want to muss her clothing or her hair or get her hands dirty or risk broken nails or calluses. She was a dainty thing, born and bred to be lovely, nothing more.

The journey had to be a hardship for her, long and tedious and uncomfortable, at times possibly even dangerous. It seemed to Donald irresponsible of the senator to bring her along. It seemed foolish of her to agree to accompany her father. He was angry at both of them for this unpleasant turn of events.

And he wondered what it would be like to see her in this setting. How would she behave at their meeting? How would she expect him to behave? Would they meet quietly and in private later? And if so, what then? Would it be like the night he had slipped into her bedroom back east? He longed for it to happen that way, and at the same time he dreaded such a thing. He found himself of two minds, and he didn't like that. He much preferred to be a man with a specific mission and a single-minded purpose with no conflicting emotions or motivations.

But considering the approaching invasion of Eva Reddels into his current situation, he found himself far from single-minded. For there was also Bethie Booker, the angel he had met on the Fourth of July.

He had tried not to think of Bethie, of the cool touch of her hand, of the smile on her pouty lips and of the way her big eyes rolled when she tilted her head to look up into his eyes. He tried not to think about what her luscious young body might look like divested of its clothing, but he could not long keep his mind off of her. And he felt guilty when he thought of her, for she was another man's wife, and Mat Donald was a man of strict principles, even if he was not, strictly speaking, a religious man.

He forced himself to think about the Sacred Hill and Buffalo Crossing. He tried to formulate just what he would say to Senator Reddels about it. Could he convince Reddels to join him in preventing Bond from acquiring it? He doubted it.

If he tried to tell Reddels of the significance of the area and its potential, Reddels would most likely insist on giving it to the old patriot for reasons of national security. The meaning of the hill and the area surrounding the hill to the local Indian tribes would mean nothing to the senator.

The only thing that Donald could think of that might possibly make an ally of Reddels on this issue was the threat to the peace of the region of having Bond or Rotison or any other white man taking the area. Osages, Comanches, Kiowas, who knows who else, would all be up in arms, and the U.S. was not ready for an expensive war in the far west at just that time. He decided that, if he should be forced to discuss the issue at all with the senator, that would be his approach. We have to keep the peace.

Then he thought of another angle. *Senator*, he said to himself, imagining a conversation with Reddels, *Senator, I am deeply concerned about the safety and welfare of Mr. Bond. Someone has given him some very bad advice, I'm afraid, and he has formed an alliance of some kind with a dangerous ruffian named Rotison, the head of a gang of villainous border outlaws. I'm afraid that he wouldn't take kindly to advice from me, but if you, sir, would speak to him about this matter—*

"Damn," he said out loud, interrupting his own thoughts. When he had left Natchitoches, he had thought that he might have to fight Indians or outlaws on this trip. When he had arrived at Jonesboro, he had thought that there would be no trouble at all. Now it was beginning to look as if he could wind up fighting Indians and outlaws after all, but the worst of it all was that he was going to have to deal with the meddling of fool politicians and an old fool patriot with dreams of empire building.

Ten

Senator Reddels and his party had not arrived in Jonesboro ahead of the *John Hart* after all, but Captain Mat Donald noted with dismay that several groups of new settlers had shown up. The tiny settlement of Jonesboro was crowded with tents and wagons. The Jonesboro merchants were, of course, delighted. Business was brisk, and the inconvenience of these boisterous newcomers would not last for long. They would all be moving out soon to establish their own homes elsewhere, some with Zeno Bond, some in other places on their own.

Donald had Sergeant Scot put the horses and Krevs's mule out to graze on good pasture and set the men to cutting firewood and loading it onto the boat. He then sought out Capitan Rey del Monte, and the two of them procured a table and chairs for themselves just outside the Jonesboro Inn in the shade of its porch. Capitan del Monte ordered wine, Donald whiskey.

"Have you had any trouble with all these new arrivals?" Donald asked.

"A few fistfights," del Monte said as he poured himself a glass of red wine. "Nothing serious."

"I hope nothing more serious develops on my side of the river," Donald said, pouring himself a glass of rich, brown whiskey.

"Are you anticipating trouble?" del Monte asked.

"I'm afraid that Mr. Bond is being led astray by his 'plainsman,' Rotison," Donald said.

"You keep your eye on that damned Rotison," del Monte said. "If I could prove anything against him, I would arrest him for you, but as it is, I would only have to let him go again."

"Yes, I know that," Donald said. "If I could prove anything, I'd catch him on the other side and arrest him as well."

"We are, as you say, in the same boat," del Monte said with a shrug. Then he raised his wineglass for a toast. "Well, amigo," he said, "here's to the women of New Orleans."

"Here, here," said Donald, raising his glass.

They drank, and del Monte added, "Would we were with them now."

"You really go for the so-called weaker sex, don't you, my friend?" said Donald.

"Week of sex, did you say? Oh, amigo, how I could go for a week of sex. You know, there is one whore on Bourbon Street—ah, she is a woman of all women. I'll never forget her as long as I live."

"You had a good night with her, did you?"

"A good night," said del Monte. "A good week. Week of sex. Oh, that reminds me, I hear that your senator is bringing his daughter with him, a lovely young thing, they say."

"You leave her alone, Rey," Donald said.

"Don't worry, amigo," del Monte said. "I also heard that she is yours."

"Well, I don't know that she's mine, exactly," Donald said, "but—"

"They told me that she has come out here to marry you."

"Oh God," Donald said, and he drained his glass of whiskey, then poured some more while del Monte laughed.

"But Mat," he said, "if you marry the senator's daughter, you can be a general by the time you reach the age of forty."

"I won't marry to get a promotion," said Donald, a pout on his face. "Besides, that's a hell of a long time to wait to be a general."

Both men laughed at that, but del Monte continued to press the issue.

"You could go back to Washington," he said, "and have ice in your whiskey. You would have a beautiful home and a lovely young wife and servants. And you could have a mistress too."

"I'm not ready to marry anyone," Donald said.

Del Monte shrugged. "Well," he said, "I don't blame you really. I saw the way that young Señora Booker looked at you on your boat."

"Wait a minute," Donald said. "I don't fool around with married women either."

"And then there's the Kickapoo preacher. She came here looking for you just yesterday. She's not a bad looking one either."

"Looking for me?" said Donald. "What for?"

"I can only guess."

"She probably wants to find my whiskey and throw it overboard," Donald said. "Krevs told me that she did that to him once."

"Threw him overboard?"

"No. His whiskey."

"Well, amigo, I think that she wants to throw you in her bed, but if you're not interested, she can throw me in my bed—or hers. I suggested that to her once though, and she behaved in a most unchristian way. She hit me."

Donald laughed and sipped at his whiskey.

"Ah," del Monte continued, "I'll get her in my bed yet." He drained his wineglass, and as he put it down on the table, he saw Cut Hand and Wright approaching with Sergeant Scot, solemn expressions on their faces. "Here comes some trouble, I think," he said.

Donald looked. He remembered both men from the Fourth of July celebration. He signaled the innkeeper for more glasses. When the newcomers had reached the table, Cut Hand poured himself a glass of whiskey and sat down. Scot mixed his with water, and Wright poured himself a glass of water only.

"Water for me," he said. "Just God's pure water."

"Something up?" Donald asked.

"Indian trouble," said Wright.

"Which side of the river?" del Monte asked.

"The American side," said Wright.

"What kind of trouble?" Donald asked.

"Iron Head's Osages have got a white captive," Wright said. "An American. Your fifteen soldiers won't have a chance alone. I'll round up all the men I can get to ride out with you."

"Hold your horses," said Donald. "Give me the whole story."

Wright opened his mouth to speak, but Donald stopped him and turned to his sergeant. "Sergeant Scot," he said.

"Well sir," said Scot, "I don't believe you've met Chief Iron Head, the Osage."

"No," said Donald, "I haven't had the pleasure."

Wright snorted.

"Well, he's got to be eighty years old if he's a day," Scot said. "It seems that the old man—well, he's got several wives, you know, and it seems that he's no longer able to, well . . .''

"I think I get your drift, Sergeant Scot," said Donald. "That's to be expected of a man his age."

"Iron Head don't seem to see it that way, sir," Scot said. "He thinks he ought to still be . . . well, virile. You know."

"I fail to see the problem here," Donald said.

"It's that Kickapoo woman," interrupted Wright.

"Sings Loud?" asked Donald. He looked at Scot.

"Yes sir," the sergeant said. "It seems as how she heard of the old man's complaint, and she took out her Bible and read to him. Anyhow, that's the way we heard the story. She read to him about how when King David had the same complaint, they sent him a teenage virgin to warm his sheets, and that fixed him all up."

"Did it now?" said del Monte.

"Well, sir," said Scot, "I don't know about that. I ain't read the book. Not that part of it anyway. But that's what they said she read to Iron Head."

"So what did old Iron Head do?" del Monte asked.

"He had them hunt him up a teenage virgin for a new wife, of course," said Scot, "and he tried it out for himself."

"And?" said del Monte.

"It didn't work," the sergeant said, "but before the old man could get pissed off at Sings Loud for misleading him like that, this Dr. Bangs showed up with his medicine wagon."

"Medicine wagon?" Donald said.

"This man and his medicine wagon showed up while you were away," del Monte said. "He calls himself Dr. Socrates Bangs, and his wagon is covered over by advertisements. Notions. Lotions. You know the kind. He came in with one of these new groups."

"He's one of Mr. Bond's settlers," said Wright, glad to get in a word.

"All right," said Donald. "So Dr. Bangs showed up. And then what?"

"Well, naturally," said Scot, "when he heard of the local problem, he saw a possibility for a sale, and he offered old Iron Head a bottle of guaranteed Youth Restorer, and the old man bought it. But he's no fool, the old man, and he don't trust white men, so he had Bangs tied to a tree, just in case the stuff don't work."

"And he's still out there tied to that tree," Wright said. "We've got to go out to the Osage village and rescue him before he's murdered."

"It would seem to me," said del Monte, "that if his remedy works, he'll be perfectly safe. If it does not, well, he probably deserves whatever they do to him."

"Mr. Wright," said Donald, "I appreciate your concern and your generous offer to help, but I can assure you that the United States Army will take charge of the situation. You can go back to your home, and you can tell the other settlers, since I'm sure the story is all over Jonesboro by now, that everything is being taken care of."

Wright stood up angrily.

"Captain Donald, Jonesboro is in Spanish Texas," he said, "and you have no authority over the settlers here. If you're not concerned with the safety of an American, we are, and we—"

Donald stood, looking up at the much taller Wright across the table.

"Mr. Wright," he said, "the Osage village is on the American side, and if you ride over there intending to start a fight with Indians, I will arrest you and anyone else who is riding with you."

"And if you arm yourselves and ride out of here looking for trouble," said del Monte, "I will arrest you first, before you cross the river."

"Senator Reddels will hear about this," said Wright, and he turned and stomped away.

81

"I'll bet he will, too," said Donald.

"And then you'll be in real trouble," said del Monte.

"Damn it," said Donald, sitting back down and reaching for his glass.

"What do you want me to do, sir?" Scot asked.

"Detail seven men to stay with the *John Hart*," said Donald, "and seven more to ride out first thing in the morning. And tell Krevs to be ready to ride out with us."

"In the morning, sir?"

"Hell," said Donald, "we'd just get lost out there riding around in the dark. Besides, it won't hurt that damned charlatan to stay tied up overnight. Youth Restorer, indeed."

Cut Hand, silent all this while, smiled softly and took a healthy slug of whiskey.

"I know Iron Head," he said.

"Will you ride with us?" Donald asked.

"If you take my advice," said the Delaware.

"Cut Hand," said Donald, "I'll be riding into Iron Head's village of two hundred or so warriors with only the sergeant here, a scout, and seven other men. I don't want the Osages to skin us alive and hang our hides out to sear in the hot sun. I thank you for your offer, and I will gladly trust your judgment and take your advice."

Cut Hand stood, and so did Donald. They shook hands across the table, and the Delaware turned and walked away. Donald sat back down with a heavy sigh. Sergeant Scot stood up.

"Well, sir," he said, "I'll be moving along now to carry out your orders, with your permission, sir."

"Good night, Sergeant Scot."

"Good night, sir."

"Oh, amigo," said del Monte, "I wish I could go with you to help, but my orders keep me on this side of the river."

"It's probably just as well," said Donald, reaching for the whiskey bottle. "Too many soldiers riding into the

Osage village might cause alarm. Let's have one more drink. Then I think I'd better turn in.''

As he poured himself another glass of wine, del Monte chuckled softly.

"What's funny?" Donald asked.

"Dr. Bangs tied to a tree all night," said del Monte, "while Iron Head tries to get a rise."

Then Donald joined him in raucous laughter.

Having said good night to Capitan del Monte, Mat Donald returned to the *John Hart*. Corporal Alan saluted him as he stepped aboard, and Donald noticed that the corporal had a silly grin on his face. He hesitated, thinking to ask the corporal what he found so amusing, but thought better of it and walked on, going up toward his stateroom on the second tier. On the way he met Sergeant Scot.

"Everything's been done, sir," Scot said. "Mr. Krevs and the men will be ready to ride with the first light."

"Thank you, Sergeant," Donald said. "Well. Now I'll say good night again."

"Uh, excuse me, sir," said Scot.

"Yes? What is it?"

"Well, sir," said Scot, embarrassed, "you have a visitor."

"A visitor?" said Donald. "At this hour? Where?"

"In your stateroom, sir. I told her she couldn't wait for you in your cabin, sir, but she just pushed right by me. She's in there, sir. Right now. Waiting."

Eva? Donald thought. He shoved Scot aside in his haste and headed up the stairs, taking them three at a time. "What the hell?" he said out loud.

Eleven

Donald reached the second tier landing and took the last distance to his stateroom door in two long strides. Jerking the door open, he saw a lady there alone with her back to him, standing looking down at something on his desk. He realized even before she turned around to face him that it was not Eva at all. It was Bethie Booker. Donald's jaw dropped in astonishment. Bethie smiled coyly and stepped toward him.

Walking up close, much too close for comfort, Donald thought, she reached up to put her hands on his chest and tilted her head back to look up into his face. Donald looked down at her and flushed hot. Bethie was wearing a low-necked dress and no underwear at all, not even one petticoat, and the dress was not tight fitting.

"Captain," she said, "I'm so glad you're back."

Donald forced himself to raise his eyes.

"Yes," he said, "well, Mrs. Booker, what can I do for you?"

He felt awkward and foolish.

"You do enforce the law here, don't you, Captain?" she asked.

Donald moved away from her. The closeness, especially with her state of dress, or near undress, was almost more than he could stand.

"Well, yes," he said. "I suppose I do. There's not much law here to enforce. What's your problem, Mrs. Booker?"

"Call me Bethie," she said.

"Yes," he said. "Well, Bethie, I can't legally arrest a man in Texas, of course. Texas, as I'm sure you know, is under Spanish rule. Capitan del Monte could, I suppose, arrest someone and turn him over to me, if there was good cause. Then, of course, I would have to take the prisoner to Natchitoches for trial."

Bethie sauntered back to the desk and picked up the picture of Murkens that was lying there. *So that's what she was looking at when I walked in*, Donald thought.

"Do you know that man?" he asked.

She shrugged. "He's not my main concern," she said.

"Have you seen him?" Donald asked, stepping toward her with a sense and a show of urgency.

"Yes," she said. "I've seen him before. Back at Kate's— Back east."

"Kate's Landing?" Donald asked. "Is that what you were about to say?"

"Yes," she admitted. "I saw him there once."

"I tracked him there once," he said, "but then I lost his trail again."

"I saw you," she said. She walked toward him again, suggestively. "And I loved you even then."

"What?" he said.

"I saw you at Kate's Landing," she said, "and I fell in love with you at once. You were so handsome and . . . dashing. You still are. I used to lie awake at night and dream about you. About you and me . . . together. I imagined that you would notice me, and love me too, and come back and take me away from—"

She hesitated.

"From what?" he said.

"From the Hunikers," she said, and her lip twisted with hate.

"Hunikers," said Donald, his face wrinkling in thought, trying to remember. There had been a family, a scurvy bunch, he seemed to recall, and a bond servant, a skinny little blue-eyed, wistful, frightened—"Bethie," he said, "you were—"

"A few years, perfumed soaps, and nice clothes make a difference, don't they?" she said.

"Yes indeed," he said. "It's amazing. But you do know Murkens, then?"

"Will you kill him if you see him again?" she asked.

"I'll arrest him," Donald said. "If he resists, and I hope he does, I'll kill him." She turned away from him, suddenly quiet. "He's not your kinfolk or anything like that, is he?" Donald asked.

She whirled back, facing him with a defiant look. "No," she snapped. Then she ducked her head. "He has been here," she said. "I've seen him here."

Donald stepped over to her and grabbed her by the shoulders. "When?" he demanded, and then he regained his composure and loosened his grip and softened his tone. "When?" he repeated.

"It was a few weeks ago," she said. "I tried to avoid him, but he might have seen me. If he did, he's gone to tell the Hunikers where I am, and they'll be coming after me. I know they will. They'll come after me and kill me, and likely Murkens will be with them. Captain, you have to protect me."

"Hold on," Donald said. "Just calm down and let me think."

She was crying, so he handed her his bandanna before

turning away to pace. So Murkens had been in Jonesboro. He could not arrest the man in Texas, but he could show the sketch to Rey del Monte and ask for his cooperation. Or he could watch for the man to cross the river, and then he could go after him himself.

Donald felt the blood rushing hot through his veins. He had been on the trail of this man for so long now that the thought of actually catching up with him, and soon, was exhilarating, but it was accompanied by a rush of ghastly memories from long ago, memories of a brutal beating, a lashing, a raw and bloody back, and a dear brother murdered. Now, at last, it seemed that the hated murderer was almost within his grasp.

Bethie rushed back against his chest and threw her arms around him, clinging to him. "You will protect me, won't you?" she said.

"If I see Murkens," he said, "I'll arrest him, but I can't take you on as a personal cause. Anyway, you have a husband to protect you."

"Tom?" she said, looking up at him, and her expression was suddenly both scoffing and tough. "Tom can't protect his own butt," she said. Donald was slightly shocked at her blunt language, but he didn't say anything about it, and she went on. "On our second day on the trail," she said, "he tried to shoot a squirrel. He kept missing, so I shot one. Then when he tried to clean it, he got sick over the sight of blood. I cleaned it and cooked it. Tom couldn't pull a trigger if it meant—"

She stopped herself as if she had almost revealed something she would rather keep secret. Perhaps she had already revealed more than she had intended. She had certainly allowed Donald to see that she was not an altogether helpless and dainty female. Donald pushed her away from him and led her to the cot.

"Sit down here," he said. He stepped back away from her as she sat obediently on the edge of the cot. She was again demure. "I think, Bethie," he continued, "that you had better tell me the whole story. Why would the Hunikers want to kill you? Why would they come all the way out here looking for you?"

"Would you let them take me away and hang me?" she asked.

"Hang you?" he said, astonished. "Of course not. But why in the world would they want to hang you? Did you kill one of them?"

She sat looking at her hands in her lap and spoke in a low voice which Donald could barely hear. "Jeth got himself killed," she said.

Donald heaved a sigh. "Tell me about it," he said.

"Well, he did," said Bethie. "He really did. He brought it all on himself. You see, there was this old hermit called Warren. Smelly old man. But folks said that he had gold hid in his cabin. One night old Warren's cabin burned down, out there in the swamp in the woods. Everybody went out there—including Jeth.

"But Jeth had come home earlier that night and left his old muddy boots. I know, 'cause it was my job to clean his nasty old boots, and I did. I cleaned them that night. And them boots had swamp mud on them. I could tell. But when Jeth showed up with everyone else out at the fire to watch old Warren's cabin burn to the ground, he was wearing a new pair of boots, and he was the one who found the old hermit's body in the ashes, too."

"Go on," Donald said.

"Well, I had cleaned his damned old boots, like I said," she continued, "and I figured he'd realize that I knew that was swamp mud that was on them, and he'd decide to kill me too to keep me quiet about what I knew. So while he was still out, I looked where he kept his things, and I found a sack of gold coins hid, and I knew then that he'd killed the old man and stole his gold and then set fire to the house."

"Keep talking, Bethie," Donald said.

"Well," she said, "I don't know if you'll remember this, but Tom was clerking in the Hunikers' store back then. And Tom liked me. He was always nice to me, and, well, I kissed him back in the storeroom once, and, well, you know, so anyway, I knew that if anyone would help me, Tom would, so I went to him, to tell him what had happened and all, but he whined around about his fat wife and spoiled little brat, and he wasn't going to do nothing, except that while I was begging him to take me and run away before it was too late, Jeth come in. He was drunk, and he come at us both with a knife and a pistol.

"Well, you know, they always kept a loaded pistol there in the store, just in case, and so when I seen Jeth the way he was, I grabbed up the store pistol, but Tom was so scared and shaking he wouldn't take it, so . . ."

"So you shot Jeth," said Donald.

Bethie stared at the floor.

"I killed him," she said.

"You shot him, and he fell," said Donald. "Did you make sure he was really dead?"

"He was dead all right," she said. "Then I told Tom that no one would ever believe it was little old me that done it, leastwise not by myself. They'd blame him, for sure, and they'd hang him too, so he decided then that he'd run away with me after all, and so we did, and we come all the way out here. I thought we'd be safe here, but now that damn Murkens has been here, and I'm afraid that he's seen me or Tom, one, maybe both of us, and he's going to bring those damned Hunikers out here. They're his cousins, you know. That's why I came to you."

Donald had not known that Murkens and the Hunikers were cousins, and he wondered what other pertinent information Bethie was holding back from him.

"Did Tom know about the money?" he asked her. "The stolen gold?"

"No," she said. "Not at first. We'd been running three days before I told him about it."

"All right," said Donald. "Go on back home to your—to Tom Booker, and try not to worry. I'll keep watch for Murkens and for the Hunikers, and I promise you that no one's going to hang you, not here and not back at Kate's Landing."

"But now you know the truth about me," she said, "and—"

"And nothing," Donald interrupted. "It will stay just between the two of us. That doesn't mean that I approve of your . . . situation, but I'll not betray a confidence. Your secrets are safe with me."

Bethie stood up and stepped in close to Donald once more, and once more she put her hands on his chest and looked up into his eyes, and once more, in spite of himself, he looked down the open dress and saw more flesh down there than he could hardly bear to look at and ignore.

"Thank you, Captain," she said.

"Thank you for telling me the tale, Bethie," he said. "You'd better run along now."

She stretched herself, reaching for his lips with her own. She pressed herself against him and pulled him toward her.

"I really did fall in love with you back then," she said. "I don't have to go, do I? Not just yet."

"What about Tom?" he said.

"Tom's brooding about his old fat wife," she said. "He's wanting to go back home to her, but he's afraid. Tom doesn't mean anything to me anyway. He never did. Don't even think about Tom. I just needed his help getting away from the Hunikers, that's all."

"And right now," Donald said, "you need my help."

"Yes," she said. "Yes, I do, but that's not why I want to stay here with you tonight. I do love you, Mat. I've loved you since that first time I saw you. I want you, and you want me too, don't you? I saw you looking down the front of my dress. You want to see more? You want to see it all?''

''Now, Bethie, I don't—''

Before he could finish the sentence, she had stepped back, jerked at a couple of strings, wriggled her whole body, and the dress had fallen to the floor around her ankles. She stood there before him stark naked. Donald flushed and broke into a sweat. God, she was beautiful. Her whole body was shapely, with nice, round curves in all the right places. Her breasts stood up round and firm, and the nipples were swollen and standing out. And the dark triangle of curly hair down below was damp, hiding promises of special joy and delight. Donald trembled. He forced himself to look up again at her face. It too was lovely. Her large blue eyes looked at him, pleading, and her lips were pursed and inviting.

Donald straightened himself up, almost as if standing at attention, and took a deep breath. ''You came here under the pretense of being Mrs. Tom Booker,'' he said. ''You introduced yourself as such, and you've been living with him as his wife. As far as I'm concerned, you are Mrs. Booker. Now, I'm going back out on the deck. Dress yourself and leave my room. Please.''

He turned and left the stateroom, careful to open the door just enough to sidle out. Then he went down the stairs and back to his favorite spot at the bow of the boat.

The damned little vixen, he thought. *How can she look so like an angel and yet be so conniving?* He leaned on the rail, aching for her sumptuous body. God, he wished she had not displayed it to him so. But it had been lovely to look at. It was not so pleasant to have walked away from it the way he had. *Damn my scruples and principles*, he said to himself. Just then Bethie, dressed again, came down from the second landing.

''Good night, Captain,'' she said, and she was smiling broadly. ''You'll lie awake all night long thinking about me and wishing you hadn't been so upright.''

91

Twelve

It was early morning when Captain Mat Donald mounted Prince Charley to ride out at the head of his small troop of cavalry. Sergeant Scot rode beside him, and a short distance ahead, on his red mule, rode the scout, Krevs. Back in front of the inn, Wright and a small group of settlers stood scowling. Just a few feet away from them, Capitan Rey del Monte sat at a table sipping his morning coffee.

Iron Head's village was not far to the northeast of the Sacred Hill, so Krevs's plan was to lead the troops to Buffalo Crossing, there to cross the river into American territory, and then to head on to the Osage village.

Although he had never met the man, Mat Donald didn't give a damn about the charlatan Socrates Bangs. He certainly knew the type, and the damned scoundrel could stay tied to that tree and rot for all he cared. Still, he knew that he couldn't allow that to happen, for the American settlers on both sides of the river would be instantly up in arms, and that was exactly what Donald had been sent west to prevent.

And he was glad to be away from Jonesboro and glad to be on horseback again instead of riding on the water. He was, after all, a horse soldier. Finally, he was glad to have the opportunity to meet Iron Head, for, after all, part of his mission was to establish good relations with all the local tribes or segments of tribes. He realized that he had been negligent in that area.

He had stopped to trade with the Coushattas on his way to Jonesboro, and he had met a lone Cherokee and a lone Delaware and the Kickapoo preacher woman. Other than that, he had as yet made no contacts with the Indians. It was about time. He only hoped that this initial contact would be a peaceful one. Damn that fake notions and potions seller anyway.

Walker woke up early on top of the Sacred Hill in spite of the fact that he had consumed a whole bottle of whiskey the night before. He had not had a vision during the night, but he did wake up with a sense of urgency and a powerful feeling that for some as yet undefined reason, he was needed at the Osage village of Iron Head.

He craved some coffee, but he didn't have any, and he didn't have the time to make any even if he'd had it. He stood up and stretched himself and was thinking of going to the cave entrance to make his way down the hill, when he heard some noises from below that did not seem to belong to the otherwise tranquil morning. He hurried to the edge of the hill and looked down.

There were horses picketed and tents being pitched. There were rugged looking men all over the place. There were campfires, and men cooking over them and making coffee. He crouched down low and peered carefully over the edge. Squinting his eyes, he looked at individuals to see if he could recognize anyone, and then, sure enough, he saw the big albino. Rotison.

So Rotison had come back, just as Walker had feared he would. He wondered what had become of Zeno Bond. Had Rotison abandoned him back at the old fool's less desirable land grant? Killed him perhaps? Or had Bond's sense of patriotism and loyalty and legality weakened? Had the old man looked at his own land and then recalled with longing the beauty and the strategic desirability of this location and tossed his scruples and his ethics to the wind? Walker searched the figures below, but he saw no sign of Zeno Bond.

Ah, well, he had to move along to the Osage town, and now that task was going to be a little more difficult. He was going to have to find his way around or through the band of renegades below. One of them had shot at him once before, and he had no doubt that any of them would kill him on sight if given the chance. He did not want to provide them with that opportunity. He uttered a brief prayer and hurried to the cave.

Down below, Zeno Bond sat alone inside his tent. His conscience was bothering him, for he had at last sided with the rascally Rotison and abandoned his legal townsite to seize and hold the area around the strategically located hill near the river crossing. He tried to push his guilty thoughts aside with sound reasoning.

This, he told himself, was by far the better location for an American settlement. The United States would expand westward, and the savages would have to give way and make room. From this place American settlers could defend themselves easily against attacks from marauding Indians, and here the Indians' lifeblood, the buffalo, came at regular intervals to cross the Red River. From here, hunters could work diligently at exterminating the great beasts and thereby weakening the tribes and bringing them more quickly to their knees.

And there was the inevitability of a war for Texas in the near future, and the strong possibility, no, probability, of attempted military invasions of the United States from the south at this very river crossing. From this spot any such attempt could be easily forestalled.

Bond told himself that Rotison had been right after all. This place must be held, for the good of the country, and even though his occupation of this land was technically illegal, he would make that right just as soon as possible. As soon as the area was secure, Bond would search out Senator Reddels, who was known to be in the region. Surely Reddels would agree with his assessment of the situation and work at securing the proper authority for Bond's new colony to be located here. If necessary, Bond would bring Reddels to the spot and show it to him. That should do the trick. If not, Bond would return to Washington to plead his case himself, in person. It was a mere formality. If he and the members of Congress with whom he had dealt had known the lay of the land to begin with, they'd surely have assigned him this spot initially anyway.

He felt much better having reasoned it all out. He was not, after all, a freebooter nor a scurvy squatter. He was a revolutionary patriot, a fighter for freedom, a pioneer, and this small technical illegality would soon be set right. Having put his mind more or less at ease, Bond stood up and stretched, then ducked his head to leave the tent.

He could smell the coffee brewing over the campfires, and he wanted some. Stepping out into the fresh air, he saw the men around him, and he was a bit dismayed at the kind of scum he was forced to surround himself with in order to achieve his grand purposes. He told himself that it would all be worth it in the long run. The ends would more than justify the means.

*   *   *

Robert J. Conley

Walker poked his head out of the lower end of the musty cavern, thankful for his first whiff of clean, fresh air, free from the smell of the rattlesnake den, and greatly relieved to have once more survived his bold intrusion into their domain. He could hear voices down below, and he could smell the coffee brewing and the bacon frying over the fires. His stomach complained vigorously to him, and he tried to ignore it.

The white men were camped just below him now, and there was no way he could take his usual route to the bottom of the hill. He worked his way through the tangle of the juniper tree, picking up his weapons and other belongings on the way. Hooking various straps over his shoulders, he prepared to move on.

The camp down below stretched along the base of the Sacred Hill beginning at a point almost directly below Walker and moving south toward the river and then west around the hill. Studying the camp as best he could from his spot halfway up the hill and hidden in tangled brush, Walker determined that there was no way he would be able to go down the usual route and sneak through the camp. Not in the daytime.

He would have to work his way slowly around to the north, to the other side of the hill, away from the camp, before attempting his final descent. He would move along the rim where the sheer rock began. And he realized that if he could see the camp below, someone in the camp could see him too, if that someone happened to look up in just the right direction at just the right time. He knew that he would have to move carefully, try to stay hidden as much as possible, and keep quiet. And that would not be easy in this thick tangle of brush and with the footing so unsure.

He started to creep along the ridge, and it seemed to him that even his lightest footstep made a crunching noise that could be heard clear to the other side of the river. He stood still and watched the camp, his heart pounding in his chest.

No one down there seemed to have noticed. He moved again.

It seemed to take forever, but at last he had reached a place on the side of the hill from which he could no longer see the camp of squatters down below. He felt a bit safer, and so he moved more quickly. A little farther and he decided that it might be safe to go down. The way there was steep, and the brush was thick. It was a more difficult descent here than his usual path back beneath the entrance to the cavern. It took longer, but he made it safely to the bottom of the hill.

Just as he was about to step out of the brush, he heard the pounding of hooves, and he stepped back quickly, his heart pounding too. From the brush, he watched as a rider from the camp passed him by only a few feet away. He had almost stepped right out into the horseman's path. He chided himself, calling himself several kinds of a fool. Of course, if Bond and Rotison were seizing the area illegally, they would have riders out circling the hill, searching the area for any sign of retaliation. He should have anticipated that.

He waited a moment, catching his breath, letting his heartbeat slow back to normal, and then he cautiously poked his head out of the brush. He looked both ways. He saw no one. Heard nothing suspicious. He stepped out into the open and ran.

When he had run as far as his bandy legs would run, when his heart was pounding once again unmercifully in his chest, when he felt like he was safely away from the camp of the renegades, he slowed to a walk. He went on a few more paces, and then he turned, and walking backwards, surveyed the land behind him to make sure there was no pursuit. He saw no sign of any, and he turned again. It seemed that he had indeed escaped the notice of the wretched crew of Bond and Rotison.

But before he could allow himself to feel too smug about this small success, he reminded himself of just where he was going. He was headed toward an Osage village, a town full of people who had been at war with his own people for as long as anyone could recall. A brutal war fueled by powerful and long-standing hatred on both sides.

And it was worse now than ever before, intensified because a contingent of Cherokees under the leadership of Diwali, the Bowl, had moved into Arkansas just a few years earlier. That move had put them very close to the Osages, on land, in fact, that the Osages claimed as their own. The old war between the Cherokees and the Osages had flared up worse than ever before. Now and then, Cherokees from the old country even traveled all the way out to the Arkansas country to help their relatives, now called the Western Cherokee Nation, fight this ancient, hated enemy they called "a nation of liars."

And here he was, walking voluntarily into the midst of this same enemy, delivering himself, as it were, on purpose into their hands, as if offering himself up as a sacrifice. It was a stupid and foolish thing to do. He knew that, but then, he reminded himself, he had not made the decision. It had been made for him when something had told him to do this idiotic thing. And he had received the message while on top of the Sacred Hill. It must have come from the spirits.

For a brief moment, as he walked along, he wondered if perhaps the spirits in this part of the country were partial to the Osages and had thus played a dirty trick on him. But he quickly dismissed that thought. After all, the worst that could possibly happen would be that the bloodthirsty Osages would kill him, and, after all, he had been dead before. It hadn't been so bad. He kept walking resolutely toward the village of Iron Head.

In the Osage village, Iron Head had not yet made his initial appearance of the day. It was still early morning, and anything could be going on inside his house. Everyone in the village was curious, for everyone knew that the old man had a new young bride with him in there, and they all knew as well why he had taken her. They knew what the Kickapoo woman had told him, had read to him from the white man's sacred book.

They knew as well why the white medicine man was tied to the tree, had been tied to it all night long, howling desperately for his freedom. They waited anxiously. If Iron Head should emerge from his grass house with a big smile on his wrinkled old face, or a smug, satisfied look, then everything would all right. The terrified white man would be released to go on his way, and the rest of the day would pass as normal, except that the old chief would be so puffed up with pride that he would be almost impossible to live with.

On the other hand, if Iron Head should come out of his house scowling, then they would know that all the proffered remedies had failed to do the trick, and that the old man had suffered humiliation all night long with his new young wife. He would start the day in a rage, and his first act would be to kill the unfortunate white man. Then perhaps he would kill the Kickapoo woman as well. No one knew what he might do after that. No matter what happened, they knew, it promised to be a memorable day in the village, and everyone was anxious.

Sings Loud stood aside from the crowd and waited and watched. She watched, though, with an aloof, special Christian haughtiness, an arrogance that told everyone around her that she knew she was above it all. If Iron Head had believed her, she told herself, had truly believed in the Word of God as she had given it to him, then everything would be all right, and her miraculous reviving of his withered tool would surely bring her many converts from among the Osages, perhaps the entire village.

If, on the other hand, the old fool had failed to heed the Word, had instead placed his faith in false medicine sold to him by the white witch doctor, he would surely fail. His tool would have remained flaccid all night long, and his young, virgin bride would still be a virgin. And it would be his own fault. It did not occur to Sings Loud that her own life could be in danger. She was doing the Lord's work, and the Lord would protect her.

Socrates Bangs had howled and squirmed off and on all night long. He had demanded his release. He had threatened the savages with swift and merciless retaliation. He had begged. None of these things had worked. He had strained against the ropes that bound him to the tree, and he had tried to wriggle his way loose, but nothing had worked. The sun was coming up, and he was still there, still tied fast to the damnable tree.

And Socrates Bangs knew that time was running out for him. The old man would have tried all night long to have his pleasure with the young virgin. With the morning light, he would come out of his house either satisfied or furious. If the latter, Bangs knew that he was not long for this world. He saw the light on the eastern horizon, and he began again to howl.

Thirteen

The sun was well up in the eastern sky when Krevs led the small army patrol into the Osage village of Iron Head. Donald took note of the cornfields and the peach orchards on the edge of the village and of the large, round, grass mat–covered houses as they rode on in. Almost immediately he saw the garish wagon of the potion peddler, the two horses, still hitched, grazing contentedly, seemingly unconcerned for the fate of their hapless master.

The wagon itself was a panel wagon, complete with enclosed living quarters, its canvas cover decorated with filigree figures and wild lettering in gold, red, yellow, and black paint. DR. SOCRATES BANGS, PHYSICIAN TO THE EMPEROR OF AUSTRIA, the largest and boldest of the lettering proclaimed. As the troops rode past the wagon, Donald read also, A POTION FOR EVERY NOTION, POTIONS TO CURE FOUL STOMACH, WATERY HUMOURS, CHOLIC, AND HYSTERIC FITS, SECRETS OF THE ORIENT GIVEN BY MARCO POLO TO THE

FAMILY OF THE ILLUSTRIOUS DOCTOR SOCRATES BANGS, and, significantly, RESTORE YOUR MANHOOD.

They rode in a little farther before halting their horses to dismount, and Osage boys came running to take the reins of the horses. Before allowing his own horse to be taken, however, Donald, in full dress uniform and plumed cockade hat, made Prince Charley prance and rear. As he swung down off the back of the big gelding, handing the reins casually to one of the boys, he noticed Socrates Bangs tied to a tree not far ahead.

"Captain," Bangs shouted in a hoarse voice, "thank God you've come to deliver me from the hands of these malevolent savages."

"Cut Hand," said Donald, looking over the large and populous town, "all of our lives are now indeed in your hands."

"Wait here," said Cut Hand, and he walked away from the group. He hadn't gone far before he was met by an older Osage man, and they greeted one another warmly. As they talked, Cut Hand glanced back over his shoulder at the waiting soldiers, and the other nodded knowingly. Donald wondered what Cut Hand was saying. Then the two of them walked back to where the soldiers still stood.

"Captain, please," Bangs shouted. "For God's sake, get me loose from here. I've been tied here all through the long night."

Donald spoke sideways to Krevs.

"Tell that son of a bitch to keep his pants on, Krevs," he said. "He could spoil everything."

Krevs fell back, then stepped aside, as Cut Hand presented Donald to the Osage who had accompanied him.

"Captain," Cut Hand said, "this is Coyote. He's Iron Head's medicine man, but he wasn't able to do the chief any good. That's the only reason Bangs and Sings Loud were both allowed to try their skills. I've already told him who you are. He'll take us to Iron Head now."

"Captain," Bangs screamed.

"Shut up, Bangs," said Krevs. "We're working on it."

Coyote said something in Osage.

"He says you're welcome here," said Cut Hand, "and he says, let's go meet Iron Head."

"Thank him for me," said Donald, "and tell him to please lead the way. We're at his disposal."

Cut Hand spoke to Coyote in Osage, and Coyote turned and started walking. Cut Hand fell in beside him. Donald motioned for Sergeant Scot to join them, leaving the rest of the soldiers there with their horses and Krevs to deal with Bangs.

All around the village, children ran and played their games, dogs barked or slept in the shade or ran with the children, women cooked over fires in front of their grass houses, calling out to each other, gesticulating, exchanging mid-morning gossip, and occasionally nodding toward the visitors in their midst.

Up ahead, Chief Iron Head himself sat in the shade of a giant white oak tree, a stout patriarch at his ease. Thick, rich, blue-gray smoke rose up from the long-stemmed pipe he held in one hand and puffed on occasionally. His visage was stern. Cut Hand took one look at the old man and spoke confidentially to Donald.

"I don't think he diddled his young bride," he said.

An old Spanish helmet was snugged down on the Osage chief's head. Donald thought that it looked terribly uncomfortable, but it did, at least, explain his name. Four women tended a large cooking pot over a nearby fire. One of them, Donald thought, couldn't have been more than sixteen years of age. Donald caught a motion out of the corner of his eye and glanced over to see Sings Loud walking toward him.

"Hello, Captain," she said. "Have you come to rescue the white faker?"

Ignoring her question, Donald said, "What are you doing here, Sings Loud?"

"The Lord's work," she said.

"The work of a pander, from what I've heard," said Donald.

"What's that mean?"

"Never mind."

Cut Hand again spoke in Osage, this time to Iron Head, who studied Donald with a wrinkled old face. Then he spoke and gestured, and Cut Hand said, "He wants us to sit."

Bangs, infuriated with the casual manner of the meeting, began to scream again.

"I demand that you release me at once," he shouted, his voice raspy. "At once, do you hear?"

"Bangs," said Krevs, "keep your goddamned mouth shut, and we just might get you out of here alive."

Iron Head ignored the screams of Bangs. He puffed his pipe calmly and spoke softly in Osage. Cut Hand translated for Donald.

"He says we'll eat with him," he said.

"Tell him we are honored," said Donald, and Cut Hand spoke again in Osage.

"What are you doing?" Bangs shouted. "This is an outrage. Kill them and burn down this village."

"Bangs," said Krevs, "if you don't keep your yap shut, I just might kill you before they do. Damn it, you could get us all killed."

Iron Head's wives dished stew out of their pot and handed the dishes around. Sings Loud sat beside Donald to eat. Donald looked at the meat in his bowl, as delicious smelling steam rose to fill his nostrils. But then, a sudden frightening thought came into his head, and he looked at Sings Loud.

"What is this?" he asked her.

"What are you worried about, Captain?" she asked.

"It's not dog, is it?" he said. "I've heard that they eat dog."

She laughed. "No, foolish white man," she said. "It's buffalo meat."

"Good," he said with a sigh of relief, and he started to eat.

Bangs watched from his tree. He almost started to scream again, but then he thought better of it. He looked at Krevs.

"Cut me loose from here," he pleaded.

"I can't do that, you damned fool," Krevs said. "If I was to just cut you loose, they'd kill you and me both. Well, actually, they'd probably skin us alive first."

"I've been here all night long," Bangs said. "I haven't had a drink of water or a bite to eat. My arms are numb from the tying, and the ropes have rubbed my poor flesh raw."

"You should have thought about all that," Krevs said, "before you tried to swindle an Osage chief."

"Please," said Bangs. "I can't take it any longer."

"The captain's doing everything he can," Krevs said. "Just be patient a little bit more."

"I'm out of patience," Bangs shouted suddenly. "I just told you I can't take it any longer. I demand to be released. Now. At once. This minute. Do you hear?"

"Shut up," said Krevs, hurrying over toward Bangs.

"Senator Reddels will hear about this," the doctor threatened, "and you'll all be cashiered. You'll be ruined, and this whole village of heathenish savages will be burned to the ground. Get me out of here."

Krevs pulled a knife from a scabbard at his belt and walked up close to Bangs. With his left hand he grabbed a handful of Bangs's hair and pulled back his head. His right hand touched the sharp blade of the knife to the fake doctor's exposed throat. Bangs flinched at the feel of the cold, sharp steel.

"This is the last time I'm going to say it, Bangs," said Krevs through clenched teeth. "You keep your mouth shut, or I'll slit your goddamned throat for you right here and now and save the Osages the trouble. You hear me?"

Bangs's eyes were opened wide. He did not answer.

Krevs pulled harder at his hair and touched the blade a little more firmly against the stretched skin of his neck.

"Answer me," the scout said, "but answer quiet. Do you believe me when I say I'll kill you?"

"Yes," whispered the terrified Bangs.

"Are you going to keep quiet now?"

"Yes."

Krevs flung Bangs's head back against the tree for emphasis, then tucked his knife away. As he turned to walk away from Bangs, he muttered, "You wouldn't be in this fix nohow if you hadn't tried to cheat old Iron Head. Son of a bitch."

Back at Iron Head's fire, when everyone had finished eating, the old chief spoke again. Then Cut Hand spoke in English to Donald.

"Iron Head asks what has brought you here," he said.

The sly old fox, Donald thought. *He must know why I'm here, with that damnable Bangs wrapped tight to a tree well within my vision.* He hesitated, choosing his words carefully.

"Tell him," he said, "that I see a white man tied to a tree. Tell him that I know the white man must have done something wrong, or he wouldn't be tied like that. Tell him that I am ashamed that a white man would come into his country and do wrong, and that I would like to take this white man back with me and punish him properly, so that other white men will know better than to come out here and misbehave."

Cut Hand translated into Osage, and a conversation developed with Cut Hand, Iron Head, and Coyote all involved. Donald waited patiently, trying to read facial expressions. Iron Head appeared to be immovable. At last Cut Hand spoke to Donald again.

"Iron Head," he said, "says he wants to keep the ugly white man a few days more and then kill him."

"Tell him for me, please," said Donald, speaking slowly and deliberately, "that it is a matter of pride and honor to white men that we punish our own criminals, and tell him further, please, that it seems a very small thing for so great a chief to do for us.''

Cut Hand spoke to Iron Head again, and then Iron Head sat as if in deep thought. The silence was ominous. At last Iron Head spoke. Cut Hand turned to face Donald.

''Iron Head says that the white man tied to the tree is a liar and a thief,'' he said. ''He says further that the man is a fool, for he must think that the Osages are very stupid. He sold Iron Head some false medicine. Coyote examined the medicine, and he says that it is nothing but water, vanilla, sugar, and a little bit of alcohol. This white man has insulted the intelligence of the Osage people.''

Donald was about to speak, but Cut Hand silenced him with a gesture.

''However,'' Cut Hand continued, ''Iron Head understands you, and he does not want to offend your white man's sense of honor and pride. You're his guest, and he's a gracious host. Furthermore, he wants always to be friends with the white men. Therefore, Iron Head says, he will let you have the honor of killing the miserable faker, if you'll do it right here and now.''

Donald sat stunned. The wily old bastard, he thought, had outfoxed him for sure. He tried to think of a response. Could he talk about the white man's need to give the fake doctor a trial? Would the Osage understand the white man's notion of justice? And even if he did understand, would he reason, rightly, of course, that no jury of white men would ever take seriously a charge of selling fake medicine to an Indian? Well, he was stumped.

''Cut Hand,'' he said at last, trying not very successfully to hide the feeling of sudden defeat that had come over him, ''you know that I can't kill Bangs. But I don't know what to say further. You offered me your help, and I placed myself in your hands. I trust you. Try something else. Anything. But I must take Dr. Bangs with me when I leave here, and he must be alive. And I don't want to offend Iron Head.''

"I'll do my best, Captain," Cut Hand said, "but that's a hell of a tough problem."

"Yes," said Donald. "I know. Try."

Walker saw the smoke of the fires of the Osage town before he could see any houses, so he knew that he was almost there. He hurried ahead. The ground was rolling hills and patches of pine forest and oak groves, and as he moved along the trail where rocky, tree-covered hills rose on either side, suddenly four young Osage men were barring his path. He stopped still, and he held his hands out away from his weapons.

One of the young men spoke, but Walker could not understand a word of the language. Slowly he raised his right hand in a sign of peace, hoping that it was as universal a sign as he had been told. He'd never tried to use it on an Osage before.

"I come in peace," he said in English. "Do any of you speak the white man's language?"

Apparently none of them did. He wondered if he should try his own language, but as he was considering the idea, one of the young Osages fitted an arrow to his bow and drew back the string. The point of the arrow was aimed just about at Walker's sternum.

Fourteen

While both Cut Hand and Captain Donald were trying desperately to come up with some kind of response to Iron Head's most generous offer, four young men came running toward Iron Head's fire, yelling all the way and driving Walker ahead of them. Sergeant Scot was the first to recognize their prisoner.

"Uh-oh," he said. "Here comes more trouble."

"What now?" Donald asked, but as he turned his head to look, he had the answer to his own question. "Walker," he said.

"There's no worse trouble on earth," Scot said, "than the trouble a Cherokee's got when he's surrounded by Osages."

Walker was shoved rudely into the space between Iron Head and Donald. He saw Donald right away and made a comically polite bow.

"Hello, Captain," he said.

"Walker," said Donald, "how did you get into this mess?"

One of Walker's captors jerked him around to face Iron Head before the Cherokee could even attempt to answer that awkward question. The Osage who had earlier aimed his arrow at Walker stepped around in front of him again, but slightly to one side so as not to interfere with Iron Head's line of sight. Again he aimed his arrow at Walker's chest, and again he pulled back the string of the bow. Iron Head spoke, and one of the young men answered. Then Iron Head spoke again. The young man started to respond, but Cut Hand interrupted. Donald leaned toward Sings Loud and whispered into her ear.

"Do you understand what they're saying?" he asked her.

"These young men caught him outside of town," she said. "Iron Head wants to know who he is, and Cut Hand is telling him." She paused a moment, listening. "Cut Hand told them Walker's name and said that he's a Cherokee. Now the young man for sure wants to kill him."

"Cut Hand," said Donald. "Tell Iron Head that I know of his war with the Cherokees, but tell him that Walker is our friend."

Cut Hand spoke to Iron Head.

"Tell him," said Donald, "that Walker is no warrior and has killed no one. Tell him that Walker is a man of peace. He died and was sent back to earth by the spirits. He's— he's a holy man."

Again Cut Hand interpreted for Iron Head, and again Iron Head sat and mulled things over in silence. He spoke low to Coyote, and Coyote answered him in equally muted tones. Then Iron Head spoke to the young men. The one with the nocked arrow reluctantly lowered his weapon, and all four, with long pouts on their faces, walked away. Walker looked at Iron Head, then back at Donald and Cut Hand.

"Sit here beside me, my friend," Cut Hand said in English. "It's all right now, at least for the moment."

Walker moved toward Cut Hand, hesitated, looked at Iron Head, then moved on over beside the Delaware and sat on the ground between him and Donald.

"Thank you both," he said. "I thought that I was about to be dead again."

"Now that we have that little crisis out of the way," Donald said to Cut Hand, "maybe you can get back to resolving my problem with Dr. Bangs."

"May I ask," said Walker, "what the problem is?"

Cut Hand and Donald gave Walker a quick rundown of the situation.

"You know," said Walker, "when I was a young man, I used to get on a horse and ride like the wind, but then I got old, and now I can't even climb up on a horse's back anymore. Why, even if someone picked me up and put me on a horse, I'd fall off. So I have to walk everywhere I go now. That's why they call me Walker."

Donald thought that Walker had gone crazy, but Iron Head was curious about what this Cherokee was talking so long about, and as soon as Walker had quit, he demanded that Cut Hand translate for him. Cut Hand did, and Iron Head roared with laughter. When he finally stopped laughing, he spoke directly to Walker, but Walker, of course, had to wait for Cut Hand's translation.

"Iron Head says that he is much older than you," Cut Hand said, "but that he can still get up on his horse unassisted, and he can still ride like the wind, and when he's riding fast across the prairie, he feels just like a young man."

"Ah," said Walker, "I envy the great Iron Head, for now things are getting even worse for me. Now my legs begin to hurt me when I walk too much. I wish I had a wagon like the white doctor's so I could ride in it."

Cut Hand translated, and again Iron Head laughed at Walker. Walker thought to himself, sometimes it is even better for one to laugh at an enemy than to kill him. It is certainly better for that enemy. Then Iron Head spoke again, and again Cut Hand translated.

"Iron Head gives you the white man's wagon and team," he said.

"While Iron Head is feeling so good at my expense," Walker said to Cut Hand, "ask him why he doesn't take the white man's wagon for himself, and in exchange for it, give the white man to Captain Donald. Tell him that the wagon is doubtless full of many good things that will please his wives, especially the young one, and it probably also has a bed inside. It would be a good thing, I think, in which to take a young bride out on the prairie where they could be alone under the stars. Very romantic."

Donald gave Walker a curious look, and Cut Hand was already talking Osage to Iron Head. Then abruptly Iron Head called for his pipe to be refilled and lit. One of his older wives took care of that chore, then handed him the pipe. He puffed it a few times, then had the woman carry it over to Cut Hand. Cut Hand smoked it, and at Iron Head's instructions, passed it along to Walker and then to Donald and on to Sergeant Scot. Finally it went to Sings Loud before being returned to Iron Head. The old chief smoked it once more, then held it out to his side. The old woman took it immediately and carried it away. Then at last Iron Head spoke again.

"This is his final answer," Cut Hand said. "He will keep the white liar's wagon and horses. You can take the white man. He's insignificant anyhow. He says, let's have no more talk about this unpleasantness. Let's eat and smoke and talk like friends."

"Tell him we agree," said Donald. "He's a very wise man. There will be no more talk of that other matter." Then to Walker, he said, "It appears that you came along just at the right time, my Cherokee friend."

"It didn't look that way at first," Walker said. "But you

may not be so happy to see me anyway when I tell you my news.''

"Oh?" said Donald. "What news is that?"

Just then all eyes were diverted to a rider coming fast on top of a hill to the southwest. Donald and his company, too, turned to look. As they watched him come closer, they could see that the rider was Indian.

"Osage?" Donald asked.

Cut Hand watched for a moment longer with squinted eyes. "Osage," he said with a nod. Iron Head stood up, a look of concern on his wrinkled old face. He waited on his feet for the rider to come in. Soon, having dismounted at the edge of the village, the man came running up to Iron Head. He was almost out of breath. He spoke falteringly in Osage. Iron Head's face turned purple with rage. He dismissed the messenger and glared at Donald. Then he spoke angrily for a long time. Donald looked at Cut Hand.

"He says that while we've been here wasting time with the no-good fake doctor," Cut Hand said, "white men have been busy taking his land and his Sacred Hill. He wants to know if you know anything about that."

Donald looked at Walker, who gave a little shrug.

"That was my news," Walker said.

"Damn," said Donald. "Is it Rotison?"

Walker nodded slowly. "And Bond," he said.

"Tell him that I knew nothing of this," Donald said. "But tell him that I will investigate the matter immediately. If there are white men on his land, I will have them moved."

Cut Hand told Iron Head, and Iron Head made his curt response. Cut Hand relayed the word to Donald.

"Iron Head says he'll give you until the leaves turn crimson," he said. "If your white friends are not off his hunting grounds and his Sacred Hill by that time, the time for the big buffalo hunt, he says he'll kill every one of them."

Donald started to reply, but Cut Hand stopped him short.

"It's time for us to go," he said, "before Iron Head

113

changes his mind. Take the white doctor and Walker with us, and let's ride out of here.'' As they walked toward the rest of the troop and their waiting horses, Cut Hand continued. "Iron Head's patience has been sorely tried," he said. "He was in a bad humor to begin with because of his failing tool. Then the white doctor defrauded him, and the Kickapoo woman read him false words from the book. He wanted to kill the doctor, but we talked him out of that. We also talked him out of letting the young men kill the Cherokee. But he has the wagon, and everything would have been all right if it had been left at that. This news about the Sacred Hill, though, was too much for him, coming when it did.''

They reached the horses and started to mount up.

"Fetch that damned Bangs," Donald said to Krevs.

As Krevs pulled out his knife, this time to cut the ropes, and walked toward Bangs, Donald noticed that Sings Loud was riding over to join them. So, he thought, she's not so sure of her own safety after all. Krevs walked over to the tree and cut the ropes, setting Bangs loose.

"Come on," he said.

Bangs started to walk toward his gaudy wagon, but Krevs grabbed him quick by the collar, nearly jerking him off his feet.

"Not that way," he said. "This way."

"But my wagon—"

"Leave it," said Krevs.

"It's my livelihood," said Bangs. "I'll not leave without my wagon."

"It's the only way you'll get out of here alive, you sorry shit," said Krevs. "Come on."

"Sergeant Scot," said Donald, "see to Bangs, and tie his hands."

"Private Jenkins," said Scot, "Dr. Bangs will ride with you."

Krevs and Scot joined forces and began tying the doctor's

wrists together. Bangs tried to resist, but the two were too much for him.

"What—what are you doing to me?" Bangs asked.

"Keep quiet, Doctor," said Scot. "It's for your own good."

"It's an outrage," Bangs protested.

"You want us to just give you back to old Iron Head?" said Krevs, as he pushed Bangs roughly toward Jenkins's horse and shoved him up behind the saddle. "Hang on, Doc," he said. "I'd sure hate to lose you out there somewhere on the lonesome prairie."

"This is robbery," Bangs said. "My wagon—it's an outrage! Senator Reddels is going to hear about this. You can be sure of that. You haven't heard the last of this. I'm a U.S. citizen, a voter. I'm a federalist and a democrat, and I'm being treated like a common criminal. I'm going to write to the president. Do you hear me? To the president!"

"Aw, shut up, Bangs," said Krevs. "I may cut your throat yet, you son of a bitch."

Then Krevs went on around to mount his patient red mule, and Mat Donald watched nervously as twelve young Osage men mounted their ponies. They were all heavily armed with bows and arrows and lances, and they sat still on horseback watching with stern faces as the white men prepared to leave.

"Sergeant Scot," Donald said, "is our company all ready to ride?"

"Yes sir," said Scot.

"Then get them moving," Donald said.

As they started on their way out of the Osage village, Donald noticed that the twelve armed Osage men followed along at a distance behind them.

"What are they up to?" he asked Cut Hand, who was riding beside him, Walker up behind his saddle.

"Don't worry," Cut Hand said. "They just want to make sure we get the hell out. That's all."

115

Fifteen

"Dr. Bangs," said Private Jenkins as they rode away from the Osage village, "I'm just a private soldier, myself, but if you don't mind my saying it to you, sir, if I was you, I'd keep myself over on the Texas side of the river from here on out."

"What do you mean to imply by that?" Bangs blustered. "I've done nothing wrong. I am the one who has been wronged, mistreated, falsely accused, abused, insulted—"

"Well, I don't know about none of that," said Jenkins, "but old Iron Head will have you killed for sure if he ever sees you again."

"We'll just see about all that," said Bangs. "I'll see that old reprobate hanged, I will. Him and his whole savage tribe. Furthermore, I'll see your cowardly, incompetent captain cashiered out of the army, and that half-savage scout of his in jail. That's what I think of your advice, young man."

Sweat ran down the face of Captain Donald as he rode along rigid in the saddle, his feathered dress hat and tight-collared dress jacket adding to his discomfort in the hot sun. Sings Loud rode slightly ahead of the others, haughty, as if she were riding alone and not with them, as if they were following her. At last rolling hills blotted out sight of the Osage town behind them, and Donald breathed a sigh of relief and unbuttoned his dress jacket. He told Sergeant Scot to allow the men the same privilege.

"It's just too damn hot," he said.

"Captain Donald," Bangs called out.

"What is it, Mr. Bangs?" said Donald over his shoulder.

"Release me at once," shouted Bangs. "I demand it."

"Captain," said Krevs, "you want me to shoot him now?"

"Go ahead and untie his wrists," said Donald, "but remind him that we are being followed by a dozen Osage warriors. If they should get the idea that we've set him free, they'll take him back to Iron Head and kill him for sure."

Krevs rode back to the side of Jenkins's horse and drew out his big knife in preparation for the cutting of the ropes that bound the wrists of the traveling medicine man. Bangs pulled away.

"Oh no you don't," he said. "I heard clearly what your captain said. If you were to release me now, those savages would kill me. I'll just pretend a little longer to be your prisoner."

"You sure about that now, Doc?" said Krevs, leaning toward him and reaching out with the knife. "You real good and sure?"

"Get the hell away from me!" Bangs shouted.

"Mr. Krevs," Donald called out.

Krevs sheathed his knife and rode up alongside Donald.

"Mr. Krevs," Donald said, "how much longer do you think they'll follow us?"

"It's hard to say, Captain," Krevs said. "They want us to know that we're being watched. Want to make sure we leave their country and that old Bangs there really is our prisoner. If I had to make a guess, though, I'd guess that when we reach that grassland up ahead, they'll turn around and go home."

"It'll be none too soon," Donald said.

He removed the cockade hat from his head and wiped sweat from his brow with a jacket sleeve. Farther north, he thought, in the Winding Stair Mountains, there must be cool breezes. But here it was blazing hot, and in just a little while, they left the shade of oaks and rode onto the grassland Krevs had mentioned, and there it was even worse. As they hit the open land, though, as the scout had predicted, the Osage riders dropped out of sight.

Out on the prairie, there was no relief from the unrelenting hot sun, so any time they came across small clumps of trees alongside creeks or water holes, Donald called a brief halt for rest in the welcome shade. Nothing was stirring on this hot day except occasional ripples of grass as dry wind blew scorching breath. At last as they neared the Red River, the sun lowered and the heat lessened somewhat. Donald could see cottonwoods and oaks ahead. They would soon be there.

Senator Reddels's entourage was a strange looking one. A small military escort of four mounted cavalrymen and a buggy with a driver and two passengers, it seemed more suited to the streets of Washington City than to the wilds of the Red River country. The wagon that followed along behind appeared to have just happened onto the rest and moved into their tracks. Actually it was a part of the whole. As the retinue hove into Jonesboro, all of the settlers, those who were resident as well as the newcomers in their temporary lodgings, came out to watch. Capitan del Monte gave the senator an official welcome to the settlement.

Bethie Booker watched from the shadow of a doorway until she was certain that there were no Hunikers and there was no Murkens among them. Then she smoothed her dress, put on one of her most coy expressions, and strolled out to meet them. She especially wanted to be introduced to Eva Reddels, for she had heard the rumors of an upcoming marriage between the senator's daughter and Captain Donald. She waited until Mrs. Wright was talking with Eva, then stepped up close and made her presence obvious. Mrs. Wright made the introduction.

"Wouldn't you like to sit in the shade of the porch at the inn," Bethie asked Eva, "and have something cool to drink? It will do you wonders after a long trip on such a hot day."

"Well, yes," said Eva. "Thank you. I would like that."

Seated at one of the outside tables, Eva Reddels fanned herself with an ivory and lace fan from the Orient. Bethie ordered them each a glass of lemonade.

"Mercy," said Eva, "is it always this terribly hot out here?"

"Oh, the nights are sometimes cool," said Bethie, "but during the daytime you'll want to stay inside, out of the sun, but near a window, for the breeze, you know. The store has some nice Betsy straw hats with wide brims, brought out here all the way from New Orleans. They help to keep the sun off, if you absolutely have to go out."

Eva tugged at her sweat-soaked collar.

"I think this ruff collar on my dress is a nuisance out here," she said.

"Oh," said Bethie, "I love your plum silk parasol."

"Mrs. Wright tells me you and your husband come from New England," Eva said.

"Oh yes," said Bethie, "but we don't dare name the town. My father didn't want me to marry Tom. He wanted me to marry someone with money. Why, if Daddy knew where we are now, he'd come after us for sure, and there's no telling what—Oh, he's really a dear, and I love him truly, but he's so . . . Well, goodness gracious, just imagine what your daddy the senator would do if you were to marry a man with no social position."

Eva laughed. "He doesn't pay that much attention to me," she said.

"Oh, I don't believe that," Bethie said. "Anyway, mine did. He spoiled me rotten, I'm afraid. I was the only child, and my daddy wouldn't even let me look at boys."

"Oh?" said Eva, and she sipped her lemonade.

"Oh, there goes Mrs. Henry Stout," Bethie said. "Do you know, she and Henry actually went all the way to Nacogdoches this year? She rode the horse and carried the baby in her arms, and Henry walked ahead of them. Oh, so much is happening at Nacogdoches, you wouldn't believe the excitement. There's a Dr. Long there right now trying to stir up a revolution to take over all of Spanish Texas as his own personal kingdom. So anyway, Henry and Mrs. Stout came back here where it's peaceful."

"I see," said Eva. Mrs. Stout had walked on past and was beyond hearing. "She's just a child herself," Eva said.

"She did marry young," said Bethie. "Henry's about twenty now, and he's strong. They say he got in a fight with a bear, and the bear knocked the gun out of his hands. Henry killed the bear with his knife. Oh, if I was you, I'd hire me a seamstress to take that ruff collar off your dress. It's pretty, but frillies can steam you to death here in Texas."

"Oh, Marie can take care of that for me," said Eva.

"Marie?" said Bethie.

"Oh, pardon me," said Eva. "Marie's my maid. I couldn't travel without her. She's a wonderful hairdresser."

Across the way, under the shade of an oak tree, Tom Booker stood talking with the Reverend Stevenson, and not far from them Senator Reddels was engaged in conversation with Claiborne Wright. Reddels was short and portly and obviously possessed with a powerful sense of his own importance. Across the river, Captain Donald and his company rode into view.

Aboard the *John Hart*, the pilot, Bolt, had seen Donald approaching even earlier than had those in Jonesboro. Surprised that the group was returning from the north, he got the boat steamed up and moved it across to the American side so that the horses and men could board. Then he took them back across to debark at Jonesboro. Donald, having learned that the senator's retinue had arrived before him, stayed in his stateroom for a short while, freshening up.

Back under the oak, Reddels, noting that the soldiers had returned, strained his eyes for a glimpse of Captain Donald.

"Excuse me, sir," he said to Wright. "I have business with the military."

He started to walk toward the boarding planks that ran from the steamer to the dry Texas ground, but just then Cotton Rotison and two of his henchmen came riding hard into town from the west, whooping as they rode, and showing no concern for anyone or anything that might be so unfortunate as to be in their path. Reddels had to jump to the side to avoid being hit by Rotison's big horse. Rotison and the other two men jerked back on their reins at the last possible moment, bringing their steeds to abrupt, skidding halts, throwing dirt and gravel.

Reddels stumbled and fell hard in a cloud of red dust, losing his cigar and his tall beaver hat. A young lieutenant, one of his escorts, came running to his aid, just as Rotison, giving another whoop, pulled a pistol from his belt and fired it into the air. The three prairie pirates dismounted and started to walk into the inn.

"You, sir!" the young lieutenant shouted, drawing out his saber.

Bethie Booker ran to the side of the fallen senator and helped him to his feet. While he harrumphed, she dusted off his clothing. Rotison, at the edge of the porch now, turned quickly, his bulk dwarfing the young officer, his scowl ferocious. The lieutenant stood frozen, sword in hand, feeling and looking foolish. Rotison grinned.

"No harm done, sonny," he said. He turned again to go inside. "Come along, boys," he said, and the two others joined him, all three laughing as they went into the inn. ''Whiskey!'' Rotison shouted from inside.

Walker came off the *John Hart* just in time to witness the episode. It reinforced his already low opinion of Rotison and his entire crew. At the same time, though, he found it amusing to have seen the pompous senator dumped unceremoniously into the street, and, since he himself had the same thought as those three ruffians, he could easily understand the sense of urgency of men in pursuit of whiskey.

He had in his own hand one of the clay-packed gold nuggets from his pouch, and as he walked down the plank, he crushed the clay in his hand. Toward the low end of the plank, he squatted, dipping the nugget into the water to wash it off. Then he proceeded on toward the inn.

Sixteen

Walker strolled past the top-hatted Senator Reddels and Bethie Booker on his way to the inn. He had not seen the senator before, but he had heard of his anticipated arrival, and he knew that this must be the man. He just had the look about him. Walker snorted softly to himself as he stepped through the doorway.

It seemed especially dark inside the inn to Walker, having just come in out of the bright sunlight. He stood still for a moment just inside the doorway, allowing his eyes time to adjust to the darkness. Jones, the innkeeper, was behind his counter. At a table against the wall to Walker's right, Rotison and his two cronies were seated with another man, a man Walker had not seen before, but he was one, Walker noted, that looked right at home with the other ruffians. One of the other two, he thought, was the man who had taken a shot at him back near the crossing, but he couldn't be quite sure of that. A bottle of whiskey sat on the table in their midst. Each man had a tin cup in his hand.

At last Walker moved across the room and carefully placed his gold nugget down on the counter in front of Jones. The storekeeper's eyes lit up at the sight.

"I want a bottle of good whiskey," Walker said.

Jones picked up the nugget tenderly, as if his fingers might mash it, and he examined it closely and lovingly, then placed it on a scale to weigh it.

"You, uh, got any more of these?" he asked. " 'Cause if you do, I'll be glad to change them into cash money for you. Cash money's easier to use, you know. American or Spanish. Your choice."

"I'm a poor man," said Walker, shaking his head. "I just want a bottle of whiskey—and my change, of course."

The man whom Rotison and his companions had joined inside the inn, a thick man with a wild brown beard going to gray and an onion-slick shaved head, watched the proceedings at the counter with keen interest. At last he stood up, slowly and deliberately, and walked over to stand just beside Walker. He leaned over, crowding Walker, to get a better look at the gold nugget.

"This Indian bring that piece of gold in here?" he asked.

"Why, yes, he did," said Jones.

"He trying to get smart with you now?" the other said.

"No," said Jones. "No, there's no trouble here at all. We're just involved in a little business transaction, that's all. Why don't you just go on back over there and sit down."

The man turned to face Walker.

"Where'd you get gold, Indian?" he said.

"Now see here," said Jones, "this is my establishment, and this man is my customer."

"Shut up," said the bully, "I'm talking to the Indian. You kill some poor settler to get this gold? Huh? Where the hell would an Indian get gold? You got any more of that gold on you, Indian?"

Walker reached for the bottle and the change in silver coins that Jones had put on the counter. "If I did have any more gold," he said, "I'd be a damn foolish Indian indeed to admit it to you, wouldn't I?"

He turned and walked out of the store, and the ruffian's face flushed with anger as he watched Walker walking away from him. Rotison burst into raucous laughter.

"The Indians hereabouts are my customers and my friends," said Jones. "I don't want you starting any trouble with them in my place."

"Aw, shit," said the newcomer. "You'd probably sell your own grandmother's ovaries for fish bait, you greedy goddamned bastard. Shit. Doing business with Indians. You sell them guns too? Huh? To use on white men?"

"Now see here—"

"Where the hell'd he get that gold anyway?" the stranger snapped.

Jones shrugged timidly. "I don't know," he said. "A lot of them carry it. Why not? It's better than money. They can use it anywhere. With Americans, French, Spanish. Everyone takes gold. And lots of gold comes up this way from down in Mexico."

The belligerent man stared hard after Walker, and he began to lovingly finger a short version of a cat-o'-nine-tails whip. Cradling the knobbed handle in his right hand, he flicked the weighted ends of the leather thongs in the air. Suddenly he swung it through the air violently, crashing the brutal thongs down hard on top of the counter. Jones jumped back, startled. Even Rotison stopped laughing.

"Come on back over here and sit down," the albino said.

"Goddamned Indian," said the other.

"Hey, there's army all over the goddamned place," said Rotison. "Remember? Come on, Murkens. Sit down and have another drink."

Russ Murkens moved back to the table and dropped heavily into his chair. He still stared at the door as if he would go on through it to follow and overtake Walker. Hardly taking his eyes off the door, he picked up his tin cup and gulped whiskey. Some of it ran down his chin. He put the cup down and swiped at his chin with the sleeve on his left arm.

"I bet he's got more of that gold," he said in a low voice.

Rotison nodded his head slowly. "He might," he said.

"Let me get ahold of him somewhere safe," Murkens said, fondling his whip, "and I'll make him talk. He'll tell me where he's getting that gold. Either that or I'll flay the hide clean off his back with this here cat of mine."

"You be careful now," said Rotison. "You want to go and call attention to yourself around here? Huh? You want to do that? Didn't you tell me that Captain Donald has been looking all over the whole damn country for you? You want to just go out and announce yourself to him? Just go on out there in the street right now, then, and yell out your name. Tell him to come on. You're here."

"Shit," said Murkens. "I'll kill him too one of these days. And it won't be long. But first I want to find out where that fucking little Indian gets his gold."

As Mat Donald walked down the gangplank from the *John Hart*, Eva Reddels spotted him and ran from the porch at the inn to meet him. A scowl darkened Bethie's face as she watched. The embrace was brief and mannerly. After all, they were in a public place with many eyes on them. Senator Reddels trudged along not far behind his daughter, mopping his brow with a handkerchief as he went.

"Mat," said Eva, "how wonderful to see you."

"I'm amazed to see you, Eva," said Donald, "way out here in the wilds. Whatever possessed you to undertake such a trip?"

"Why, to see you, Darling," she said. "But you sound almost disappointed."

"No," said Donald. "No, it's not that. It's just that . . . well, it's great to see you, of course, but I'm just not sure that this is the right place for you to be."

"Mat, my boy," roared the senator, interrupting the conversation in good time for Donald, "how are you?"

"I'm doing well, Senator," said Donald. "The more relevant question is how are you and Eva?"

"Wonderful," said Reddels. "Just great. The entire expedition has been exhilarating. I haven't felt better for years. I have great news for you, my boy. For all of us. Great news."

"Oh?" said Donald.

"The Act of March the Second, which created the Arkansas Territory, you may recall, became effective on July fourth last," the senator said. "We are now standing in Arkansas Territory."

"Excuse me, Senator," said Donald, "but we're on the Spanish Texas side of the river."

Reddels had, of course, already met Capitan del Monte, and he looked quickly around to make sure the Spanish officer was not standing nearby. Then he spoke to Donald in a lower voice.

"Well, just across the river," he said, "is for sure Arkansas Territory. There's no doubt about that. Here where we're standing . . . well, let's just say, right here is in doubt. Boundaries are in dispute, shall we say. Personally, I contend that the United States owns all the land from here to the Sulphur River."

"I see," Donald said.

"Do you realize, Mat," the senator continued, "just exactly what territorial status means? It means a governor, and numerous government jobs. It means that economic opportunities and opportunities for advancement will abound."

"Daddy," Eva said, "Mat doesn't want to talk politics just now."

"Not talk politics, hell," said Reddels. "Everything's politics. But you two young people go on and talk. I'll get out of the way. I need to mix and mingle and talk with the folks here anyhow. Great to see you, son. Great. You're looking good.''

Reddels turned and walked back toward the inn, where small crowds of settlers were gathered. Eva took Donald's arm, and they started to stroll along the riverbank.

"Mat," she said, "I hope you won't think that I'm being too forward."

"What," he said, "by taking my arm?"

"No, silly," she said, "by what I'm about to say to you."

"Were you about to say that we should go aboard the *John Hart* to the privacy of my stateroom?" he asked. "That would be rather forward, I suppose, but I think that I could find it in my heart to forgive it."

"No," she said. "Not that. There's no real privacy here anyway. If we were to go to your stateroom . . ."

"We could close the door," he said.

"And everyone here would know we were in there with the door closed," she said. "And everyone would talk about what we were doing, whether we were doing it or not."

"We would be doing it," he said.

"Besides," she said, "you'd lose all control of yourself and absolutely ruin my coiffure. I remember it well."

"I'd just about forgotten, myself," he said. "It's been so long. I could use a reminder."

"Now stop it," she said, "and pay attention to me. What I have to say is important."

"All right," he said. "You have my undivided attention."

"You know that Daddy has always wanted me to marry well," she said. "I mean, you know, someone in a prominent position."

"Uh, yes," he said. He had hoped that the subject of marriage wouldn't come up so quickly. "I suppose so. I mean, I suppose that's only natural."

"Mat," she said. She stopped walking and turned to look him in the face. "Now pay close attention. Daddy has agreed to recommend you for a high position. Just as soon as our engagement is formally announced, he'll have you released from the Army and appointed secretary to the new governor of the Arkansas Territory.''

So that's what the old bastard was getting at, Donald thought.

"And oh, Darling,'' she continued, "if you still want me, you can say farewell once and for all to these dangerous and tedious patrols. We'll have a fine home and servants and—''

"I'm not a clerk, Eva,'' he said, turning away from her to stare off toward the far side of the river.

"You won't be a clerk,'' she said. "You'll have a score of clerks to do your bidding. You'll be the man nearest the governor, and when the governor goes on trips outside the territory, you'll be the one who'll take his place. You might even wind up being the next governor. Oh, just think of it, Mat. It will be wonderful.''

Donald continued looking away from Eva. He wanted her badly. He told himself that he loved her, but he knew that he wasn't ready to settle down. And certainly not in that way.

"I can't take that job,'' he said. "I'd be no good at it. False smiles and folderol.''

"Mat, do you love me?'' she said.

"Yes,'' he said. "Of course I do. You know I do. I've tried not to love you, but I can't stop it. I dream of you at night. I see your face and hear your voice. I think about you all the time. If that's not loving you, I don't know what is. But I won't ask you to marry me. Not yet. I won't leave this patrol, Eva. Andy Jackson gave me a job to do, and I promised him I'd do my best. I have to stay here.''

"General Jackson can't hold you to that promise,'' she said. "And he wouldn't want you to miss this opportunity. Not if he really cares about your future. Mat, it's the opportunity of a lifetime.''

"Not for me," he said. "I'm a soldier. I'm not a tea sipper or a paper pusher. I won't leave the Army, Eva. It's all I know. It's my whole life."

Eva stood looking down with a pout on her face.

"Daddy's offer is very generous," she said.

"Yes," he said. "I realize that."

"Well, you'd better think it over," she said. "You did . . . enjoy me in Washington. You can have me again just as soon as you start acting sensible."

"I can't change myself, Eva," he said. "If I could, I would for you, but I can't. I am who I am."

Eva stood silent for a moment, her face flushing hot.

"Walk me back to my father?" she said.

"Of course," said Donald.

She took his arm again, but it was formal this time, not warm and loving, he could tell, and as they walked toward the inn, Donald himself began to question his ardently professed love, for he realized that he was mainly bemoaning the very real likelihood that he had just ruined all chances he'd had of getting Eva alone in his stateroom. He admitted to himself then that his main regret was that he had just tossed away a chance at a casual romp in his bed.

Seventeen

That night Captain Donald again had a special dinner served aboard the *John Hart*, but this time not everyone was invited. Senator Reddels and his daughter were the special guests, and Capitan del Monte was also included. Secretly, Donald hoped that the presence of del Monte would temper the senator's bold predictions about the future of Spanish Texas.

Eva made a point of keeping her distance from Donald. He had expected it, and, he admitted to himself, he was more than a bit relieved to find that his expectations had been correct. He wasn't feeling up to any more talk about his future. He was quietly annoyed, though, when he noticed that Eva was, as it appeared to him, flirting with Capitan del Monte. He thought about intruding on their conversation, but then he decided against it. Senator Reddels was alone, and Donald had been waiting for an opportunity to confide in him. He walked over to Reddels's side.

"Good evening, Senator," he said.

"Evening, Mat, my boy," the senator said. He seemed cheerful enough, Donald thought. Eva must not have told him about their conversation beside the river earlier in the day. "Very nice of you to have us aboard," the senator continued. "Very pleasant. Dinner on the river. And your whiskey's good too."

"I'm glad to see that Sergeant Scot has seen to your needs," said Donald.

"Ah yes," said Reddels. "Yes indeed."

"Senator," said Donald, "there's a certain rather touchy matter that I've been wanting to take up with you."

"Ah," said Reddels, "about my daughter?"

"No sir," said Donald. "Not that. Not just now. It's government business."

"Oh?"

"You know that Zeno Bond is out here with a land grant and the intention of establishing a new colony," Donald said.

"Yes, of course," said Reddels. "He'll be the harbinger. Others will follow his example. He's a great man, a great American."

"Yes sir," said Donald. "I'm sure he is. However, he's allowed some questionable frontier types to attach themselves to him, and I'm afraid that he's been misled by them."

"Oh?"

"Instead of settling on his own grant of land, in league with a man called Rotison," Donald continued, "Mr. Bond has seized land that is not his. And it happens to be land that is, well, very special to several tribes of local Indians. If Mr. Bond stays where he is, I'm afraid it will almost certainly mean war and possibly the deaths of a number of colonists. Now, my charge from General Jackson was to maintain the peace out here, and—"

"Mat, my boy," said Reddels, throwing an arm around Donald's shoulders, "I know Andy Jackson, and I'm sure that he told you what he had to tell you at the time. So let's not worry just now about what old Andy said.''

''But sir—''

''Now Zeno Bond,'' the senator continued, ''let's talk about Zeno just a minute.''

''Yes sir.''

''Zeno is a great American hero,'' the senator said. ''One of the shining stars of the American Revolution. A patriot in our War for Independence from the tyranny of Great Britain. An illustrious and shining example of the pioneering spirit that has already made our young country great.''

''But sir,'' said Donald, ''Mr. Bond has a grant of land. He should settle there. Instead, he has chosen an entirely different location, miles from the place where he can legally settle.''

''A small matter,'' said Reddels. ''It can be fixed.''

''I'm afraid that won't satisfy the Indians,'' Donald said. ''Chief Iron Head of the Osage told me just yesterday that if I fail to move the settlers from his land, he'll kill every one of them.''

''Now, Mat,'' the senator said, the look on his face stern, ''that's precisely the sort of thing you can't allow. I know you have a small troop out here, but you are in charge of U.S. forces in this region—for now, at least. And you can't allow a savage Indian to intimidate the Army of the United States of America.

''If the Indians, Osage or any other,'' Reddels said, ''dare to harass Zeno Bond and his colony of American settlers, then you must protect those settlers with all the power at your command. I'm sure that you could muster a good many civilian volunteers from right here in Jonesboro to bolster your forces, if need be.''

''Yes sir,'' said Donald. ''I know I could. They've already volunteered themselves, but that's not the point.''

''That's exactly the point,'' Reddels snapped back. ''Our country is marching west, and men like Zeno Bond are leading the way. You see that he's kept safe from the savages if you have to wipe out every savage in the whole damned region. Now, that's enough of that. Let's change the subject. I want you to prepare quarters for me and Eva and her maid here aboard the *John Hart*. Oh yes, and Mrs. Booker will be joining us as well. Can you see to that, Mat?"

"Mrs. Booker has a home and a husband in Jonesboro," Donald said.

"We'll be heading for Zeno Bond's settlement first thing in the morning," Reddels said, "and she's expressed an interest in the project to me. I told her she could come along."

"Without her . . . husband?" Donald asked.

"Her husband wasn't mentioned," said Reddels.

"Then you'll all be staying aboard tonight?"

"Yes," said Reddels. "If it's quite convenient."

Donald thought that it was not at all convenient, but he could tell that Reddels was already becoming irritable with him. He figured he'd pushed his luck with the senator about as far as it would go. Goddamn a politician, he thought.

"It might not be very comfortable, sir," said Donald, "especially for the ladies. I have livestock aboard, you know."

"I don't think you'll need the horses, Mat," the senator said. "My own mounted escort will follow along on the riverbank."

"I see," said Donald. "Well, I'll, uh, I'll get Sergeant Scot right on it, sir."

Dinner was served just then, and Donald found it a welcome interruption. He did manage to collar Scot while everyone was still eating and inform him of the senator's plans.

"It will take some shuffling around of the crew members and of the men, sir," Scot said.

"Just do the best you can, Sergeant," Donald said.

"Yes sir," Scot said. "So we'll need a room for the senator, one for Miss Reddels and her maid, and another for Mrs. Booker. Is that right, sir?''

''That's correct, Sergeant,'' Donald said. ''And leave the horses at pasture, but bring Krevs's damned old mule with us.''

''The mule, sir?''

''You heard me right,'' Donald said. As Scot left to carry out his orders, Donald thought, *There's going to be trouble now for sure. Reddels is a stubborn fool and will never back down. With him on their side now, neither will Rotison and Bond. And to top it all off, old Iron Head is every bit as stubborn as they are.*

He ate the rest of his meal mostly in silence and in deep thought. He muttered brief replies to any questions or statements spoken directly to him. Among other things, he was mulling over the practicalities of an unconventional idea he'd heard proposed once by another officer regarding the use of a mule in combat. He didn't know if it had ever yet been tried, but he thought that he might just get the opportunity to experiment with it on this trip—especially if his dire premonitions turned out to be accurate.

Just as Donald was finishing his meal, he noticed a Spanish soldier come aboard and report quietly to del Monte. The soldier then left, and del Monte beckoned Scot. Scot, in turn, moved over to whisper in Donald's ear.

''Capitan del Monte would like a few words in private with you, sir,'' he said, ''at your convenience.''

Donald poured himself another whiskey and pushed his chair back from the table to stand. He walked over to the soldier who was serving the table and got the wine bottle. Carrying the bottle to where del Monte waited, Donald filled the capitan's glass.

''Join me for a quiet drink?'' he said.

Del Monte stood up and picked up his glass.

''Thank you,'' he said, and the two young captains walked away from the crowd to stand alone near the rail on the port side of the steamer. Donald thought that he would chide del Monte for the earlier scene with Eva, but del Monte spoke first.

"Mat," he said, "I'll be leaving in the morning with my entire force for the Sulphur River."

"What's up?" Donald asked.

"I have just now received a message that your countryman, Dr. Long, has seized Nacogdoches," del Monte said. "His intention, apparently, is to take over all of Texas as his personal empire. I've been ordered to take my command and help gouge him out of there."

"I'm sorry to hear that, Rey," said Donald, heaving a sigh, "but I'm not really surprised."

"Your own army should have stopped him before he ever left the jurisdiction of the United States," del Monte said. "This sort of thing is very bad for relations between our two countries."

"I'm sorry, Rey," said Donald. "I really am."

"Oh, I'm not angry with you, amigo," del Monte said, "but your leaders who permit and even encourage land pirates such as this Dr. Long are disgraceful."

Donald shot a glance in the direction of Senator Reddels, and said, "I couldn't agree more. I've got one of them right here with me now, and I'm afraid that he's going to cause some problems before he's gone."

"This Dr. Long," del Monte continued, "has with him four hundred men. He promises each so-called soldier in his mob ten sections of land and such loot as they can scavenge along the way."

"That's a lot of land," Donald said, "but I'm sure you'll stop him."

"Si, amigo, but not, I fear, without some loss of life," del Monte said. "Madmen! We will kill them, of course, but when will the madness end? How many must be killed because of these land-grabbing promoters?"

Donald shook his head.

"I don't know, my friend," he said. "I just don't know." And he thought about Zeno Bond and Senator Reddels and the whole notion of the Manifest Destiny of the United States. He wondered what role he himself might eventually be forced to play in this relentless, sweeping pageant. He wanted the adventure. He craved the glory, but, he asked himself for the first time in his life, at what cost?

"Ah well," del Monte said, "I'll take my men with me in the morning, and we'll join others at the Sulphur River and see what we can do against this bold invader."

"Rey," said Donald, "I know this Dr. Long is an American, but he's a criminal, and you're my friend. I wish you success, and I hope to see you safely back here soon."

Del Monte suddenly changed his mood. He smiled broadly at Donald and slapped him on the shoulder.

"I'll be back before you know it," he said, "for I have a mission here too. Since you refuse to do it, I must get Señora Bethie Booker in my bed before she goes crazy with desire. Her Tom is not doing his job, it seems."

Just then Sergeant Scot made a sudden appearance.

"Pardon the interruption, sirs," he said, "but Sings Loud just came aboard."

"Ah, that one," said del Monte. "She's another reason I must return. I have much unfinished business with her too."

"What does she want?" Donald said.

"She heard we're going upstream in the morning," said Scot, "and she wants to ride along. She says she has urgent business that way."

"Put her in the cabin with Mrs. Booker," Donald said.

"Yes sir," said Scot, and he turned to carry out the order. Del Monte broke into a good-natured laugh.

"Good, amigo," he said. "They'll scratch out each other's eyes. On second thought, that will be very convenient. Keep them together like that for me if you can. I'll hurry back now for sure."

Eighteen

It was midnight, and the quarter moon in the big sky over-head painted the world white with black shadows. Majesti-cally silver in a powder-blue sky, it topped dark waves with light and frosted the tops of buildings and of the steamboat rocking idly there on the waters of the Red River.

Walker lay still at the water's edge. Waves sloshing the bank nearby washed over his empty bottle and reached out toward his motionless form. His miraculously unbroken eye-glasses lay just beside his head.

An old red hound ambled out from the transient camp, and, sniffing blood, moved to inspect the still form there on the riverbank. It snuffled at Walker's bloody scalp and face. It whimpered. Walker stirred just a bit. He rolled over on his back slowly and raised his left arm, pointing accusingly at the stars above. He fought against gray nausea, felt in-credibly light, disembodied even, and then he drifted back into the world of nowhere.

An owl hooted deep in the woods south of the river, as

Corporal David Alan walked toward the gangplank, returning to the boat after an evening of courting in the settlement. The sound of Alan's footsteps crunching sand and gravel seemed to fill the still night air. He stepped up on the low end of the long plank, about to board, and he heard the whimper of the hound.

He stopped, stood still, and looked around. Then he saw the hound, and he saw that it was snuffling at something there on the bank. He stared a moment. It appeared to be a human form, prone at the edge of the water. Deciding to investigate, Alan walked toward the shape. He could soon see that it was indeed a human form.

"Go on. Get," he snarled at the dog, and it ran away, its tail between its legs. Alan moved closer, and he recognized Walker. He saw the bottle being washed by the river's waves. "Drunk," he said. He squatted and picked up the bottle, taking a sniff. The smell of whiskey was still strong. He tossed it out into the river, turned, and looked at Walker. He thought about leaving him there. It would serve him right, he thought, but he recalled that Walker seemed to be a special friend of Captain Donald.

He could pretend that he had never seen the man, he told himself, and he started to stand, but just then, he noticed in the moonlight that something was wrong. He squinted. He moved closer. He saw the blood on Walker's face. He touched Walker's shoulder, gingerly at first, then more firmly.

"Sir," he said. "Sir, are you all right?"

Walker stirred and moaned.

"Sir, is anything wrong?" Alan asked.

Walker's eyelids moved slightly, trying to open, allowing him to see through tiny slits the tall, dark leather cap with the cockade, the linen vest with leather stock rising around the neck. At last he recognized the face of Corporal Alan.

"I'll live to drink again," he said in a weak voice. "Will you take me to Captain Donald?"

*   *   *

At the inn only one table was in use. Chairs had been stacked on other tables for the night, and Jones, the innkeeper, dozed on a quilt-covered couch. Cotton Rotison, Murkens, and Joe Ranik had been joined at their table by Socrates Bangs. Murkens was surly, pouting. He swung an arm out and slapped at the bottle on the table.

"Give me that bottle," he slurred. Grasping it just in time, he lifted it and found that it was empty. "Damn," he said.

"I'll get another one," said Ranik, and he got himself to his feet and staggered toward the bar.

"The little bastard had some gold," Murkens muttered. "I seen it, all right."

"You seen one lousy nugget," said Rotison. "That's all. Maybe that's all he ever had. And keep your voice down, will you? It's bad enough you went and done what you done. Don't be talking about it."

"Hell," said Murkens. "He's just a damned Indian. Who cares?"

"The goddamned Captain cares, that's who," Rotison said. "That Walker's his pet Indian. I told you about that. And I told you we don't want no trouble here in Jonesboro. Not just yet anyhow."

Ranik returned with a bottle, and Murkens snatched it away from him, refilling his own cup and spilling a quantity in the process.

"Shit," he said. "Pet Indian. I know the son of a bitch has more gold."

"Did you go through his pockets, Russ?" asked Ranik.

"Indians don't have pockets, you dumb shit," Murkens scoffed. He reached inside his shirt and pulled out a small leather pouch which he tossed out on the table. "I searched him all right. This is all I found."

"What is it?" Ranik asked, reaching for it.

Rotison slapped Ranik's hand and picked up the pouch.

He pulled it open and spilled its contents, Walker's clay-packed gold nuggets, out onto the table.

"Clay marbles," said Murkens. "That's all."

"Hell," said Rotison. "What'd you keep the damn thing for?"

Murkens shrugged. "I don't know," he said.

"Marbles?" said Ranik.

Socrates Bangs wrinkled his nose. He picked up one of the "marbles" and rolled it absentmindedly between his fingers.

"The Indian has gold hidden somewhere," he said. "You say he bought whiskey with a gold nugget. You should have followed him to his hiding place instead of beating him half to death."

"I followed him for awhile all right," Murkens protested. "He didn't go nowhere."

"Say, wait a minute," Bangs said. He looked down at the clay-wrapped nugget in his hand. "This is awfully heavy clay, don't you think?"

Rotison grabbed one of the clay balls up from the tabletop, as did Murkens and Ranik.

"Let's see," said Rotison.

"It is heavy," said Ranik. "What kind of clay you reckon that is?"

"Shut up," said Rotison. He stared at the clay ball in the palm of his hand. Then he raised his hand, flipped it over, and slapped it down hard on the tabletop. Slowly he moved his hand to reveal the gold nugget there in the middle of pieces of cracked clay. He smiled. He chuckled. The others began to chuckle with him.

"Gold clay," Rotison said. "That's what kind of clay. Gold clay."

The chuckling turned to happy laughter, until Socrates Bangs managed to shush everyone.

"Stop it," he said. "Stop. We have to keep this quiet."

"He's right," said Rotison, shooting a sideways glance

141

at Jones over on the couch. Everyone got very quiet then, and Jones suddenly snored into the silence. Rotison relaxed a little, but when he spoke next, it was with a low voice. "Keep it quiet. Joe, did you say that this is the same little Indian you took a shot at down by Buffalo Crossing?"

"Well, Cotton," said Ranik, "you know, one Indian looks pretty much like another one to me, and he did startle me jumping up like that, but, well, yeah, I think it was the same one."

"Yeah," Rotison said. "And I think that was him we seen up on top of the hill too. The river crossing and the hill. Now what do you reckon he was doing up on top of that hill?"

"He has a gold mine there," said Bangs, his eyes glittering with the thought. "You men were fools to split up with old Zeno Bond. He's got control of the hill now. The crossing too."

"Watch who you're calling fools, Bangs," said Rotison, glaring at him. "There was good cause. Too many new settlers came in to join up with him, and we lost control. That's why."

"My apologies, Mr. Rotison," said Bangs. "I was just, uh, overly excited, shall we say, at the thought of the gold mine on the hill."

"You really think there's a mine on that hill?" Murkens asked.

"Well," Bangs said, "the Osages have gold. I saw it. I didn't think too much of it at the time. I just thought that it was Mexican gold. But now we know that this Cherokee has been on the hill, and he too had gold. They say that the hill is a special place to the Indians. They all go there."

"And they've all got gold," Rotison concluded. "It must be."

"Tell me," said Bangs, "is Zeno Bond's colony well supplied? Could he hold out against a strong Indian attack?"

Rotison laughed out loud. "He's an old fool," he said, "and he's a sitting duck."

"Do you have enough men to take the place away from him?" Bangs asked.

"I could round up enough," said Rotison, "but it takes supplies. Food and powder and bullets. And that takes money. Have you got money, Bangs?"

"No," said Bangs. "Of course not. The damnable Osages confiscated everything I own."

"Well, let's see now," Rotison said, scrunching up his face in deep thought. "There's lots of pilgrims comes this way and lots of swamp where bodies can disappear. 'Course, that would take time. Maybe we could just jump his claim."

"You mean just openly attack?" said Bangs.

"Sure," said Rotison. "We could take him. His supplies would be enough to get us started with, hold us out till we grab up all the gold and get out with it."

"Oh, Mr. Rotison," said Bangs, "obviously you know nothing about mining."

"Why?" said Rotison. "What's wrong?"

"It takes work and patience to get gold out of the ground," Bangs said. "It takes planning. Sometimes it takes water sluices. The gold might be in nuggets, or it might be scattered around in small bits. Whatever form it's in, we want to get it all. It might take years. We'll have to fight off Indians. We'll have to set up a permanent operation."

"Who made you the skipper of this outfit?" Murkens said menacingly.

"I'm the king of this hill, Russ," said Rotison, "and I'm telling you to listen to the doc. He's right. He knows what he's talking about. We have to go quiet and careful. If there's a gold mine up there on that hill, it could make us all rich men."

"We kill old Bond?" Murkens asked.

143

"Carefully," said Bangs. "There are many ways a man can die."

"Accidental like," said Rotison. "And then we bury him with tears in our eyes, out in the open in front of everybody, with Dr. Bangs here preaching a sermon over him. We act like good citizens from here on out. We don't want the Army coming after us."

Socrates Bangs chuckled. "If you do this like I tell you," he said, "the Army will actually have to protect us. We'll let them kill the Indians for us."

"You see what I mean, you slobs?" Rotison said. "Listen to the doc here. We're going to be respectable citizens. Rich, respectable citizens."

"I have to go piss," said Murkens, and he stood and staggered to the back door of the inn. Rotison scooped up the gold nuggets from the tabletop and returned them to the pouch. Suddenly the front door of the inn was thrown open, and Mat Donald stepped in, followed by Sergeant Scot and two troopers. Donald held a pistol in his hand. Scot and the troopers each held a rifle at the ready. The room was dark, lit by only one candle on the table. Donald saw the pouch on the table in the dim light.

"I'll take that pouch," he said.

"What's the meaning of this?" demanded Bangs.

"That pouch was stolen from a friend of mine," Donald said.

Bangs picked up the pouch casually.

"This?" he said. "Why, it's nothing. Some clay beads or marbles or something. That's all. Why would anyone steal such a thing? As a matter of fact, Mr. Ranik here found the pouch on the ground outside the inn. We have no idea to whom it may belong."

"It belongs to Mr. Walker," said Donald, stepping in close and taking the pouch from Bang's hand. "I'll see that it's returned to him."

"I saw that drunken Indian staggering around out there,"

said Rotison. "Likely he dropped it. Then I guess the drunken fool accused us of stealing it from him."

"Besides, Captain," said Bangs, "we're in Spanish Texas. You have no authority here."

"Right now I have the authority of these guns," said Donald. "Any of you feel like putting it to the test?"

Rotison shrugged. "If that there pouch belongs to your little old Indian friend," he said, "give it back to him. Hell. No harm's done. We're all good citizens here." He shot Bangs a meaningful look.

The back door opened, but Murkens saw the soldiers and stopped still, the door only cracked. He lurked in the darkness just outside, watching. Donald hesitated a moment, wishing he could do more, but he knew he had no authority, and he had no proof. Walker had not been able to identify his assailant, and Ranik could have picked the pouch up off the ground.

"Let's go," he said, and he and the soldiers left the inn. Murkens slipped back inside quietly and rejoined the others. All of them glared at the door.

"When can I kill him?" Murkens asked.

Nineteen

The little but crowded settlement of Jonesboro was bustling the next morning as it had never bustled before. The soldiers and the boat crew of the *John Hart* were busy getting ready to be underway. Groups of settlers were making ready to move north or west, some were even planning on southerly moves. Captain Donald's none-too-welcome passengers, Senator Reddels and his daughter and Bethie Booker, all having spent the night aboard the steamer, were disembarking for a final taste of dry land and a quick shopping spree before the actual journey upriver.

Reddels, Eva, and Bethie all went into the store, Bethie to buy a new hat. She had decided at the last moment that she needed an extra. She paid for her hat and left the store before the others. As she was walking back toward the boat, Cotton Rotison stepped out from around a corner to confront her. He whipped the slouch hat off his head and held it in both hands over his chest.

"Beg pardon, Mrs. Booker," he said, his voice low and

confidential. "I hear tell you're going down the river today with the senator."

"I don't believe we've been introduced," said Bethie.

"The name's Rotison, ma'am," he said, "and I ain't got time for the niceties. Besides, I think you know who I am. The way I see things is like this: Old Zeno Bond has got hold of some land that ain't his by rights. Captain Donald's going to try to kick him off it. The senator'll likely side with Bond, but I'd like to hedge that bet somewhat."

"Whatever are you getting at, Mr. Rotison?" Bethie asked.

"I want to see that Bond's colony stays put right where it's at," said Rotison. "I got a good reason. And I figure you've got some influence with the senator. You help us make sure that the senator sees things our way, and I'll see that it's worth your while. You can count on that, little lady. You got my word."

"You certainly don't have the appearance to me of a man of means," Bethie said. "Just how, if you don't mind me asking so bold a question, do you intend to make it worth my while?"

Rotison heaved an exasperated sigh and looked furtively around to make sure no one else was near enough to overhear what he had to say.

"Mrs. Booker," he whispered, "there's gold on that hill out there, and I've got a plan to get at it. You help me out, and you'll come in for a nice share. Are you with me now?"

Bethie hesitated a moment, as long as she dared. It sounded like the opportunity of a lifetime.

"I'll see what I can do," she said.

"And I'll see you later," said Rotison, "out at the colony."

Down at the far end of the street, Captain Mat Donald approached a scraggly group of would-be settlers who appeared to be making ready to move out.

147

"Where are you folks headed?" he asked.

"Zeno Bond's colony," said one, a scrappy looking man in his early thirties with patches in his clothes.

"Listen to me," said Donald. "All of you. Zeno Bond is going to have to move his colony. He can't stay where he is right now. I strongly urge all of you to wait here until Mr. Bond is properly located before moving your families and all your personal effects. If you go out there now, you'll only have to move them again. I'm on my way out there myself today to move him out."

"We ain't waiting, Captain," the scrappy man shouted from the crowd.

"Mister," said Donald, "I'm asking you politely and for your own good to wait awhile longer. Just a little while. Right now, Zeno Bond and the others with him are out there on Indian land."

"Me and the wife has got five kids, Captain," the man said. "We got to get our cabin built before winter sets in so they'll have proper shelter. Hell, we're living here in a tent with holes in it. We have to get wood cut now, so it'll be seasoned proper and seal up right. We talked all this over with Mr. Rotison, and he's ready to take us out there now."

"Rotison is a renegade," said Donald. "He'll tell you anything for his own purposes, and Bond does not own that land. He'll have to be moved. I'm sorry, but that's the way it is."

"Hell, Captain, we ain't scared of no Indians," the man said. "Maybe you and the Army are, but we ain't. Mr. Rotison says that nobody shouldn't ought to let Indians scare them off of good land."

"Captain," said a worn looking woman standing beside the man, "my man don't mean to be rude with you, but we have to get settled for the sake of our children. You understand."

Donald looked at the woman and at the five hungry looking children huddled there around their parents. He looked around the crowd. There were other families there too. All of them had desperate looks on their faces. Damn these entrepreneurs and land pirates, he thought. Damn all politicians and speculators.

"It's for the sake of your children," he said, "that I have to keep you away from the crossing. I've told you why. I mean to see that Zeno Bond moves his settlement to the proper location, the land that the government assigned him. Now you can wait here as I suggest, or you can be turned back later. Good day to you."

As Donald turned to walk away from the small but now hostile crowd, he could sense their hatred toward him building up, and his face flushed hot. Then he noticed Bethie and Tom walking toward the boat, Tom loaded down with supplies. Wondering what the hell they were up to now, he hurried to catch up with them.

"Tom," he said, panting just a little from his trot, "I didn't know you were going with us."

"I wasn't planning to," Tom said, "but Bethie wants us to join up with the Zeno Bond settlement."

"Kind of sudden, isn't it?" Donald asked, looking at Bethie.

Bethie gave a coy shrug. "Come on, Tom," she said.

"This isn't the right time, Tom," said Donald.

Tom hesitated, looking from Donald to Bethie.

"Senator Reddels thinks different," said Bethie.

Just then Reddels puffed up beside them.

"Mr. Booker," he said, "Mrs. Booker. Good. Let's get aboard. It'll be time to shove off soon. Good morning, Mat."

Reddels and the Bookers hustled up the ramp and boarded the boat, as Donald stood watching them. "Damn," he said. He glanced back toward the inn, and there he saw Bangs, Rotison, and Ranik leaning casually against the front wall. They were looking in his direction and grinning.

"The captain don't look too happy this morning," said Ranik.

"He don't know the half of his troubles to come," Bangs said.

"Cotton," said Ranik, "what if the Booker gal double-crosses you?"

"When I get her out there at the crossing," said Rotison, "I'll get rid of that sissy husband of hers and show her what a real man can do. She'll stick with me, all right. Besides, she's a greedy little bitch. I can tell that about her. She'll come across."

"Well, all right then, but what if she can't swing old Senator Reddels over to our way of looking at things?" Ranik asked. "What if she can't do that no matter how hard she tries?"

"Then we'll offer him some of the gold too," Rotison said.

"You mean bribe him?" Ranik asked.

"Hell, he's a senator, ain't he?" said Rotison. "Ain't that what you're supposed to do with a senator?"

Ranik shrugged.

"We have to be real careful," said Bangs, "but at the same time, we can't drag our feet neither. That old heathen Iron Head gave Donald an ultimatum. If whites are still at the crossing when buffalo killing time gets here, then he's going to attack. Donald wants to get the whites out of there before then."

"He ain't got but fifteen soldier boys out here," said Rotison.

"He could send for reinforcements out of Natchitoches," said Ranik. "Couldn't he?"

"Not in time," Rotison said. "By the time he could get in his request for help, old Reddels could get to Andy Jackson, and who do you think old Andy's going to listen to anyhow?"

"What we have to do, gentlemen," said Socrates Bangs,

"is prevent Captain Donald from convincing Bond to move, and then when Donald is out of the way, take control of the colony away from Bond. Then we'll have the leisure to find the gold and to start mining it. It's that simple."

"What about when the Indians attack?" Ranik said.

"Don't worry about that. We'll be ready for them," said Rotison.

They stood there watching as the *John Hart*'s stacks began to belch smoke and Captain Mat Donald boarded the boat. Crewmen pulled the planks aboard, and soon the steamer was chugging its way west, headed for Buffalo Crossing. Russ Murkens stepped out of the inn to stand beside Rotison.

The scruffy settler who had been arguing with Donald earlier came walking over to the inn. He stopped in front of Rotison.

"That Captain Donald told us we can't go out there," he said. "He told us that Bond is going to have to move his settlement anyhow. He said he'd keep us away from that place."

"Don't you pay no mind to that upstart captain," Rotison said. "There's a U.S. senator on that boat too, and me and him has an understanding. That captain is just being picky because old Bond's paperwork ain't quite right, but the senator's going to make it right, and the captain's going to be looking for another job. Trust me."

"Then we're going?" the man asked.

"You get everybody loaded up and mounted up," said Rotison. "We'll be heading out in ten minutes."

The man turned and ran back toward where his family and the others were waiting. Rotison spoke to Murkens without turning to look at him.

"I'd say you can go on ahead and kill that damned meddling Donald just anytime now," he said.

Murkens grinned and went back through the door to the inn.

"Come on," said Rotison. "Let's get this thing going." He started walking toward the anxious, waiting settlers. Bangs and Ranik followed.

The day was damnably hot, and the mood aboard the *John Hart* was tense. Bethie Booker pouted because she had been assigned a room with Sings Loud. Tom was to sleep on the deck with the crew. She didn't care about that, but she had thought that she would have a private room, and she especially didn't want to have to share one with "some old squaw." Reddels grumbled about the heat and kept calling for whiskey. Eva stayed in her room with her maid. Donald did everything he could to avoid any direct contact with Senator Reddels, with Eva, or with Bethie. Other than all that, the first day out on the river was mercifully uneventful.

When darkness came at last, it brought little relief from the heat, but it did bring the journey to a halt. The boat was tied up for the night. Captain Donald went to his room alone, grateful for the opportunity for privacy, closed the door, and stripped himself completely naked because of the almost unbearable heat. He stretched out on his bed, trying to relax and looking out at the full moon through the small open porthole across the room to his left. The boat drifted, tugging at its ropes, and a slight breeze wafted through the tiny porthole. It wasn't enough to do any real good.

In spite of the heat and all the problems on board and those he knew he would face ahead at the crossing, Donald found himself thinking about Eva. He longed for her embrace, but he would not leave the army for her. He still questioned what he had thought was his undying love for her, hesitant still to write it off as nothing more than animal lust. Perhaps, he thought, he really did love her after all, but he just didn't love her quite enough.

A river bird called from somewhere downstream. A panther yowled off in the distance, and great horned owls hooted from woods on the American side of the river. The

John Hart swayed gently in the drought-lowered waters of the Red River, and Donald recalled with a sense of irony the heavy rain they had endured on their trip in from Natchitoches. That seemed like it had been ages ago. Then he heard something stir among the cottonwoods on shore, and he sat upright for a moment. Then he lay back down. It was probably just some animal scurrying around out there. Anyway, there were men on watch on deck.

The breeze faded, and in the momentary stillness, Donald heard light footsteps just outside his door. Twisting on the bed, he reached quickly for the Model 1811 North and Cheney pistol hanging in its holster just beside the bed. He clutched the handle and eased the pistol out. It was quiet again, and he wondered if he had only imagined the sound. He sat still in his bed, listening, the pistol cocked and ready in his hand.

Twenty

There was a clacking sound in the night air as someone lifted the latch to Donald's cabin door. He fingered the flint on his pistol with his left hand to make sure it was still in place, as he eared back the double-necked hammer with his right thumb.

"Who's there?" he said.

"Don't shoot. It's only me," said Bethie, stepping in and shutting the door quietly behind herself. Donald sat dumbfounded for a moment, just long enough to give Bethie's eyes time to adjust to the change in light. "My," she said, "just look at you." She giggled, as Donald, suddenly realizing the full situation, jerked a sheet around himself. He still held the cocked pistol in his right hand. "Silly," she said, "why don't you put that pistol away? Are you going to shoot me?"

"I might have," Donald said. "I ought to. What do you mean walking in here in the middle of the night unannounced like that?"

"Did you want me to tell someone to announce me?" she asked coyly. "I could do that. Then everyone would know that I was coming here to see you in the night."

"No," he said. "I mean, yes, you should be announced before coming to see me, but no, you shouldn't have come in the middle of the night like this. Now go on back to your room, please."

She walked toward him, and he could see that she wasn't dressed. Not really. She wore a flimsy gown, and he could easily see the outline of her body beneath it. She walked across the room and sat beside him on his bed.

"Well," she said, leaning toward him to make sure that he had a good look at her pointed young breasts, "either go ahead and shoot me or put it away."

Careful to hold the sheet around him with his left hand, Donald turned and shoved the pistol back into its holster. In his nervous situation, he neglected to ease the hammer back down.

"Mrs. Booker," he said.

"I'm not Mrs. Booker," she said. "Not really. Remember?"

"Well, Bethie," he said. "You shouldn't be here."

"I couldn't sleep," she said. "And that . . . woman you put into my room snores. Besides, I need to talk to you."

She put a hand on Donald's bare shoulder, and he gulped hard. If she was trying to arouse him, she was doing a good job of it. He was glad that the sheet covered up the surefire, telltale sign of her success, which was rising up down below.

"What—What do you want to talk about?" he stammered.

She scooted closer to him and slid her arm around his shoulders. Her breasts pressed into his side. Donald felt himself going hot all over, as she whispered so close to the side of his face that he felt her breath against his cheek.

"It can wait," she said. She put her other hand on the

side of his face and turned his head toward her, then kissed him full on the lips. Donald's arms went around her in spite of his better judgment and his moral code. After all, his brain raced, she was not really a married woman. And Eva had as much as told him that he would not again get her in his bed until he had resigned from the Army. He had responded to her that he would not leave the Army. Therefore, though neither one of them had come right out and said it, things were over between them.

And here was Bethie in all her youthful female loveliness offering it all to him. She had come to him, ready and willing, more than that, anxious. He reached for a ripe breast and mashed it in his hand as their tongues probed each other's mouths. Bethie pulled back.

"Just a minute, Captain," she said, and she quickly stood and wriggled out of the gown, letting it drop to the floor. Donald didn't have time to drink in the sight of her, for she was back beside him on the bed in an instant. He threw the sheet back, and their bodies were pressed together. They were kissing again, and her hand slid down his chest and belly, and farther. "Oh, my," she said. "You didn't really want me to leave at all, now did you?"

Donald lay on his back, spent, exhausted, staring at the ceiling of his cabin. Bethie was beside him. God, he thought, she was good. Much better than anything he had ever had before. She had done things to him and with him that the snooty Eva had never done, probably would not do. His thoughts were really muddled now. He wondered if he could love Bethie. He knew that he could have a hell of a good time with her.

She wasn't at all like Eva. She would be able to take life with a soldier, adventures in the West. She wouldn't be after him to become a secretary to a goddamned governor. But what would they do about Tom? Even though Tom wasn't really her husband, she had brought Tom out here. She had tricked the poor man, and now, it seemed, there was no turning back for him. But Bethie was really something. That much was sure. She purred and turned on her side, kissing him on the cheek. He reached for her, but she suddenly sat up.

"Now we can talk," she said.

"Oh," he said, "well, yes, of course."

"Why are you so dead set against Zeno Bond's colony?" she asked.

Donald stammered. The question was totally unanticipated. It seemed abrupt and thoroughly out of place. It wasn't really a subject he wanted to discuss, especially naked and in bed with a naked woman. He tried to clear his head and gather his thoughts.

"I'm not against it," he said. "The man has a legitimate grant of land, and he's located his colony in the wrong place. That's all."

"Oh," she said, leaning over and tickling the hairs on his chest with a finger, "what difference does it make just where he's located? There's room out there for the whole world."

"It makes a great deal of difference to the Osages and other Indian tribes," Donald said.

"Well, just who the hell cares what they think?" she said. "Mat, I'm joining up with Mr. Bond's colony. This is important to me. Don't you care about that?"

"Bethie," he said, "Andy Jackson sent me out here to keep the peace, and the only way I can do that is to keep settlers off of Indian land."

"Well, if you listen to the Indians, it's all their land, ain't it?" she said.

"Well, I—"

"Well, ain't it?" she said. "What do you want anyway, Captain Mat Donald? You want everyone in the whole land to pack up and move back to England or Ireland or wherever they come from?"

"No, Bethie," Donald said. "That's not the point. There's nothing I can do about what's in the past. And really, what I have to do now has nothing to do with how I might feel about anything. I have my orders. That's all."

"Well, orders can be changed, can't they?" she said.

"Of course they can," he said. "It happens all the time."

"Well, I have it on very good authority," she said, "that your orders are going to be changed. So that's not a problem, now is it? Why don't you just sit quiet and wait then until that happens?"

"Until my orders are changed," he said, "I have to act on the orders I have."

"Oh," she said, "you're so exasperating. Maybe you really are afraid of the Indians like Mr. Rotison says."

"Have you been talking to that lying renegade?" he said, sitting up and glaring at her.

"He's not a renegade," she said. "He's a pioneer, and he's a real man too."

Donald sat up straight and slapped his own head with both hands. "God, Bethie," he said. She flounced away from him, dropping her legs over the edge of the bed and putting her feet on the floor. Suddenly she let out a short, startled scream.

"Look out!" she said.

Donald looked and saw a face at the open porthole, a bearded face and a shaved head. As the man at the porthole poked a hand clutching a pistol into the room, Donald grabbed Bethie and rolled them both off onto the floor. The pistol flashed in the darkness and roared out in the small cabin. The sound blasted eardrums, bounced and echoed, and the acrid smell of gunpowder filled the air.

Donald scrambled to his feet and grabbed for his own pistol, but just as he turned to fire, the face at the porthole vanished, and Donald fired the already cocked pistol too soon, burying the lead uselessly in the wall beside the porthole.

"Damn," he said.

There was shouting and the pounding of running feet outside on the decks. There was a loud splash and the sudden bark of rifle fire. "Over there," someone shouted. There was the noise of rapid hoofbeats and of something large crashing through the cottonwoods and willows on the riverbank, and there was another rifle shot.

Donald hastily pulled on his trousers, as someone pounded on his cabin door. Bethie scooted her naked self under the bed.

"Captain," Sergeant Scot bellowed just outside the door.

Donald glanced down to make sure that Bethie was hidden. He stepped over and jerked open the door. Scot was standing there wide-eyed with a lantern in one hand and a pistol in the other.

"It's all right, Mr. Scot," he said. "The man missed me. Did he get away?"

"He jumped overboard, sir," Scot said. "He must have had a horse waiting. Corporal Burns got off a shot, and I did too, but I don't think we hit anything. What happened here, sir?"

"He shot at me through the porthole," said Donald. "A man with a beard and a shaved head. I never saw him before that I know of."

"I seen one like that in Jonesboro once," said Scot.

"Well," said Donald, "double the guard for the rest of the night. With daylight we'll search the bank just in case there's any sign."

He was about to send Scot on his way when Eva came scurrying toward the door in her robe and slippers. She pushed her way past Scot and in through the door, throwing her arms around Donald.

"Oh, Mat," she said. "Mat, are you all right?"

"Yes," said Donald. "Someone took a shot at me, but he missed. Unfortunately, my return shot also missed. The man has apparently escaped unharmed."

Taking advantage of the space Eva had created, Scot stepped into the room and held up the lantern. There were

159

feathers strewn about the room—and a nightgown was on the floor beside the bed.

"He killed your feather pillow, sir," said Scot, quickly moving the light. "It's a good thing you moved when you did."

"Yes," said Donald. "Well, thank you, Mr. Scot. That will be all."

"Yes sir," Scot said, and he turned to see to the watch down on deck.

Eva's eyes were on the flimsy nightgown there beside the bed. Donald saw where she was looking. He opened his mouth as if to say something, but, of course, there was nothing to say. Eva gave him a hard look, then turned and left the room without another word. Donald stood for a moment, then shut the door.

"You can come out now," he said. He picked the gown up off the floor as Bethie came crawling out from under the bed, and he held it out toward her. "Here," he said, "put this on and go on back to your room." Then he noticed that she was trembling. "It's all right," he said. "It's all over."

She stood shaking for another moment, trying to get some words out. He was angry with her, because he had almost thought that he could fall in love with her. Then she had revealed the real reason she had come to him. She was trying to persuade him to leave the Bond colony alone. That was all. Even so, she looked so frightened and so vulnerable, standing there naked and trembling. He stepped over to her and put the gown over her head, pulling it on down to cover her—more or less. Then he put his arms around her and held her close. God, he thought, she still felt good.

"It's all over, Bethie," he said. "It's all right."

"That was him," she said in a small and trembling voice. "He's here."

"Who, Bethie?" he asked her. "The man at the porthole? Who was he?"

"It was Murkens," she said. "He's here."

Twenty-one

The sun was low in the eastern sky, and a light southwest breeze left over from the night still blew cool, speaking of untrammeled grassland, dust, and sweet Texas prairie. The welcome smell of fresh coffee drifted aft to fill his nostrils as Donald came down the stairs from the second tier of the boat. Sergeant Scot must have been ready for him, for he met the captain at the bottom stair with a steaming cup of coffee.

"Good morning, sir," Scot said.

"Good morning, Sergeant," said Donald, taking the cup and sipping the hot, black liquid tentatively. "And thank you."

Donald moved on to the rail at the bow of the boat. Over his first cup of morning coffee, he mulled over the hectic events of the night before. He'd had a young and beautiful woman come calling and practically throw herself at him, and he had actually tried to throw her out of his room. He really had.

But in the end, of course, she had won the battle, and what a time he'd had for himself in the losing of it. He had even thought for awhile that he was in love again, or might be, and then she had displayed her true colors in the nick of time.

However, she had saved him from a surprise attempt on his life, and then he had discovered that he had actually seen the hated Murkens. It had been Murkens who had made the attempt. In the years since Donald had seen the man before, the wretch had shaved his head and grown a beard, effectively turning his face, ugly enough to begin with, upside down.

God, Donald was glad that Bethie had been there. Not only was it she who had seen Murkens and shouted the warning, thereby saving Donald from Murkens's cowardly, skulking murder attempt, but also she had been the one to identify the man for him.

He recalled with a shudder how Murkens's shot had hit the pillow where his own head had been lying just seconds before. Yes indeed, he thought, Bethie's shout had saved his life. There was no doubt about it. As angry as he was at her for her motives and methods in seducing him, he still owed her, and in a big way.

But, damn it, the hated Murkens was so close. There was something in Donald that wanted desperately to turn the command of the *John Hart* over to Sergeant Scot and just go out alone and chase after the bastard, but then, he had allowed Senator Reddels, the pompous ass, to talk him into leaving the horses behind. Of course, he told himself, he could pursue Murkens on Krevs's red mule.

Hell, he would pursue him on foot, barefoot across the desert, if need be, but he knew that all this was vain fantasy. He could not allow his personal quest to interfere with the business of his military mission. But Murkens had taken a shot at him, and there was Bethie's identification of the man as well as his own. If he got a chance, he could arrest him on a legitimate charge that would stick in any court.

Except, in order to make it stick, he and Bethie would both have to admit in open court that they had been in the room alone together in the middle of the night, and that might not be such a good idea. There was also the question of jurisdiction. The shot had been fired on a boat in the middle of the river between U.S. territory and Spanish Texas. Donald wasn't at all sure just who had jurisdiction in such a case. Whose was the river?

But if he should ever come across Murkens again, he told himself, then damn jurisdiction and other such troublesome complications. He would just kill the son of a bitch. Keep it simple. It really wouldn't matter where the killing took place, Arkansas Territory or Spanish Texas. No one would question him. No one would press charges. Or would they?

Suddenly Donald asked himself just what was Murkens doing out here anyway, and the only answer to that question that came to him had to do with the Rotison gang. Was Murkens involved with them? He must be, Donald thought. They were birds of a feather, and there was no other attraction for Murkens in the area.

Donald listened as the *John Hart*'s engine chugged to life, and he turned to watch smoke billow from the tall stacks as the boilers began to build up steam. He walked over to the deck chair by the nearby table and sat down with his empty cup. Soon the boat began to move, and soon he was surprised to see Eva walking across the deck in his direction. He had thought that she would never speak to him again after last night. As she approached the table, looking aloof, Donald stood and offered her a chair.

"Good morning," he said.

"Good morning, Mat," she said.

Sergeant Scot appeared almost magically with another cup and the coffeepot. He poured a cup for Eva and refilled Donald's cup. Then he faded politely away. Donald thought about offering an apology, perhaps an explanation. Instead

163

he quietly sipped his coffee and avoided her gaze.

"Is your latest playmate back in her own bed now?" Eva said at last, coolly.

"Eva," said Donald, "if you have just set the tone of the conversation to follow, I would just as soon it not progress any further."

"Oh dear me," she said. "I am sorry. I suppose women like that do serve their purposes."

"Women like what?" Donald said, feeling the need to bite back. "Do you mean women who go to bed with men who are not their husbands?"

Eva flushed hot, and Donald could tell that he had hit his mark. He almost felt guilty for that small victory, and he briefly considered apologizing but decided against it. Let her stew, he thought. She picked up her cup and sipped some coffee, then placed the cup carefully back down on the table.

"Well," she said, "at least it wasn't her husband who shot at you."

"No," he said, "it wasn't, and quite frankly, Eva, had she not been there, I'd be dead right now."

"Oh?"

"The bullet went right where my head had been lying on the pillow," he said. "It was she who saw the face in the porthole, and she screamed just an instant before he fired. That's what saved me. That's all that saved me."

"Well," Eva said, "in that case, I suppose I should be grateful that you were . . . thus engaged. It's ironic, isn't it?"

"Yes," he said. "I suppose it is. But Eva, in our last conversation, you very strongly implied that there could no longer be anything between us. That—"

"Is that what you understood from me, Mat, Darling?" she said. "Well, of course, then that explains your actions of last night. Now I understand. My goodness, how could I have left you with such an impression? I'm terribly sorry, darling. All I meant to say was that until you resign from the Army—"

164

"That's all you need to say," said Donald. "I've told you that the Army is my career. It's my life. I have no intention of resigning and becoming a government clerk or a politician. So if those are your terms, then there's no more to be said."

"Mat," she said, her voice suddenly almost maternal, "you'll get it out of your system. All little boys want adventure, but little boys also grow up. You'll have to settle down one day." As he started to open his mouth to protest, she added hastily, "Would you get me another cup of coffee, please?"

"Certainly," he said, and he stood and picked up the two cups, then headed toward the galley. At another deck table, closer to the galley, Sergeant Scot was seated with Senator Reddels and the scout, Krevs. Scot saw Donald approaching with the cups and jumped up to refill them for him. Donald thanked the sergeant and started back toward the table where Eva was waiting. Out of the corner of his eye, he saw Bethie emerging from the cabin she grudgingly shared with Sings Loud.

Donald was only a few feet away from Eva when a loud shot rang out from the south shore and a heavy lead ball tore the cup from his left hand. He flung the other cup away and ran to Eva, pulling her out of her chair and down onto the deck. He reached for his pistol before he remembered that he hadn't bothered strapping it on that morning.

Back at the other table, Sergeant Scot had jumped up and was shouting orders. Krevs pulled the terrified Reddels to the deck. Bethie hit the deck without any assistance. Soldiers took cover, readied arms, and looked for something out there to shoot at. Donald saw Corporal Alan searching the south bank in vain for a target for his rifle. He ran to the side of the corporal and took the heavy Springfield out of his hands.

Aiming for the spot from whence he figured the shot had come, Donald fired. Sergeant Scot, seeing where Donald

165

was aiming, fired his pistol in the same direction, and two other soldiers fired rifles. For a moment after, there was empty silence.

Then there was a sudden pounding of hooves, and a horse and rider appeared on the far side of the cottonwoods riding south well out of rifle range. Donald stared hard after the man. There was no point in more shooting, none in pursuit. *Damn Reddels for talking me into leaving the horses behind,* he said to himself. *Damn me for listening to him.* Sergeant Scot stepped up beside Donald.

"Do you recognize him, sir?" he asked.

Donald stared at the diminishing figure in the distance and shook his head slowly.

"No," he said, "but I don't think it's Murkens again. He looked like a bigger man than that."

"Rotison?" Scot said.

"Could be," said Donald. "See to the men, Sergeant. I'll check with the passengers."

"Yes sir."

As Scot turned away, Donald shot a glance at the aft table and saw that Bethie and Reddels were huddled up together there in deep conversation. She's cold, he thought. That's the second time she's got right down to business after a close call. He turned his own attention to Eva. Walking over to where she still crouched on the deck, he gave her a hand up.

"Are you all right?" he asked.

"Yes," she said. "I'm all right, but Mat, that man tried to kill you."

"Yes," said Donald. "He did."

"That's the second attempt," she said.

"Yes," he said, "and the second shooter."

"You mean it wasn't the same man as last night?" she asked, incredulous.

"That's what I mean," he said.

"Mat," she said, "what's this all about? Who wants to kill you so badly? And why?"

"I don't know, Eva," he said, "but I intend to find out."

He had an idea that it had something to do with the illegal settlement at Buffalo Crossing, but he kept that thought to himself.

"Mat," she said, "how in the world can you really want to remain in a situation like this? Your life is in actual danger. Doesn't that mean anything to you? This is the very reason you need to—"

"Eva," he said, "this is not the time for such talk. If you're sure that you're quite all right, I've got to get back to my command."

Back at the aft deck table, Bethie and Reddels were still huddled together. Scot and Krevs had both gotten up to look around. There really wasn't that much to be done. Only one shot had been fired at the boat, and no one had been hurt. The shooter had gotten well away. Still, guards were posted with orders to keep their eyes peeled. Two different men had taken potshots at the captain. Others might try.

Eva had started to join her father, but when she saw him in the company of Bethie, she turned in a huff and went back to her room instead. Marie would be good enough company for her.

"Such a terrible lot of excitement, Senator," Bethie was saying. "I hope you weren't hurt."

"I got a fright," Reddels said, "and that's for sure, but I think I'm all right. Yes. Yes. I'll be just fine. I'm fine."

"It's just terrible," Bethie said. "Whatever do you think is going on around here?"

"It seems that someone is out to assassinate Captain Donald," Reddels said. "First there was that shot last night, and now this."

"But whatever for?" Bethie asked. "Why would anyone want to kill poor Captain Donald?"

"I don't really know," Reddels said, "but I wouldn't be at all surprised if it turned out to have something to do with his rather vocal opposition to Zeno Bond's colony. I can well understand the fervor of the colonists. Of course, that's no reason for attempted murder, and I in no way condone it myself. It's just that, as I said, I can understand their patriotic zeal."

"Yes," Bethie said, resting her chin on her palm, her elbow on the table, and leaning toward Reddels. "I can understand that too. Why, my Tom and I are on our way out there right now to join up with Mr. Bond's colony. But, of course, you already knew that."

"Yes," the senator said. "Yes, I did, and I wholeheartedly approve, as I think you already know."

"But Senator," she said, "do you think that Mat—I mean, Captain Donald—will really stand in our way?"

"I've tried to talk to him," said Reddels, "but he's absolutely bullheaded concerning that issue."

"But isn't there something you can do? After all, you're a U.S. senator," she said. She looked into his face admiringly.

"My dear," he said, "a U.S. senator cannot directly issue orders to an Army officer. Captain Donald has his orders from General Andy Jackson, who, by the way, is a good friend of mine, and he's apparently damned determined to act on them until they're changed. I suppose I shouldn't condemn him for that. He's a good soldier.

"What I can do is appeal directly to General Jackson himself, and if that doesn't work, then I shall have to appeal to my fellow congressmen back in Washington City, and if I must, then I assure you, my dear, that I will do exactly that."

Bethie moved even closer to Reddels, and the senator could smell her perfume and feel her hot breath as she spoke into the side of his face. He pulled out a handkerchief and mopped at the sweat that popped out on his brow.

"But Senator," she said, "all that will take time, and I'm just afraid that there isn't much time to be wasted."

"Why, just what are you getting at?" he asked.

She leaned in even closer, and her lips touched his ear and tickled it as she whispered softly to him.

"There's a gold mine on that hill," she said. "The Indians know it, and Mr. Rotison knows it. If we don't latch right on to that area now and hold tight, someone else could come along and take it for themselves."

"You say Rotison knows," Reddels whispered. "Who else?"

"Rotison," she said, "and me . . . and you."

Twenty-two

Paddle wheels churned shallow water as the *John Hart* moved along at its top speed of five miles an hour, the eleven-inch–diametered cylinder of the engine making powerful sixteen-inch strokes, and the fireman throwing wood into the furnace to maintain constant steam in the boiler. Scot joined Donald at the bow.

"The pilot says the river's getting mighty low, sir," Scot said. "We'll be crawling when we hit Garfish Bend. We could sure use some rain."

"Careful wishing for rain," said Krevs in a loud voice. He was standing not far off and had overheard Scot's remarks. "You crawl along in shallow water, but Lord God, you get actual devastation when it comes a gully-washing, stump-moving rain out here."

"Tall tales," said Scot.

"Half of them's true," Krevs said.

Donald pointed to a cabin on the north bank, abandoned,

its roof caved in. "Look at that," he said. "I wonder what happened there."

"Oh," Krevs said, walking over to stand closer to Donald and Scot, "that was old Dubois's place. Nothing much happened. He just got sick of being a river rat and moved off up into the hills. He was gone quite a spell before anyone knowed he was gone."

"That reminds me," said Donald. "Have either of you seen Tom Booker lately?"

"I ain't," said Krevs.

"I remember seeing him early yesterday," said Scot, "but come to think of it, sir, I haven't seen him since then either."

"Sawyer ahead," said Krevs.

Just at that moment, Reddels approached the small group, and he overheard Krevs's announcement. "Sawyer?" he said. "What's that?"

"It's an entire tree," said Krevs, "that's loose in the water. Likely it was swept in when a bank caved in. Its roots or branches or something's stuck in bottom mud. If we was to hit the damn thing, it could tear the whole damn bottom out of this flimsy little boat and leave us all to wade out of the river and walk home."

Reddels looked ahead squinting his eyes.

"I don't see anything," he said.

"You can't see it," Krevs said. "It's under the water."

"Then how do you know it's there?"

"Looky yonder," said the scout, pointing. "The surface of the water has a different pattern."

"Oh yes," said Reddels. "Yes, I can see that."

"It's caused by the sawyer," Krevs said.

The *John Hart* slowed and veered to the left, staying in the current as much as possible, the pilot deftly avoiding the trap which lurked just below the surface. Trees on the high bank cast oblique shadows as the boat chugged safely past the nearly hidden danger. Reddels breathed a sigh of relief.

"Well," Donald said, "I still wonder where Tom Booker has got to. Sergeant, would you check around for him?"

"Yes sir," said Scot.

"Uh, one moment," said Reddels. "There's no need. Mr. Booker is not aboard. I believe that he's gone to join Mr. Rotison to ride on ahead into the colony."

"He was traveling with us," said Donald. "When did he get off the boat? And why?"

"I, uh, believe that he disembarked during all the confusion this morning following the gunshots," said Reddels. "I believe that he did so on the advice of his, uh, wife."

"That doesn't make any sense," said Donald. "What—"

"I'm sure I don't know," said Reddels. "The lady must have had her reasons."

"Damn," said Donald.

"Mat, my boy," Reddels said, throwing an arm around Donald's shoulder and pulling him away from Scot and Krevs, "forget about Mr. Booker. There's something that I've been meaning to talk to you about. I believe that I made you a most generous offer. I did it not just for your sake, but also for the sake of my Eva. I'm sure you know that. Mat, the position of Secretary to the Governor of the Arkansas Territory is not to be sneezed at. It's an important position, and it will lead to even bigger and better things."

"Yes sir," said Donald. "I'm sure that all that's true. And I don't question your wisdom or your motives. I do appreciate the offer—but I'm just not suited for the position. I'm a soldier, sir. And that's all I'll ever be."

"We adapt and conform, Mat," said the senator. "We all do, and you can do it as well as anyone else. The man who marries my daughter will have to—"

"That's just it, sir," Donald said. "I've already told Eva that I can't think of leaving the Army, not even for her. I've already told General Jackson that I want to go west on the next possible expedition. When my assignment here is over with, I expect that to happen. And I'll not pass up the chance.''

Reddels gave Donald a look of disbelief, and he was about to say something, when the river curved, throwing them completely into the shadow of towering trees on both banks. The engine slowed to a low beat as the river twisted sharply southwest, and tall, rocky banks rose on each side. Donald looked anxiously up toward the tops of the high banks.

''Better take cover, sir,'' he said.

''What?''

''Sharpshooters up there could pick us off easily,'' Donald said.

''Indians?'' said Reddels.

Donald shrugged. ''Indian or white,'' he said. He didn't need to say anything more. Reddels hurried off toward the safety of his cabin, and Donald smiled to watch him scurry away. Sings Loud came out of her cabin just then. She stood still for a moment, watching the senator with a look of disapproval on her face. When he had slammed the cabin door behind himself, she walked over to join Donald at the rail.

''What's he so scared of?'' she asked.

Donald, still smiling, looked up. ''Someone up there might shoot him,'' he said.

''I get it,'' she said. ''You just wanted him to go away. Right?''

''You're right,'' Donald said. ''Was that a bad thing for me to do?''

''Not bad,'' she said. ''Not too smart either. You could have just tossed him overboard. That way, he wouldn't come back later.''

''I take it you don't care for the senator,'' Donald said. ''Is that a proper Christian attitude?''

''He's a hypocrite,'' she said. ''Got that little blond-

173

headed white woman in his cabin. Humph. And his own daughter just next door, too. The Devil's going to get that old white man for sure. He might as well get him today as next year.''

Donald turned and stared in the direction of Reddels's cabin, trying to imagine the senator and Bethie behind that closed door together. The old bastard, he thought. And Bethie. Damn her too. So that was why she had run Tom off the boat. And Reddels pretended like he didn't know.

"Sir, she can turn and turn and turn again," Donald said.

"Huh?" said Sings Loud. "Why you calling me *sir*?"

"What?" said Donald. "Oh. No. That's just a line from an old play."

"Oh," she said, and they stood side by side in silence watching the river ahead.

Tom Booker rode behind the others, eating their dust. He was trying to figure out just what Bethie expected him to do with this bunch anyway. She had told him to join them and ride on to the colony to alert Zeno Bond that they were coming and wanted to join up with him. But that was where the steamboat was headed anyway. Why couldn't he have just stayed aboard? He couldn't figure her out, but neither could he argue with her, so he had left the boat and met up with Rotison and the others, just like she had told him to do.

They were a rugged bunch, all heavily armed. Mean looking, all of them were dirty and unshaven. They were a loud, boisterous, profane, and drunken lot, and he was thoroughly uncomfortable in their company. He consoled himself somewhat by saying that they would soon reach the crossing and go over to meet up with Zeno Bond and his settlers. After that it wouldn't be long before the boat arrived, bringing the soldiers and the senator—and Bethie. He guessed that he could stand it that long.

Up ahead, Rotison called a halt. When the dust had

cleared a little, Booker moved ahead to find out what was going on. They had arrived at the river, and Booker assumed they were at the crossing. Then he saw for the first time what it was that had given the crossing its name.

Dust filled the air all around, stretching north and south for miles, and a large herd of buffalo filled the crossing and stretched as far as he could see on both sides of the river. He was stunned by the sight and the sound and the smell. He had heard of these vast western buffalo herds, but nothing had prepared him for the actual sight of one.

"My God," he said aloud. "There must be thousands of them."

"Hell," said Ranik, who was standing nearby, "this ain't such a big herd. I've seen millions at a time."

"Build a fire," said Rotison. "We're going to be here for awhile. We might as well settle down and brew up some coffee."

"What the hell we have to stop here for?" said Murkens. "The air stinks of beef and shit."

"We stopped here," said Rotison, "because we're headed just over there." He pointed to the hill on the other side of the river. "That damn herd is just where we have to go in order to cross the river. So we're stopped. Got to wait it out. That's all. Quit your bellyaching and help build the fire."

"As long as I have to stop for the shaggy, stinking goddamn things," Murkens said, "I think I'll kill me a few of them."

"You'll do what the hell I tell you to do," Rotison snapped back. "Put your rifle down and build the fucking fire."

Murkens scowled but did as he'd been told, and Booker cringed at the language of the sorry looking men he had allowed himself to be attached to. He thought about leaving their company, but he wasn't at all sure he would know what to do or where to go without them. It also occurred to

175

him that if he tried to leave, they might kill him. He looked around and started to help gather sticks for the fire.

The fire was built and the coffee was brewed. Booker had a cup along with all the rest. Rotison pulled a bottle out of his coat pocket and reached over toward Booker.

"Little whiskey in your coffee?" he asked.

"No," said Booker. "No, thanks."

Rotison shrugged and poured the whiskey into his own cup. "Suit yourself," he said. "Ever' man to his own taste, howsoever peculiar it may be."

Later, while Booker sipped at his second cup of coffee, wondering just how much of this vile company he could stand, he saw to the east along the river the smoke from the *John Hart*'s stacks. It was none too soon for him, and he watched anxiously until the boat came slowly into view. It was already late afternoon, and the herd in the crossing had thinned. Most of the great beasts were now in Texas. A few stragglers remained on the other side of the river. Rotison ordered the men to mount up.

As they rode across the river, great shaggy beasts shied away when the mounted man-beasts came too near for their comfort, and Booker marveled even more at their appearance close up.

On the north bank after the crossing, they veered northeast, toward the eastern side of the prominent hill, and therefore away from the stragglers at the eastern edge of the herd. Soon they rode up to Zeno Bond's tent settlement, and the old patriot himself stepped up to meet them.

"Mr. Booker," said Bond, "welcome to my fledgling colony. But where is your lovely young wife, sir, and what are you doing in this company?"

Booker dismounted, feeling a tremendous sense of relief to be in decent company again. He walked toward Bond, smiling.

"Bethie is on board the steamboat, sir," he said. "They'll be here soon. I only rode in with these—gentlemen because

Bethie thought it was important that I get here as soon as possible and alert you to the arrival of the boat.''

Bond looked toward the river and saw the smoke from the stacks.

"So," he said, "the Army's coming to pay us a visit, is it?"

"Yes," said Booker, "but Senator Reddels is also with them, Mr. Bond."

Bond's tense expression relaxed a little. "Good," he said. "Good." Then he looked at Rotison. "I'm a little surprised to see you back here, Mr. Rotison," he said. "I thought that you had found our company too restrictive for your tastes."

Rotison swung down off his horse and stepped up squarely in front of Bond to tower over him.

"Well now, Mr. Bond," he said, "me and the boys has thought it all over since we pulled out on you, and, uh, well, we decided, me and the boys, we decided that we made a bad decision. We want to come back and join up with your colony here."

"Are you quite sure of that, Mr. Rotison?" Bond said. "The rules have not relaxed here. And I hired you originally as a scout and a guide. I never really thought of you or your men as settlers."

"Hell, Mr. Bond," Rotison said, "everyone's got to settle down sometime, ain't he?"

"I suppose that's true," Bond said. "Mr. Rotison, I welcome settlers to this colony, but I demand adherence to the rules. I insist on good behavior from them all, and that includes decent language."

"Well, uh, I'll watch the boys real good, Mr. Bond," said Rotison. "We can be just as civilized as the next folks."

Bond looked back toward the river. The rising smoke was no longer moving west. The steamboat had stopped.

"I believe that the Army has arrived," Bond said. "We'll have visitors soon. We must prepare for them."

Twenty-three

Captain Donald had Sergeant Scot detail two men to stand watch on board the boat. The pilot and the other boatmen remained aboard as well. Then the rest of the soldiers along with the passengers disembarked and walked the distance to Zeno Bond's camp at the base of the Sacred Hill. Donald enjoyed watching Reddels puff and moan from the exertion. *Serves the pompous ass right*, he thought, *for making me leave the horses behind.*

When they reached the camp, Donald was a little surprised to find that Bond had prepared a feast for their arrival. A crude but stout table was set up near the base of the hill, and two buffalo calves turned on spits over hot coals. Over open fires, bread fried in skillets of grease, pots of red beans boiled, and coffee brewed. In spite of Donald's anticipation of an unpleasant visit at Bond's camp, he found the smells of cooking welcome and inviting.

He noticed that Bethie greeted Tom rather coolly, and he saw Rotison shoot him a glance and sidle back to the far

178

edge of the crowd. Trying not to be obvious about it, he looked around the faces, searching for Murkens, but he found no sign of the man. Senator Reddels puffed up to meet Zeno Bond and pumped the old man's hand vigorously.

"Mr. Bond, sir," he said, "it's a great honor and a distinct pleasure to make your acquaintance. I have long looked forward to our meeting."

"Senator Reddels, I presume," Bond said.

"Oh, yes sir," said Reddels. "Pardon me, please. In my excitement I forgot to introduce myself. And may I present my daughter, Eva?"

Eva stepped up beside her father.

"How do you do, Mr. Bond?" she said.

"It's a pleasure to meet you both," Bond said. Then he raised his voice to add, "I invite all of you to partake of our humble fare."

Everyone was seated and served, but Donald noticed that the Rotison gang held back, lurking at the far edges of the camp. He still saw no sign of Murkens. The meal was good, and the diners all ate their fill. Then Bond stood up at the head of the table, obviously prepared to make a speech. All conversation at the table ceased.

"Ladies and gentlemen, settlers and visitors," Bond said, "my apologies for the crude fare and the rude setting, but this is only the beginning, the beginning of a great undertaking. Ten years from now, no, less, when we again sit down together on this very spot, you'll find yourselves seated at a table of polished teak from the Orient, covered with Damascus cloth and set with delicate chinaware and silver. In place of these rude tents will be a town, and there, just there, will be my castle."

"Excuse me, Mr. Bond," Donald interrupted, "but this is U.S. territory, and you are squatting here illegally. Your land grant is elsewhere."

179

Bond held up his hand asking Donald to hush up and wait his turn.

"This land will ever be U.S. territory," he said, "with the grand old flag flying free. I pledge my sacred oath on that. I have fought and bled for this country, and I love it with all my heart. I'll take this raw land and build my trading post, my plantation, and my town. I'll replace these wild herds of buffalo with domesticated cattle. I'll plow and plant these fields. You'll see buildings of masonry, brick, and stone where now you see tents, and you'll see citizens riding carriages down cobblestone streets with lampposts on the corners."

Reddels suddenly and alone applauded vigorously.

"Bravo!" he shouted. "Bravo. A wonderful American ambition, sir. Mighty are the pioneers who bring light to the darkest land."

"You can't stay here, Mr. Bond," said Donald, rising to his feet. "Not only are you here illegally, but you and all your people are in grave danger of an attack by the Indians."

Bond smiled at Donald as if at a foolish child.

"There's no problem, young man," he said. "As long as the savages come in peace and behave themselves, they are welcome at my table. The trading post will be established largely for their benefit and will thrive on trade for their furs."

"But they don't want you here," said Donald, "trade or no trade, and this is their land."

"Their land?" Bond bellowed suddenly. "I fought and bled for this land, sir. The savages are nomads who roam over land but do not own it."

"I'm sorry, Mr. Bond," Donald said, "but I'm here representing the United States Army, and my orders are to maintain the peace. Your presence here is a direct threat to that peace."

Suddenly, from his lurking spot in the background, Cotton Rotison rose to his full gigantic height and spoke out in a loud voice.

"You got fifteen soldier boys, Captain," he said. "We got three times that many settlers here. Now just how are you planning on making us move?"

Sudden confusion panicked the old patriot. It could be seen on his face.

"Wait a minute," he shouted. "Mr. Rotison, sit down. We will not raise arms against the United States Army, and I will not tolerate threats against my beloved country from settlers in my camp."

Reddels stood up.

"Now listen to me," he said. "There's no call for things to go that far. I am a United States senator, and I say there's no need for us to be fighting among ourselves. We're all American citizens."

"We ain't all that," Sings Loud muttered to herself.

"Now my suggestion," Reddels continued, "is that we appeal to Army headquarters at Natchitoches for a ruling on this matter."

"But there's no time for that," said Bethie.

"When will the Indians attack?" the senator asked.

"In the fall," said Donald, "but—"

"There's plenty of time for a trip down the river and back," Reddels said.

"I'm satisfied to leave the matter up to the wisdom and the authority of Army headquarters," Bond said. "They'll make the right decision, I'm sure."

"Then it's settled," said Reddels. "Now let's all talk about something else."

"It ain't settled very good," Sings Loud said almost to herself from where she was seated next to Krevs.

Krevs turned and spat tobacco juice on the ground. "No ma'am," he said. "It sure ain't."

He stood up and walked away from the table, and others followed his example. The meal was done, the speechmaking was over, and the argument had been put on hold. Donald was frustrated. Had it not been for the presence of the damned senator, he thought, he would have won this confrontation. As commander of the U.S. troops in the area, he was the final authority. But Reddels was a U.S. senator, a lawmaker, and his opposition undermined Donald's authority. He stood up disgusted, and as he turned, Eva was right there in front of him.

"Will you walk with me, Mat?" she said.

"I'm not at all sure your father would approve," he said.

"Never mind him," she said. "I feel like taking a walk, and I certainly don't want to go out there on my own."

Donald hesitated. The sun was low in the western sky, and it would soon be dark. Donald was furious with Eva's father, and he wasn't at all sure any more how he felt about Eva. He certainly had no idea how she felt about him. Each time they spoke, she seemed to have a different attitude, just about opposite the last one she had expressed. He was getting more than a bit tired of it, but he didn't want to be rude nor cause a scene, and, of course, he couldn't allow her to walk alone after dark. He offered his arm, and she took it. As they strolled away from the table, he thought that he could see the senator watching them, and Bethie, and Sings Loud. *Hell*, he thought, *everyone's looking at us*.

They walked to the river in silence. Gray-brown plovers ran before them, hunting insects. Swallows circled overhead, eating mosquitoes. A long line of ravens flew east to spend the night in tall trees along the shore. Out in the river, a large fish jumped half out of the water, making a loud splash, and somewhere over on the Texas side, a panther screamed. Eva clutched Donald's arm tight.

"It's all right," he said. "That was clear over in Texas."

He wondered, though, if it was really all right. He wasn't afraid of panthers or bears, but he had been shot at twice. Murkens was somewhere about. He knew that. And Rotison and his gang were right back there in the camp at the base of the hill. Here he was alone with Eva on the banks of the Red River. The nearest help were the two guards on board the boat. He felt foolish and vulnerable.

"Mat," Eva said, "why are you doing this?"

"You said you wanted to walk," he said. "Do you want to go back now?"

"That's not what I meant," she said. "You're deliberately aggravating Daddy."

"No, Eva," he said, "I'm not. I'm following my orders, and he's deliberately interfering. That's what's going on, in case you haven't noticed."

"Mat, you're wrong," she said. "Your orders are going to be changed anyway. We both know that. When Daddy talks to General Jackson, Zeno Bond will get the approval to stay right where he is."

"But the—"

"And Mr. Bond says lots more settlers are coming out here to join him," she continued. "When they see how strong the settlement has become, the Indians will back off."

"They won't," said Donald.

"Well, it's not your problem anyway," she said. "Daddy wants you to turn your boat around and take us back to Natchitoches. There he'll talk to General Jackson. You'll have new orders, and all this will be out of your hands. At the same time, Daddy can get you transferred wherever you want to go. If you don't want to be the governor's secretary, you can stay in the Army and get a transfer to Washington or Virginia or some place else where things are peaceful. And if you still want me, I'll marry you. I'll be a soldier's wife."

She was standing close to him and looking up into his face. In the moonlight, she was beautiful, and Donald felt himself softening. He wouldn't have to leave the Army to have her after all. He would only have to give up his dreams of adventure in the West. He recalled Capitan del Monte's advice. Marry her and become the youngest general in the Army. The senator could pull it off. He would pull it off—for a son-in-law.

He put his hands on Eva's shoulders, and he was about to kiss her tenderly on the lips. He was about to tell her that they'd head for Natchitoches first thing in the morning. He was about to ask her when she would like to have their wedding plans announced. He was about to do all those things, when he saw the full moon over her shoulders, back behind the Sacred Hill.

It was huge, and it was bright, and then across its face moved the small dark silhouette of a man walking on top of the hill. Donald knew who it was. It could be no one else. It was Walker.

Twenty-four

Zeno Bond had offered his guests accommodations for the night, but Donald declined, saying that he and his men were needed back on the boat. Senator Reddels declined as well on behalf of all the civilian passengers.

"We're all settled into staterooms already," he said, "and we might as well make use of them, rather than impose further on your most generous hospitality."

So they returned to the *John Hart* there at the crossing, prepared to spend yet another night on the river, all except Sings Loud, who chose to stay at the settlement, because, she said, she had seen no other preacher there. As they were settling in, Reddels's small mounted military escort showed up there on the north bank. The horses were lathered. The men were sweat-soaked and dirty. Reddels leaned into the starboard railing to shout at them.

"Where the hell have you been?" he squealed.

The captain in charge sat heavily in his saddle, his chin

resting on his chest. "Sorry, sir," he said. "We, uh, sort of got lost."

"Sergeant Scot," said Donald, "detail a couple of men to look after their horses and bring the men aboard."

"Yes sir," said Scot.

When the four soldiers came aboard, Donald stopped the captain. "Did you run into any trouble?" he asked.

"No, Captain," said the other. "We rode out north a ways to get onto the prairie. The going along the bank gets pretty rough in places. And I guess we just kind of lost our bearings for awhile. We did run into a camp of immigrants out there."

"Where were they headed?" Donald asked.

"Zeno Bond's colony, they said."

"Damn," said Donald. "How many of them?"

"Well, I'd say somewhere between fifty and a hundred," the captain said. "Closer to a hundred. That's men, women, and children."

"Captain, I'll want to borrow a horse from you in the morning," Donald said.

At last everyone was settled in for the night. Sentry schedules were established, and the rest of the night was calm. No shots were fired from anywhere toward the boat, and no women invaded Donald's privacy during the night.

The next morning, he had his coffee, declined breakfast, mounted the borrowed horse, and set out in search of the new party of settlers the senator's escort had stumbled across. In spite of the fact that the four soldiers had gotten lost, they did manage to give Donald decent directions to the settlers' camp.

Donald figured that the immigrants would have broken camp by the time he got to them, so he anticipated their route to Buffalo Crossing and set his own to intercept them on the trail. He was having enough trouble with Zeno Bond as it was. He did not want the illegal colony reinforced if he could help it, and he sure as hell meant to try.

It was noon before he spotted the wagon train. When the settlers saw an Army officer approaching, they called a halt to their long line of wagons and waited for him. One man on horseback rode a little forward to meet him.

"Hello," said Donald. "I'm Captain Mat Donald, commander of the U.S. forces out here."

"Charles Davis," said the other. "We're sure glad to see you. But you're alone. Where's the rest of your troops?"

"They're back at the river," said Donald. "I rode out alone to meet you because I want to ask you to turn back."

"Turn back?" said Davis. "What the hell for? Injun trouble?"

"No," Donald said. "At least not yet. You're planning to join the Zeno Bond settlement?"

"That's right," Davis said. "Mr. Bond told us that there's plenty of good land for all, and we've got twenty families here that needs it."

"Mr. Bond is probably correct," Donald said, "but right now, he's illegally squatting on the wrong land. I'm engaged in moving him to the proper land, and I suggest that you take your people back to Jonesboro to wait for the relocation to be completed."

"Well, Captain," said Davis, "I reckon it'll take your whole troop of cavalry to turn us around. We set out to join up with Mr. Bond, and we mean to do just that. If he packs up to relocate, well, we'll just have to follow him along, I reckon, but we ain't turning around now. No sir."

Donald wore himself out arguing, but all to no avail. At last he turned his horse around and rode back to the *John Hart*. He was met by an anxious Krevs.

"Captain," the scout said, "we've got to get this boat turned around and headed back east right away, lessen you want to be stuck out here waiting for the next rain."

"What's wrong, Krevs?" Donald said.

"If the river drops any lower," Krevs said, "when we

187

hit Garfish Bend them paddles'll be trying to churn red mud.''

"I see," Donald said. He gave the horse to a private to tend to, and he boarded the boat. Senator Reddels almost immediately puffed up to him, fanning himself with his sweat-soaked handkerchief.

"Mat," the senator said, "I've pussyfooted around with you long enough. Now I'm telling you. You've got a volatile situation here. Zeno Bond is not going to budge, and frankly, I don't blame him. If you try to pry him loose from his camp with just your fifteen soldiers, Rotison's bunch and Bond's settlers will cut you to shreds. If you fool around longer with them, the Indians might attack. You've got to turn this boat around and head for Natchitoches. Get a decision on the whole matter from headquarters. If the higher-ups agree with you about where Bond puts his colony, I promise you, I won't say another word about it. But if they give him the right to stay put, then you're going to need reinforcements to protect them from Indian attack.''

"You're right, Senator," Donald said. "We'll put about first thing in the morning.''

Donald walked away, heading toward his cabin, leaving the senator dumbfounded. Reddels had just taken a deep breath in anticipation of further argument. Donald's quick and unexpected acquiescence took him completely by surprise.

West of the Sacred Hill, small groups of stragglers from the mighty buffalo herd stomped and bellowed. On top of the hill, Walker sat as in a trance. At the settlement, axes rang loud, and men, women, and children concentrated on building log cabins. The midday sun glowed like a furnace in a brassy-blue, clear sky, but near the western horizon, two thunderheads loomed.

Donald sat alone in his cabin feeling like a defeated man. He had done everything he could think of to do. He had argued with Reddels, Bond, Eva, Bethie, and other individual settlers. He had made speeches to the crowds of settlers. He had threatened Rotison and others of his bunch of renegades. And all of them, the ladies, the senator, the crazy old patriot, and the border ruffians had joined forces and were lined up against him.

There was nothing left for him to do. He couldn't fight them with only fifteen soldiers. And even if he could, he knew better than to fight American settlers. And he didn't want to fight them. On the long, lonely return ride on the prairie, following his meeting with Davis, he had thought it all over.

So all right, he told himself. *Let the politicians have their way. Let the generals make the decisions. That's the approved way to get things done. If the settlers insist on staying, and if the commander at Natchitoches approves their staying, just why the hell should I stick my neck out?* Why the hell, indeed?

He thought, with a twinge of guilt, about Iron Head and his people, who depended on the buffalo herds for their livelihood. And they weren't the only ones. He thought about the significance of the Sacred Hill to the various Indian tribes. And he thought about Walker and his mission.

But he was alone among his own people with these thoughts, and it was his own people he had to live with, and it was among them that he had to make his career. He was only one voice, and it was not being listened to. It was too bad about Walker and Sings Loud and Iron Head and all the other Indians, but, he told himself, it was out of his hands. There was nothing he could do.

He hoped that he would find General Jackson still in Natchitoches. Then, if the decision went in favor of Bond and all his allies, as Donald was almost certain it would, he would ask the general to relieve him of his command and send him somewhere out west as a part of some expedition. He would try to put all this behind him.

The next morning, Donald's thoughts had not changed. His mood was still sullen and depressed. He ordered the *John Hart* steamed up and turned around. He stood at the bow of the boat, leaning on the rail, looking not ahead but down at the red waters, and feeling like he had just suffered a major defeat.

Twenty-five

From his vantage point on top of the Sacred Hill, Walker
saw the *John Hart* steaming its way back east. He knew that
Captain Donald and his soldiers were on board, and he knew
that the camp down below had not been moved. He also
knew that Donald had intended to moved the settlers. All
that taken together could mean only one thing. Donald had
failed. And that meant trouble.

He went again to the entrance at the top of the rattlesnake
cavern, and again he offered his prayer. As he moved cautiously into the musty darkness and listened to the soft rustlings and the ominous rattles, he said his apologies to the
inhabitants of the darksome den for having to once again
disturb their privacy. And once again he made his way
safely to the other end and out to welcome fresh air.

As he did the last time, he worked his slow way around
the hill to a spot away from the camp before making his
descent. He moved through the tangle of brush that grew
beneath the trees and stepped out into the open. He did not

see Ranik and Murkens. He heard the voice of Ranik behind him.

"Look what we got here," Ranik said, and before Walker could even turn around, Ranik had reached all the way around him with both his arms, pinning Walker's own arms to his sides and holding him in a tight squeeze. Murkens then stepped around to look Walker in the face. A broad grin opened in his beard when the bald-headed white man recognized the Indian.

"This is the gold-toting Injun," he said. "Ain't it?"

"I reckon it's him," said Ranik.

"Remember me?" said Murkens, and he slapped Walker hard across the face. Walker's eyeglasses flew off and landed in the grass near the brush. Walker saw spots dancing before him.

"I'm sorry," he said, "but you white people all look alike to me."

Murkens slapped him again.

"You know me, all right," he said. "We met in the inn when you was spending your gold."

"Hey, Russ," said Ranik. "See if he's still got that bag of gold nuggets on him."

Murkens pulled the bandolier bag loose from Walker's shoulder and dumped its contents onto the ground. Sure enough, the small bag was among them. He picked it up and checked the contents. The nuggets were still there, some of them still coated with clay.

"We'll keep this just between the two of us," Murkens said.

"Yeah," Ranik agreed. "Do we kill him now?"

"Hell no," said Murkens. "Don't be stupid. He knows where that gold mine is."

Gold mine? thought Walker. What gold mine could they be talking about? Did they think that he had a mine just because he had a small bag of nuggets? That was a stupid assumption even for a white man to make.

"Now, Injun," said Murkens, "you can make this hard or easy. All we want from you is the way to that gold mine. We'll beat it out of you if need be. If you tell us where it's at, we'll let you go unharmed."

Walker thought that the white men must believe him to be as stupid as they were, if they really expected him to buy that line. They meant to kill him no matter what. They just wanted to find out something from him first. The location of some imaginary gold mine. How could he stall them, he wondered. Murkens slapped him again, and his head spun.

"I'm trying to be nice to you," Murkens said.

"Say, Russ," said Ranik, "had we ought to go get Cotton and tell him about this?"

"Why should we tell him what we find out for ourselves?" Murkens said.

"He's got all those men at the settlement," said Ranik. "What if we do find out how to get up there to the mine? He'll still have control of the whole damn area."

Walker's brain was fuzzy from the slapping, but he began to put these things together. The gold mine they were seeking was on the hill. Now the imbeciles wanted him to show them the way up. For some reason, they had decided that he was getting his gold on top of the Sacred Hill. That was it. It had to be.

"You just leave all that to me," said Murkens. "Right now I just want this little bastard to talk."

Out of patience, Murkens swung a hard backhand right that Walker thought had taken off his head. That was the last thought he had before he drifted off into oblivion once again. His body went limp in Ranik's arms

"Russ," said Ranik, "you've killed him."

Murkens grabbed a handful of Walker's hair and lifted the head to look into the now expressionless face.

"Ah, hell," he said, "he ain't dead. Just passed out."

"Well, don't hit him no more," said Ranik, "or you'll

kill him for sure, and then we'll never find out what he knows.''

Murkens snorted, let Walker's head drop, and looked around, spying a lone tree out a short distance from the woods that crowded the base of the hill.

"Bring him over here," he said, and while Ranik held up the small body, Murkens tied it to the tree. "We'll leave him hang there," he said, "till he comes around. Then we'll just sit here and wait. When he gets hungry and thirsty enough, he'll talk."

The two brutes then sat in the shade of the trees at the base of the hill, staring at Walker. Murkens pulled a bottle of whiskey out of his coat pocket and took a long drink. He glanced at his scurvy partner, hesitated, then offered it to him. Ranik took it and turned it up.

"Here," said Murkens, grabbing for his bottle. "Not too much now."

Walker's body still sagged against the ropes that held him up, but his brain and his senses came back to life. He told himself to play dead. Then maybe his tormentors would go away and leave him to rot.

"Hey, Russ," said Ranik. "I got an idea."

"You ever had one before?" Murkens taunted.

"Listen," said Ranik. "Get the Indian drunk. Then he'll tell us anything. That's how the government gets them treaties signed, ain't it? Get them all drunk?"

"I ain't wasting my whiskey on him," Murkens said. "If he don't come around pretty soon and tell us what we want to know, I'll just strip his skin off with my little cat here."

Murkens fondled his short whip and sipped more whiskey.

"It'd work, I bet," said Ranik in a pout.

It grew quiet then, except for an occasional belch or fart from Ranik or Murkens, and Walker was wondering just how long he would have to play dead. Then he heard, or perhaps he sensed, that someone else was around. More than one. And they were quiet. Slowly he rolled his head to one side and opened his eyes just a little. And then he saw them. Osage. Two of them.

He thought that they were two of the young men who had wanted to kill him that time but had been stopped by Iron Head, and he wondered what they would do now. Would they help him or let the white men have him? He had no idea what to expect of them.

The Osages were moving along the tree line at the base of the hill, coming toward Ranik and Murkens from the northwest. They could see Walker all right from where they were. He couldn't tell if they knew the white men were there or not, but he thought that they must. Otherwise they wouldn't be moving in so cautiously.

Murkens's head dropped in a doze, and Ranik picked up the bottle. He stood up slowly, watching to make sure that Murkens still slept. Then he stepped over to the tree where Walker was tied. He moved the bottle back and forth under Walker's nose.

"Hey, Indian," he said. He kept his voice quiet so as not to wake Murkens. "Indian. You want a drink?"

Walker could smell the rotgut whiskey, and he could tell that the stuff was so vile and cheap that he would not want a drink, even if he had gone without whiskey for two weeks. He still played dead.

"Hey, Indian," said Ranik. "Come on. I'm trying to help you here. Have a drink of whiskey on me. It'll do you good."

Murkens stirred, then sat up quickly.

"What the hell are you doing?" he said.

"Aw, Russ," said Ranik, "if we get him drunk, he'll tell us where the gold mine is."

"I told you not to give him my whiskey," Murkens roared, and he came suddenly to his feet and rushed at Ranik. Ranik dropped the bottle and braced himself for the clash. Just as the two men were about to smash together,

Murkens put out his two hands and bashed Ranik in the chest, knocking him over backwards. Ranik howled as he landed hard, and he reached for the pistol at his belt.

Out of the slits of his eyes, Walker saw the Osage fit an arrow to his bowstring, saw him draw back the string and let the deadly missile fly, but just before it hit, Murkens moved aside to avoid Ranik's aim. The arrow drove itself into the ground between Murkens and Walker.

Murkens pulled out his own pistol, and Ranik turned to fire at the Osage. Flame leaped from the barrel of the flint-lock pistol, and smoke filled the air around Walker and the bandits. It was a lucky shot, for it was a long shot for pistol range, but the ball from Ranik's pistol tore into the Osage's chest, and he pitched forward—dead. The other Osage ran as Murkens fired a wild and useless shot after him.

"Damn," said Murkens, and he grabbed up his long rifle and started to run after the escaping Osage. Ranik did the same. Walker realized that this might be his only chance, and he started to wriggle there against the tree trunk, loosening the ropes that bound him.

In the camp, Zeno Bond and the others heard the shot. Rotison anticipated Bond's reaction and ran to his side.

"I'll mount up and go see what's up," he said.

"Do that, Mr. Rotison," Bond said, "and report back to me immediately."

Rotison quickly saddled up a horse, mounted, and rode hard out of the camp. Bond watched him go, then turned to Tom Booker, who was standing nearby.

"Mr. Booker," he said, "follow him and keep an eye on him. I don't trust that man."

Riding northeast around the hill, Rotison came across the body of the young Osage. He looked around and, seeing no immediate danger, dismounted to investigate further. He saw the ropes there on the ground beneath the tree, and he saw the bottle, and the arrow sticking in the ground. Looking around more, he saw other things that the two renegades had left lying around carelessly on the ground. Whatever had happened had happened right here. Someone had killed an Indian. He wondered who and why. He wasn't ready for trouble with the Indians, not until he had taken over from old Bond. Then Tom Booker came riding up.

"What the hell are you doing here, Booker?" Rotison demanded.

"Mr. Bond sent me," Booker said. "In case you needed any help."

"A fat lot of help you'd be," Rotison said, just as Murkens and Ranik came lumbering back from their chase. He waited until they were close enough to hear. Then, "What the hell's going on here?" he asked.

"We was minding our own business," said Murkens, "when this damn Injun here took a shot at me. Ranik got him, but there was another one with him. We chased after him, but he got away."

Rotison walked over to the ropes on the ground and gave them a kick.

"What's this here?" he said.

Ranik gave Murkens a furtive look.

"Aw, hell," said Murkens, "we caught that damn little Indian with the gold nuggets, and we had him tied there. We was trying to get him to tell us the way to the mine."

Rotison took a deep breath and let it out slowly. "And you let him get away," he said through clenched teeth.

Booker backed slowly away. He had a feeling that he was listening to something that could be dangerous for him to know about.

"Hold on there, Booker," said Rotison. "Where the hell do you think you're going?"

"I don't think you need me here," Booker said. "I thought I'd just go back to camp and tell Mr. Bond about the Indians."

197

"And the gold mine?" said Rotison.

"I don't know anything about a gold mine," Booker said.

"You don't, do you?" Rotison said. "Your pretty little woman sure as hell knows about it. Didn't she let you in on the secret?"

"I don't know what you're talking about," Booker said. Rotison laughed.

"She's smarter than I thought she was," he said, and then his expression grew sullen again, and he added, "or else you're lying to me."

Just then Walker, wearing his glasses, appeared on the rim of the top of the Sacred Hill. He lifted his arms over his head and gave out the gobbling cry of a male wild turkey. The four men down on the ground beneath the hill jumped and looked, and then they saw him there.

"He ain't human," Ranik said.

"The hell he ain't," said Rotison. "If he can get up there, so can we. You two dumb bastards climb up there and find the way."

Ranik and Murkens crashed into the bramble at the base of the hill to begin their search. Rotison faced Booker again.

"And you," he said. "I'll be the one to report to Bond. You ain't seen nothing. If you say one word to old Bond or anyone else about what you seen and heard out here, one word I say, I'll skin you alive myself. You got that? Now get your ass on out of here."

Booker mounted up and rode fast, feeling lucky to have escaped with his life.

On top of the hill, Walker was kneeling at the top end of the rattlesnake den, looking down into the dank pit.

"My friends," he said, "there may be some disrespectful white men coming your way. Watch out for them."

Twenty-six

Murkens and Ranik climbed the hill together until they arrived at the top of the vegetation and saw that there was nothing above them but sheer rock. There was no way to continue the climb.

"It'd take ropes and grappling hooks," Murkens said, "and even then I ain't sure we could get up there."

"That little redskin got up there," said Ranik. "I seen him up on top. What'd he do? Fly?"

"Well, he damn sure didn't climb straight up that wall," Murkens said. "There's got to be another way up. You work your way around to the north. I'll go south. If he can get up there, so can we, by God."

Ranik started inching his way along the ledge, and his foot slipped. "Shit," he said.

"Shut up and keep going," Murkens said.

"Who made you the boss hog?" Ranik snarled.

"Rotison told us to find the way up, didn't he?" said Murkens. "Well then, let's find it."

Robert J. Conley

As he inched his way south, Murkens could hear Ranik muttering for awhile longer. He could also hear his clumsy steps loosening rocks and gravel, and he cursed the man under his breath for an oaf and a fool. He also cursed his own bad luck that had brought Rotison around before he had managed to get the information out of the damned Indian and keep the location of the gold mine to himself. Of course, Ranik had been with him, but he'd have killed Ranik at the first opportunity.

Perhaps, he thought, as he bellied along the rock wall, he could still keep it to himself. If he were to find the way up before Ranik, he could just keep quiet about it and figure out a way later to get the gold out and not share it with the rest.

It wasn't long, though, before Murkens was about to decide to give it up as a hopeless cause. The crawl along the side of the hill was tedious, and it was beginning to feel like so much hard work, a thing that he was not used to and had a particular aversion for. A tangled juniper tree blocked his way, effectively closing off the narrow pathway along which he traveled.

He stopped and looked around. The path was particularly dangerous at that point. It would be easy to take a hard tumble. Then he noticed that there was a way down to the bottom that looked easy, especially compared to the way he and Ranik had climbed up. He thought about taking it, going down and forgetting the whole thing.

Then it occurred to him that if he had discovered the best access up and down to the halfway mark, that was probably the Indian's path. And likely Bond's camp being down below had forced the Indian to take a more treacherous path up and down. He was mulling this over in his thick skull, when his foot slipped, and he grabbed in desperation for a branch of the juniper tree. His weight bent the branches, and as he was pulling himself back upright, he saw the cave.

He caught his breath, and his eyes opened wide. ''By

200

God,'' he said to himself. He wondered if it could be. He'd known of caves that opened at both ends, that wound their ways through the ground like tunnels. This could be the secret way the Indians had to the top of the hill. He pulled at the twisted branches of the juniper, breaking some of them off and tossing them behind himself to clear his path. Then, panting greedily, he moved into the dark hole.

"Captain," said Sergeant Scot from his position at the bow of the *John Hart*, "Spanish flags ahead."

Donald walked over to stand beside Scot. As the boat chugged along, tents came into view. It was a Spanish military camp on the Texas side of the river.

"I wonder if it's Capitan del Monte returned," said Scot.

"It might be," said Donald. "Damn it, Scot, we'd better stop. See to it."

"Yes sir," said Scot, and he hastened to give the orders. As the boat slowed and moved toward the south bank, Reddels jumped up from the aft deck table where he had been sitting and sipping whiskey to rush forward for a confrontation with Donald.

"What are we doing?" he demanded.

"We're pulling over for a talk with the Spanish there, Senator," Donald said.

"There's not time for that," said Reddels. "We have to get on to Natchitoches as quickly as possible."

"Senator," said Donald, "there's trouble brewing back there at the crossing. Neither Indians nor bandits respect borders. Capitan del Monte, or whoever is in charge there, deserves to be informed."

"Our business is not to inform the military of a foreign government," said the senator. "I demand that we continue on our way."

Donald turned and walked away from Reddels, and the boat stopped and was secured by the crew. Donald and Scot went ashore and walked to the Spanish camp together. Rey del Monte saw them coming and walked out to meet them.

"Amigo," he said, "I was hoping to find you out here."

"Rey," said Donald. "It's good to have you back. Did you manage to put down the rebellion in the south?"

Del Monte made a throat-slitting gesture with the forefinger of his right hand across his own throat.

"They'll never learn, amigo," he said. "How are things with you?"

"Not so good, I'm afraid," Donald said. He gave del Monte a quick rundown of the situation that had developed in his absence, how Bond had settled below the Sacred Hill and therefore antagonized the Osages of Iron Head's village, how Reddels had sided with Bond, the whole story. "And now," he said, "it seems that I have no choice other than to make a trip back to Army headquarters at Natchitoches for a final decision. I, of course, will recommend that Bond and his settlers be moved. The senator, damn his soul, will ask that they give the old bastard permission to stay where he is. It's out of my hands, Rey. I hate it, but there's nothing more I can do."

Del Monte stroked his chin in deep thought. "I see," he said.

"The senator is angry with me right now for stopping to inform you about the situation," Donald said. "He says we don't have time for that, and that it's not our business to keep you informed."

"I'm glad that you did, amigo," del Monte said, "and I'm sorry if it causes you trouble with your own politicos. By the way, how is our Señora Booker?"

Donald flushed, and del Monte grinned.

"Be careful, Mat," he said. "Her cousins have come to look for her. They might force you to marry her, if you have compromised her honor."

"I don't think that's possible," said Donald. "Anyway, she and Tom have joined up with Bond."

"They are at the illegal settlement then?" del Monte asked.

"Yes," said Donald. "Listen, Rey, I'd like to stay and visit, but I really have to get going. The senator's already hot under the collar, and I'm sure he's planning to fill General Jackson's ear with tales of my incompetence and insubordination."

Donald turned to walk back to the boat, and del Monte called after him.

"Good luck to you, amigo," he said, "and if I see those Hunikers again, I'll tell them they can find their pretty cousin at Buffalo Crossing."

Donald stopped abruptly and turned back to face del Monte. "Hunikers?" he said. "Did you say Hunikers?"

"*Sí,*" del Monte said. "That's the name they gave me. Is something wrong?"

Krevs was the first to spot the rider coming hard toward them over a rise on the north bank. In another minute, he recognized Tom Booker, and he knew that something must be wrong, the way Booker was mistreating his horse. Krevs met Booker, talked with him briefly, then conducted him across the river to where Captain Donald was still visiting with del Monte.

"Captain," said Krevs, "you need to hear this."

"What is it?" said Donald. "Mr. Booker, what are you doing out here?"

Booker was still panting from his fast ride, but he did his best. "Captain," he said, "I'm afraid there's going to be big trouble at Mr. Bond's settlement." He paused to try to catch his breath.

"What's happened?" Donald asked, impatient.

"Ranik and Murkens," Booker panted, "have killed an Indian. I think it was an Osage. There were two of them, and the other one got away. At least, I think he did."

"Goddamn," said Donald. "How did it happen?"

203

"I didn't actually see it happen," Booker said. "I was in the camp when we heard the shot. Mr. Rotison said that he would investigate, and Mr. Bond told me to follow. He said he didn't trust Mr. Rotison. So I rode after, and when I caught up with Mr. Rotison, he was standing over the Indian's body. Apparently, Murkens and Ranik were in pursuit of the other one. When they returned, they said that they had captured, what was his name, your Cherokee friend?"

"Walker?" Donald said.

"Yes," said Booker "They had captured him and tied him to a tree. They were trying to make him divulge the location of a gold mine when the Osage shot an arrow at them. They killed the one and chased the other, and while they were gone, Walker escaped."

Donald was in a muddle. He had been in a hurry to get to Natchitoches, largely because of the insistence of Senator Reddels. Reinforcements were needed, the senator argued, and Donald had reluctantly agreed, in the event the Osages should attack. Now, because of the stupidity of Murkens and Ranik, the Osage attack was likely to come soon. Bond and all the settlers at Buffalo Crossing were in grave and probably immediate danger. Reinforcements or no, Donald decided, he had to get back to warn them.

"Rey," he said, "may I leave Senator Reddels and his daughter here with you? I need to go back to the hill, and I can't deliberately take them into danger."

"Of course, my friend," said del Monte. "We're on our way back to Jonesboro anyway, and we'll be glad to take them along."

Donald thanked del Monte and returned to the boat. He gave Reddels a quick report on the latest developments and told him of del Monte's offer.

"No," said Reddels. "I insist that we continue on our way to Natchitoches."

"Didn't you understand me?" Donald said. "Mr. Bond and his settlers are in danger of attack soon."

"What difference will fifteen soldiers make?" the senator said.

"Nineteen," said Donald. "I'm taking your escort into my command."

"I protest," the senator blustered.

"Protest all you want, Senator," said Donald, "but get yourself and your daughter off this boat immediately."

"There's no need for you to go back there, Mat, my boy," said Reddels, changing his tone. "Zeno Bond has plenty of settlers as well as Rotison and his men. They can drive off the Osages without the help of the Army."

"I don't know that," said Donald, "and I can't take that risk. Even if nineteen more fighting men won't make that much difference, a timely warning might. Now I must insist that you and Eva get off here and allow Capitan del Monte to escort you back to Jonesboro."

Reddels crossed his arms over his chest and set a determined pout on his face. "I refuse to budge," he said, "and if you dare lay hands on me or on my daughter, I'll see you court-martialed."

"Very well," said Donald. "You leave me no choice. I'll just have to take you back into the middle of the fight along with the rest of us."

"What?" said the senator.

Donald ignored him. "Sergeant Scot," he called. "Get the boat underway and turned around again. We're going back to Buffalo Crossing."

"You can't do this," Reddels said. "You can't—We might all be killed."

The engines started chugging and the boat started to move slowly. Reddels ran toward the starboard railing.

"Let me off here," he shouted. "Let me off."

"Sergeant Scot," Donald said. "Let the senator and his daughter get off the boat."

"Yes sir," said Scot.

The *John Hart* held position while the planks were laid

out for Reddels and Eva, and as they disembarked, Eva cast Donald a cold hard look. As soon as those two were on dry ground, the planks were pulled up again, and the boat was gotten underway. Donald hoped that he would be able to forestall a disaster.

Twenty-seven

Ranik came down from the hill in the same spot from which he had gone up. He was scratched and bruised from slipping and sliding along the narrow, brush-tangled trail, and he was in a foul mood. Huffing and puffing from his climb, he found Rotison waiting impatiently for him there by the tree where they had tied Walker. The body of the unfortunate Osage was still lying where it had fallen. Murkens was nowhere to be seen.

"Well?" said Rotison.

"I didn't find a damn thing," said Ranik. "Not a damn thing. It don't look to me like there's any way in hell to get up there from down here."

"The Indians know how to get up there," Rotison said. "There's a way."

"Maybe they know how to fly," Ranik said.

"There's a way," Rotison insisted.

"Well, maybe Murkens'll find it then," Ranik said. "Me and him went different directions."

"Ah, maybe so," Rotison grumbled. "He ain't come back yet. Maybe he's having better luck than you did. We'll wait for him here. I mean to find the way up there and get that gold mine."

The *John Hart* returned yet again to Buffalo Crossing, and Donald, Scot, and two other soldiers, accompanied by Tom Booker, walked to the settlement to confront Zeno Bond. Bethie saw them coming and ran up to stand just behind Bond. When Donald told him why they had returned, old Bond refused to accept the story of some of Rotison's men having killed an Osage.

"Nothing's wrong here, I tell you," the old man said. "It's only a cheap trick to get me to abandon my colony. That's all it is. A cheap trick."

"But Mr. Bond," said Booker, "I saw the body. Remember? You sent me to follow Mr. Rotison because, you said, you didn't trust him."

"Mr. Bond," said Donald, and he took a deep breath. This was getting to be tiresome. "There were two Osages out there today. Murkens and Ranik killed one and chased the other, but the second one escaped. At least so far as we know. When he gets back to Iron Head's village, do you think for a minute that Iron Head will wait for his deadline to attack? One of his people has been killed. He'll attack in full force, and that real soon. Believe me. If you're not worried about your own safety, think of the women and children here. You've got to clear out."

"The Army should protect me here," Bond declared staunchly. "We are a colony of United States citizens, and as such—"

"Mr. Bond," said Donald, "I have nineteen soldiers with me. That's not much protection. If I run to Natchitoches for reinforcements, by the time we get back here, you'll all be dead."

"I need to think," said Bond. "I need some time to think this through."

"You don't have time," Donald said. "The Osages could be gathering to attack right now."

A short distance away, lurking behind a tent, Socrates Bangs listened to the discussion. Then, unnoticed by anyone, he slipped away again.

"Mr. Bond?" said Booker.

Bond turned suddenly and decisively on Booker. "Mr. Booker, did you leave Mr. Rotison and the others out there where this alleged incident took place?" he asked.

"Yes sir," said Booker. "They were still at the scene when I left."

"Go back out there and find Mr. Rotison and bring him here to me," Bond said. "I'll get the whole story straight from his mouth."

Bethie, who had stood silent all this time, stepped forward. "I'll go with you, Tom," she said. "We'll get to the bottom of this."

As Tom and Bethie started to walk away, Bond smiled at Donald, one of his paternalistic smiles. "You'll see, young man," he said. "Everything's under control here. Everything's going to be just fine."

Donald started to say something to stop them from leaving. They might not be safe out there with Rotison, Murkens, and Ranik. He corrected himself. Tom Booker might not be safe. Bethie would probably do just fine for herself. She always did, it seemed. Still, it didn't seem right to let them go alone. Bond had turned away from Donald and was pacing. Donald leaned toward Sergeant Scot and spoke low.

"Take these two men with you," he said, "and follow them."

"Yes sir," said Scot. He spoke low to the other two soldiers, and the three of them followed Bethie and Tom Booker, at a distance. Donald waited a moment, watching them go.

"Mr. Bond," he said.

Bond whirled around to face Donald, as if he had been startled.

"What is it?" he said.

"Mr. Bond," said Donald, "you've got to gather all these people together here so we can inform them of the full situation. They're going to have to get ready to leave this place very soon now."

"I will wait for Mr. Rotison's report on the story," said Bond.

Sings Loud had been watching the entire proceedings and listening with interest from a spot by a nearby fire, where she sat sipping coffee from a tin cup. Glancing over to make sure no one was paying any attention to her, she put her cup down on the ground, stood up, and walked into the bushes at the base of the hill.

"Hey, look," said Ranik, pointing to the approaching Bookers, Tom and Bethie.

"Keep your yap shut," said Rotison. "I'll deal with this—whatever it is."

He crossed his arms over his massive chest and waited in silence until the two newcomers were close enough for conversation.

"Booker," he said, "I thought you run off for good. What brings you back here?"

"Mr. Bond sent me back," said Booker. "He wants to talk to you."

"To me?" said Rotison, trying to seem innocent. "Whatever for?"

"He wants to hear what you have to say about what happened out here, I think," said Booker. "Captain Donald has returned, and he wants us all to abandon this place right away."

"We went all through that with him before, didn't we?" Rotison said.

"That was before an Indian was killed," said Booker. "Captain Donald says the Osages will attack us now for sure."

"Now, I wonder how Captain Donald heard about that dead Indian," Rotison said. Booker opened his mouth as if to respond, but Rotison stopped him from speaking. "Well, never mind that now," he said. "If Mr. Bond wants to see me, then I'd better get back there right away. Ranik, you and Booker stay here and keep watch. Mrs. Booker can go back with me."

Just then, Sergeant Scot rounded a curve and saw the group there ahead. He stopped quickly and motioned the two soldiers behind him to do the same. Then the three of them slipped into the brush at the base of the hill to watch and listen.

"Why should I stay?" said Booker.

"Well now, them Indians might come back," Rotison said. "You want poor Ranik here to get caught out here all by himself?"

"Why should anyone stay here?"

"Murkens is up on the hill," Rotison said. "If someone ain't here when he comes down, he won't know what happened or where to go."

"Well, I—"

"He's right, Tom," said Bethie.

"Well, all right then," Booker said. "But I hope it's not for long. Captain Donald's trying to get everyone packed up to move out."

"I reckon Murkens'll be down off that hill soon enough," said Rotison. He turned to give Ranik a look and a knowing wink. "While you're waiting, Ranik'll take good care of you. You'll be safe enough." He looked at Bethie and smiled. "Shall we go?" he said. "We don't want to keep old Mr. Bond waiting, now, do we?"

Rotison and Bethie started walking back toward the tent settlement. Without knowing it, they walked right past Scot and the other two soldiers. They also walked past Sings Loud, who had worked her way through the woods all the way from the camp. With Bethie and Rotison on around the curve and out of sight, Ranik turned to face Booker, a sneer on his ugly face.

"I wonder how Captain Donald knew about the dead Injun," he said.

"I told him, of course," said Booker. "I thought it was important for the military to know about the situation here."

"Oh, did you now?" Ranik said. "I seem to recall, now that I think back on it, that Mr. Cotton Rotison told you to keep your sissy yap shut about anything you think you might have saw or heard out here. Do you recall that remark from old Cotton?"

"I remember," said Booker, "but I am not aware that Mr. Rotison holds any position of authority. Mr. Bond is in charge of this settlement, and Captain Donald is in command of the military. I'm not obliged to take orders from Mr. Rotison."

"Oh, you ain't?" Ranik said.

"No," said Booker. "I'm not."

Suddenly and without warning, Ranik bashed Booker in the jaw with a powerful blow from his big right fist. Booker flew over on his back, landing hard. Blood trickled from a corner of his mouth, and a black bruise showed on his jaw.

"I'll show you some authority," Ranik said. "How's that for goddamned authority? Huh? Get up, and I'll give you some more. You want authority, do you? Come on, Booker. I think I'll just beat the brains clean out of your head."

Back in the brush, Scot whispered a quick order.

"Take him, men," he said. Scot and the two troopers were out of the bushes quickly, with weapons trained on Ranik, ready to fire, but Ranik was totally unaware of the situation. He was too much involved in his vicious tormenting of poor Tom Booker to hear the rustlings behind him. He had moved in close and reached down for Booker, intending to pull him to his feet, so he could knock him down again.

"Hold it," Scot shouted.

Ranik stopped still and looked back over his shoulder. He saw immediately that he had no chance. Two rifles and a pistol were already trained on him, and even the pistol could have made the shot. He lifted his arms up over his head.

"Don't shoot," he said.

"You're Ranik?" Scot asked.

"Uh, yeah. Ranik. That's me. Did I do something wrong, Captain?"

"It's Sergeant, Ranik," said Scot.

"Oh, well, whatever," Ranik said. He gave a nervous chuckle. "Sorry. But anyhow, there's nothing wrong here, Sergeant."

"We'll see about that," said Scot. "Right now, you're under arrest, Ranik. Make a wrong move and you're a dead man. Keep him covered, men." Scot moved in to disarm Ranik, as Booker got slowly to his feet. He stood rubbing his already swollen jaw. "You all right, Mr. Booker?" Scot said.

"I'll be all right," said Booker.

"Then let's all go back to the camp right now and see Captain Donald," Scot said. "Move it, Ranik."

When the small group had vanished around the curve, Sings Loud came out of hiding. She had watched it all from behind the trees at the base of the hill. She stepped out into the clearing and looked at the body of the young Osage, and she said a silent prayer. Then she heard a slight rustling behind her and turned just in time to see Walker coming out of the brush.

"What are you doing here?" she said.

"I was up there," he said, pointing toward the top of the hill.

"The captain's back," she said. "He's trying to get those men to leave again."

"They'll listen to him if they know what's good for them," Walker said.

Sings Loud shook her head slowly.

"I don't know," she said. "That old man's crazy, I think."

"There's going to be trouble," said Walker. "I have to try to stop it."

"What will you do?" she asked.

"I should go see Iron Head," he said, "but I can't talk his damned language."

"I can," she said. "I'll go with you, if you'll watch your language."

"I apologize for that slip of my tongue," Walker said. "It often happens when I'm talking the white man's talk. Shall we go then?"

"Let's go."

And the Cherokee mystic, Uwas' Edoh', known as Walker, and Sings Loud, the Kickapoo Baptist preacher, took off together, side by side in an easy trot in the direction of the Osage town.

Twenty-eight

"There's a dead Indian out there, all right, Captain," said Scot.

"Shot?" Donald asked.

"He's been shot all right," Scot said. "He's got a big hole in his chest. It looks like he fired an arrow before he was hit."

"Is he an Osage?"

"Well, sir," Scot said, scratching his head and wrinkling his brow, "I ain't no expert on these matters, but I'd say he was an Osage. Yes sir."

Donald looked at Ranik, still with the soldiers' guns trained on him.

"I didn't kill that redskin," Ranik said, "but even if I did, so what? Like the sarge said, he shot first."

"So who killed him?" Donald asked.

"It was Murkens who done it," said Ranik. "The Injun shot his arrow at us for no reason, and then Murkens shot

215

him. That's all. Tell these damn soldier boys to take their guns off me."

The mention of Murkens's name made Donald's blood run hot and his heart pound in his chest. A large part of him wanted to forget all this other nonsense and chase after the hated bastard.

"Where is Murkens?" he asked.

Ranik shrugged. "I don't know," he said. "He left. You going to let me go now?"

Donald turned to Scot. "Mr. Scot," he said, "what about it? Do you have any reason to hold this man?"

"Yes sir," said Scot. "I think so. We ain't holding him because of the Osage."

"What's it all about then?" Donald asked.

"We found this one," said Scot, "Ranik's the name he goes by, beating up on Booker here. I don't know yet what it was all about, but that's why I put him under arrest, sir, for beating on Booker the way he was doing."

"Good work," said Donald. "We'll sort it all out later. Take him aboard as a prisoner when we're ready to leave here."

"Yes sir."

"Now, wait a minute," Ranik started.

"Shut up," Scot snapped.

"Right now," Donald continued, "we've got to get these settlers moving."

"Now, just hold on there, Captain Donald," said Bond. "I don't believe we've resolved this situation quite yet."

"Mr. Bond," said Donald, raising his voice, "I've wasted all the time I'm going to waste arguing with you. I'm taking command here right now, and I'm ordering this settlement abandoned. I want everyone to pack up and get across the river immediately. Once they're on the other side, they will all start on their way back to Jonesboro. Those are my orders."

Bond sniffed a deep breath in through his nostrils and

drew himself up as tall as he could manage. Just about everyone in the settlement had gathered around by this time to listen anxiously to the arguments and to find out what was going to happen to them.

"Very well, Captain," Bond said. "I will not fight the United States Army. I fought and bled for its right to exist, and I will not raise a hand against it now. However, I surrender this land to you, only for the present and under strong protest, and when we have arrived at Army headquarters in Natchitoches, I mean to lodge a serious complaint against you with your superiors, and I will testify against you at your court-martial."

"That's your privilege, Mr. Bond," said Donald, "and I'm sure you'll exercise it. Right now, let's get everyone going."

"And," Bond said, in his best oratorical manner, turning to face the crowd that was gathered there, "we will return once again to this very spot of earth, bringing along with us the proper approval from our beloved government, and we will yet make our homes right here."

"Move along," Donald ordered.

Rotison faded back in the crowd and sidled up to Socrates Bangs. "Help me gather the boys," he said.

"We're not going along with the herd, I take it," said Bangs.

"Hell no, we ain't," Rotison said. "We ain't giving up on that gold this damned easy."

Walker had to slow his pace. He had run just about as long as his body would take it. Sings Loud slowed down so as not to run off and leave him.

"I could sure use a drink of good whiskey," Walker said.

"That's what's wrong with you," Sings Loud said. "You drink whiskey and you cuss. You need to change your ways. Start reading your Bible."

"I don't have one," Walker said.

217

"I have an extra one I'll give you," she said.

"I don't think I'll bother reading it," Walker said. "I don't mean offense, but I have my own ways."

"Heathen ways," she said. "You'll change your mind when you're roasting in hell, but it'll be too late then."

"I already died once," said Walker, "and I didn't go to hell that time. I don't think I'll worry about that."

"Have you caught your breath yet, you old heathen?"

Walker didn't bother answering her. He just broke into an easy lope, and she did too.

Donald's attention was so completely on the settlers as they moved into the crossing that he didn't notice Rotison and his men mount up and ride off in the other direction. He was anxious to get the families to safety. If Iron Head's Osages were already on their way to attack, they could still cross the river and pursue the settlers, of course, but Donald was hoping that they would be satisfied that he had managed to move the intruders out.

"Sergeant Scot," he said, "As soon as all of them are across, get the men all on board. Oh, and invite Mr. Bond to ride along with us."

"Yes sir," said Scot.

Bond grudgingly accepted the invitation. Though he hated to admit it, his old bones ached from too much travel, and the riverboat would be much easier on him than would be horseback riding. It also occurred to him that the *John Hart* might not stop at Jonesboro, and he wanted to be along for the ride on into Natchitoches. Bethie and Tom Booker were also on board.

Reddels's escort of four mounted soldiers, having been commandeered by Donald, was also taken on the boat, horses and all. With the entire population of Bond's colony, Rotison and crew excepted, across the river and moving east toward Jonesboro, Donald at last got back aboard and ordered the boat once again turned around.

"If he keeps this up much longer," Krevs said to Scot, "we'll all get dizzy with the spinning around."

Donald stood on deck at the bow of the boat and watched the settlers moving along the south bank of the river. They were a wretched looking lot, he thought, and he felt sorry for them. *But, damn it*, he told himself, *they should have listened to me*. If they had only waited a little longer at Jonesboro, as he had asked them to do, then he could have easily moved old Bond to the proper location. The settlers could have followed, and there would have been no trouble. They could all be busy by now, he thought, building their new homes.

He told himself that Bond and Reddels were both fools and Rotison was a villain. They were the ones to blame for the misery of this flock of sheep. Even so, he was the one the settlers were blaming. He knew that. He was the object of their hatred. He could feel it. He it was who had told them they had to move. Bond, Reddels, and Rotison had all defended their right to stay put.

Soon the settlers were out of sight. The riverbanks having become wooded, they had been forced to move a little south before continuing their eastward way toward Jonesboro.

Well, Donald thought, at last he had his way, but he wondered what it would all be worth in the end. What would happen when they arrived at Army headquarters in Natchitoches? Bond, a well-known and highly respected patriot, would level all kinds of charges against him, and he would be supported by a United States senator.

Donald's only defense would be that he had followed orders. That in itself should be enough. A soldier is always supposed to follow orders. But for some reason, in this case, Donald had a feeling that it would not be enough. He had a feeling that Bond and Reddels together would sway the opinion of the authorities at headquarters.

And even if his defense should work, even if his actions should be seen by the authorities as justified because he had been following his orders, it was almost a foregone conclusion that the orders would be changed. Bond would get his new grant of land, and the colony would go right back where it had come from. The Osages would attack, and the Army would be sent to subdue them and protect the settlers. All of his effort would have been for nought.

Damn me, he said to himself, *if I joined the Army for this kind of silly intrigue.* He glanced over his shoulder to see Bond standing on the second tier, straight and stiff, head held high, his hands folded behind his back, looking for all hell like he was the captain of the boat.

With that backward glance, Donald noticed too that a storm seemed to be brewing to the west. Then, as if in answer to his thoughts, lightning flashed in the dark and still distant clouds, followed by a low and far-off rumble of thunder. *Maybe we'll outrun it*, Donald thought. He looked forward again, and then he saw there in the water ahead two large trees floating on the surface, each one alone big enough to do major damage to the flimsy boat. Just then Sergeant Scot stepped up beside Donald.

"Mr. Scot," said Donald.

"Yes sir," said Scot. "The pilot seen them already, sir. He thinks we can steer between them easy enough."

The passage between the two trees was narrow, and Donald thought that getting between them would be like threading a needle. But as the boat crept closer, it looked as though they would actually make it. Then, too late, he saw the rope. He shouted at Scot, and Scot shouted at the pilot. There was no need for the shouting. Just about everyone had seen it at the same time.

Engines were reversed. Water splashed. Scot shouted orders, and soldiers ran for their weapons and their posts. Zeno Bond clutched the rail of the upper deck and stared hard ahead. The *John Hart* ran into the rope, moved ahead a little farther, then reversed itself. The rope having been stretched

220

as far as it would go, it flung the boat backward, helping the reversed engine do its job. Once they had backed out of the trap, the engine was cut. They were adrift on the water.

Donald looked around quickly to make sure that his men were ready for whatever might be about to happen. The two trees tied together were a deliberate trap. There was no other way to look at it. The settlers were plodding along somewhere on the south bank. Bond was on board. Reddels was with del Monte, either back at Jonesboro or on the way back. Rotison and his gang were out loose, and the Osages might be anywhere and up to anything.

Scot had the men all ready, so there was nothing for Donald to do but be ready himself. He scanned the banks on both sides of the river. They were thick with willows and tall cotton trees. There were plenty of places to hide. Still, he saw no one, heard nothing. Perhaps no one was out there at all. Perhaps the trap had been set just to slow them down, just to harass them. But why?

Donald knew that someone was going to have to get off the boat and into the river to cut the rope before the boat could get underway again. But he didn't want to expose anyone to danger from the banks. He wanted to make sure first that there was no one there. Even so, he couldn't just wait like this forever.

Suddenly a shot was fired. Donald looked quickly in the direction of the sound, and he caught a glimpse of Rotison with a still-smoking rifle in his hands, just dropping back down out of sight. Some of the soldiers had seen him too, for there were several shots fired from the boat into Rotison's general vicinity. There was no way to tell if any one of them had hit its mark.

Scot called out, "Cease fire," for there was nothing to shoot at, and he didn't want ammunition wasted. Donald looked around to see if any damage had been done by Rotison. Then he saw, up on the second deck, Zeno Bond still standing, but wavering and clutching at his chest. As Donald watched, the old patriot's knees buckled, and he crumpled slowly into an insignificant looking heap there on the upper deck.

Twenty-nine

The silence on the Red River was long and deathly still. Donald crouched on the deck of the *John Hart*, pistol clutched in his hand, his eyes searching the north bank for any sign of the albino renegade Rotison or any of his cronies. A soldier had gone to the second tier of the boat to check on Zeno Bond. He knelt down beside the pitiful bundle of rags and bones, looked up, and called out, "He's done for."

Just then whooping and shouting and shooting erupted from the woods along the northern bank of the river. Donald caught brief sight of Rotison and then of Socrates Bangs. He wasn't able to get off a good shot at either one of them though. He did find another target, and he squeezed off a round just as one of the gang was getting ready to fire his own shot toward the boat. The man screamed and slapped at a red blotch that had suddenly appeared on his face, then fell back.

"You got one, sir," said Scot.

"There's plenty more," said Donald. "Enough to go around."

Frightened but fascinated, Tom Booker huddled in the doorway to the cabin that was occupied by Bethie, his pretended wife, and watched wide-eyed as bullets spanged here and there into the walls and the deck of the boat. Bethie was inside the room.

Then, as suddenly as the fighting had erupted, it stopped, and once again an eerie silence prevailed. Once again, the renegades were all hidden. The soldiers on the boat looked around to no avail for something out there at which to shoot.

"Take it easy, men," Scot said. "Don't fire unless you have a target."

"Do we have any casualties, Mr. Scot?" Donald asked.

Scot took a quick accounting of his men. He could see them all from where he crouched.

"Only Mr. Bond, sir," he said. "He's dead, but no one else is hit."

Donald wondered if Rotison had deliberately killed old Bond, or if the shot had been a random one that just happened to hit the old man. It would have made more sense, it seemed to Donald, had Rotison tried again to kill him. Why kill Bond? Simply because Bond had agreed to go along with Donald and let the military sort things out?

Whatever the reason, he thought, the old fool Bond brought it on himself, and as he thought it, he felt a little guilty for having had the thought. After all, the poor old man had been a hero of the War for Independence. But then he had gotten more than a bit dotty in his old age, and he had sure caused plenty of trouble on this occasion. Once more, Donald scanned the still north bank for any sign of movement. Then he saw a dirty white handkerchief tied on the end of a stick emerge slowly from behind a thick tangle of bush.

"Hold your fire," he said calmly, and Sergeant Scot repeated the order in a roar.

"Captain Donald," a voice called out.

"Who's there?" Donald called back.

"It is I, Dr. Socrates Bangs, Captain Donald. Well now, I seem to have turned the tables on you, wouldn't you say?"

"We'll see about that," Donald said. "You can't get away with attacking the United States Army, Bangs. You're at least smart enough to know that. You and the others surrender your arms."

"No, I don't think we'll do that, Captain," said Bangs. "You know, there's military authority and then there's civil authority, and the military doesn't have any business messing around with civil matters."

"I know all that, Bangs," Donald said, "but what's it got to do with us now?"

"You're harboring a fugitive from justice on that boat of yours, Captain," Bangs said. "I have out here with me right now a Mr. Josiah Huniker and his brother, Joshua, carrying with them a civil warrant for the arrest of Mrs. Elizabeth Booker for the wanton murder of their brother, Jethro, and for the theft of a sum of money that had belonged to the deceased."

Tom Booker heard the dreaded name of Huniker with horror. His jaw dropped.

"Bethie," he said. But she had heard too. She grabbed Tom and pulled him back into the cabin, shutting the door. She clutched the lapels of his coat and pulled him toward her, shaking with fear.

"They've come after me, Tom," she said. "They mean to kill me."

"If they can get to us," Booker said, "they'll kill the both of us. That's for sure."

"Tom," she said, "get a gun. Get a gun and stand guard. Keep them away from me."

"Captain Donald will keep them away," Tom said. "Try to calm down, Bethie."

"What if he can't stop them?" she said. Then, almost

225

hysterically, she screamed, "Tom, get a gun, goddamn you!"

Back out on deck, Donald called back to Bangs.

"Bangs," he said, "you tell those Huniker brothers that their civil warrant, if they even have one, carries no weight out here. You're in Arkansas Territory now, and so far, the only local authority here is military. If they have a complaint against Mrs. Booker, or anyone else, they can report it to me. Now put down your weapons and show yourselves with your hands held up high."

"This is a citizen posse, Captain Donald," Bangs said, "and we have no intention of giving up our duly constituted authority to the military, much less our weapons. Give us Mrs. Booker and the money she stole from the Hunikers. Then we'll allow you to pass peacefully on down the river."

"Does he think we're big enough fools to believe that?" Scot said.

"Dr. Socrates Bangs, you phony son of a bitch," Donald roared, "I gave you your last chance. In three more seconds we're going to blow you and your white flag all the way to hell. Mr. Scot."

"Fire at will," Scot shouted.

Socrates Bangs tried to dig a hole like a gopher, as every gun on board the *John Hart* was fired in his direction. In the midst of all the blasting, Donald thought that he heard someone on shore yelp with pain, and he hoped that it was Bangs.

It didn't take long, though, for the outlaw posse to start to return fire. Soon it sounded like a small war had broken out there on the Red River, but the bullets from both sides were not finding their marks. No one was really taking careful aim at anyone else, for men fired wildly and huddled low to avoid being hit.

Donald looked anxiously toward the storm clouds approaching from the west. He longed for what Mr. Krevs would call a real gully washer, that might temporarily dampen the spirits of the gang on the banks and give him at least a chance to free the boat and get it moving along again. Otherwise, he wasn't at all sure how he was going to get out of this one.

The fight slowed down to a long standoff with an occasional potshot being taken from one side or the other. Still, no one else was hit. The day dragged on. Overhead the sun was hot, but when the dark clouds came closer, they brought with them some welcome cool air. Then, drifting underneath the sun, they darkened the whole world in shadow. Donald felt the first few drops of rain, and he thrilled at the anticipation of more.

But once the decks of the boat were slick from a light sprinkling, the clouds moved on, totally disinterested in the petty human drama that was being played out along the thin red ribbon which meandered along beneath them. The sun once more beat down, and the sky was clear and blue. There was no storm. And there was no more sign of a storm approaching. And the standoff continued in that way until darkness fell.

Donald sat on the deck of the boat in shadow. Soldiers were on watch. No one from the bank had fired at the boat since the sun had gone down. No one on board had fired a shot. Even if they made it safely through the night, Donald thought, morning would bring nothing more than the same situation. He had to come up with a plan of action. Sergeant Scot crept up and knelt beside him.

"Coffee, sir?" he asked.

"What?" said Donald, and then he saw the cup, the steam coming off its top. "Oh, yes," he said. "Thank you."

He took the cup, and Scot started to leave, but Donald stopped him.

"Mr. Scot," he said, "wait a minute."

"Yes sir," Scot said, and he sat down on the deck beside his captain.

"Mr. Scot, we have to send someone over the side to cut that damn rope," Donald said.

"Tonight, sir?" Scot asked.

"Whoever goes over will stand a better chance in the dark," said Donald. He sipped hot coffee.

"I'll send Corporal Alan," Scot said. "He's a strong swimmer and a bold lad."

"That's good," said Donald.

"Anything else, sir?" Scot asked.

"Yes," said Donald. "I need two men who can put on a good show."

"A show, sir?"

"Yes," Donald said, "and a damned convincing one."

"Well, sir," Scot said, "Corporal Burns is a right cutup, he is. Always mocking and carrying on. He did a funny impression of the senator, he did. Had us all laughing till our sides hurt."

"He'll do," said Donald. "One other."

"Jarvis, sir," said Scot.

"Good," said Donald. "Give Burns the key to Ranik's locks, and have the two of them report to me."

"Right away, sir," said Scot, starting to get up.

"And Scot," said Donald. "Break out that cannon."

"Yes sir."

Scot scurried off into the darkness, and Donald sipped his coffee. He heard a rustling beside him and turned to see Bethie coming slowly toward him.

"Bethie," he said. "What are you doing out here on deck?"

"I had to see you," she said. "They're out there."

"Yes," he said, "I know."

"The Hunikers are out there, and they mean to kill me," she said.

"That's why you need to stay inside your cabin," he said. "It's much safer."

"Mat," she said, "you promised me that the Hunikers

wouldn't get me. You promised to protect me, and you've got to keep that promise."

"I'm doing my best," he said, "but you'll make it much easier for me if you get back inside the cabin and stay there until this is all over."

Corporal Burns and Private Jarvis showed up, hunkering down in the shadow with their captain. "You sent for us, sir?" Burns asked.

"That's right, Burns," said Donald. "Now, Bethie, do like I said. Get back inside that cabin and stay there. Stay there until I tell you to come out. Go on now."

Bethie looked from Donald to Jarvis and Burns, then began scooting her way back to the cabin. Donald heaved a heavy sigh.

"Sir?" said Burns.

"Yes," said Donald. "I have a job for you. I want you two to get drunk."

"Sir?"

"Well, not actually," Donald said. "I want you to pretend drunkenness. Can you do that?"

"I think so, sir," said Burns, "but—"

"Just listen," said Donald. "Those renegades out there think that they have us pinned down. I want them to think that rising water's setting us loose and we're going to be underway with first light. You understand?"

"Yes sir."

"Repeat what I said."

"The water level's rising and we'll be underway with first light," said Burns.

"Correct," said Donald. "Now here's how we make them believe that. The two of you get drunk and happen by our prisoner. You know where he is?"

"That Ranik, sir?" Burns asked.

"Yes," said Donald.

"He's in irons and chained to a post in the stables, sir," said Jarvis.

"Yes," said Donald. "So you two are drunk, and you happen to go near him. In your drunkenness, you talk about the rising water and our plans to be underway with first light. Make sure he can overhear."

"Yes sir," said Burns, grinning. "I get it."

"Yeah," said Jarvis.

"Then you, Jarvis, go on your way," Donald said. "Burns, you stay there. Fall down if you have to, to make it seem real. Let Ranik take over from there. He'll try to find a way to get you to turn him loose. Don't make it too easy for him, or he might catch on, but let him go in the end. You got it?"

"Yes sir," said Burns. "I got it. So that's why Sergeant Scot gave me the key to the irons."

"That's right," said Donald, "but don't give it up too easy."

"Right, sir," said Burns.

"Jarvis?" said Donald. "You have your role straight in your mind?"

"Yes sir," said Jarvis. "You can count on us, sir. We'll get the job done."

"I know you will, men," said Donald. "Now get to it."

Thirty

The whiskey bottle was filled with strong tea, but it had the right look, and Corporal Burns started to giggle from way back by the galley. Jarvis picked up on it easily, once Burns got him started. Both men adopted a rolling walk, one that made it look as if they might topple over at any moment. They rolled toward the stairway that led up to the second tier.

"Wait a minute," said Burns. "Where do you think you're going?"

"I don't know," said Jarvis. "No place in particular."

The speech of both men was slurred, as if by too much drink.

"Well," said Burns, "those stairs go up to the captain's room. You don't want to go up there and let him catch you like this. Do you?"

"No, no," said Jarvis. "Hell no."

"Here," said Burns, shoving the bottle at Jarvis. "Have another drinkee." Jarvis took the bottle and tipped it up.

"And stay away from Captain Fancy Pants."

Jarvis spluttered and broke into drunken giggles.

"Captain Fancy Pants," he repeated. "Captain Fancy Pants. Don't get caught by Captain Fancy Pants."

"Hush now," said Burns. "I see old Scotty over there by the rail. Be quiet."

"Old Scotty Pants by the rail," Jarvis whispered.

"Come on," said Burns, taking the bottle back from Jarvis. "Shh. Follow me."

He threw his arm around Jarvis's shoulders, and the two of them staggered together into the stable area. Burns dropped heavily into a sitting position on the deck just beside Krevs's mule. He pulled Jarvis down with him.

"Hey," Jarvis protested.

"Shush," said Burns.

"Let me have another pull at that jug," said Jarvis.

Burns handed the bottle back to Jarvis and giggled.

"Aren't you afraid you'll get drunk?" he said.

"I got to get drunk," said Jarvis. "I been on this damn river too long, and now we're just stuck here. Got to get drunk."

"Oh," said Burns. "It's all right. I heard Captain Fancy Pants talking to that pilot. That little bit of rain we had— it's causing the river to rise after all. Must have been more rain in the west or something. Anyhow, they say we'll get out of here in the morning."

"Oh, yeah?" said Jarvis. "That's good."

Jarvis drank, then began struggling to his feet.

"Where the hell are you going?" said Burns.

"I have to go piss," Jarvis said. "I need to be ready to go in the morning."

"Don't fall overboard," said Burns, laughing.

Jarvis staggered away, and Burns sat alone for a moment, alternately singing to himself and giggling. Then, "Hey," he said. "Son of a bitch took my bottle with him. Got to go get him."

He got himself up on his feet and stood swaying for a moment. Then he started to walk, but he lurched instead, almost stumbling into Ranik where he was chained to the post nearby.

"Oh," he said. "Excuse me, sir."

"Hey, soldier," said Ranik.

"Are you talking to me, sir?" Burns said.

"Yeah. You," Ranik said.

"I'm sorry, sir," said Burns, "but I have a very important mission to perform. I don't have any time for chitchat."

"I know what your damned mission is," Ranik said.

Burns appeared to be astonished.

"You do?" he said.

"Your buddy took off with your bottle," Ranik said. "You can get him later. Listen to me just a minute, will you?"

"Well," said Burns, "all right. One minute."

"I got a ten-dollar gold piece in my pocket," Ranik said. "That'll buy a lot of whiskey. I'll give it to you if you get me loose from here."

"Oh," said Burns, "I don't know about that."

"Come on," Ranik said. "No one'll ever know who done it."

"Ten dollars?" Burns said.

"Yeah," said Ranik. "In gold."

"Let me see it first."

Ranik tried to get a hand in his pocket, but he couldn't manage it because of the chains.

"It's right in there," he said. "I can't get to it. You get it out."

Burns reached forward and fell against Ranik. "Excuse me," he said. He righted himself and shoved a hand deep into Ranik's pocket, coming out at last with the coin. Because of the darkness, he held it close to his eyes to examine it.

"Well, come on," Ranik said. "Get me out of here."

"I don't trust you," Burns said. "If I turn you loose, you might kill me before you run."

"You've got my gold piece, you bastard," Ranik said. "Get me loose from here."

Burns fumbled in his own pockets for the key he had gotten from Sergeant Scot. He held it in front of Ranik's nose.

"Here," he said. "This will unlock you."

"Well, do it," Ranik said.

"I don't believe I will," Burns said. "Hold out your hand."

Ranik turned a hand up, and Burns placed the key in his palm. "That's all you'll get from me," he said, and he turned and staggered away.

Ranik had a struggle, but he finally managed to get the key into the lock and turn it. The big, heavy padlock clacked, and Ranik waited, afraid that someone might have heard the noise. Then he slipped the lock out of the chain links and carefully lowered the chain to the deck. Looking all around, he crept to the edge of the deck, slipped under the rail, and lowered himself down into the water. From a dark shadow against the lower cabin walls, Donald watched him go.

It was a few minutes later when Sergeant Scot and Corporal Alan moved stealthily to the port side of the deck. Alan was stripped to his underwear and carrying a sharp hunting knife.

"Go over here," said Scot. "Then work your way around to the bow. Be careful. They might be watching from the other side."

"Okay, Sarge," Alan said.

"And Alan."

"Yeah?"

"When you go to cut that rope," Scot said, "be real careful. Don't let yourself get tangled in the rope or the

234

trees. Go slow and easy. We want to get loose here, but we also want you to get safe back aboard. Any sign of trouble, get your ass back around here. I'll be waiting here for you."

Alan slipped quietly over the side and into the water, just as Krevs and two soldiers walked up to Scot and knelt on the deck there beside him.

"Now, Scot?" Krevs asked.

"Is Captain Donald ready?" Scot asked.

"He's raring to go," said Krevs.

"All right," said Scot. "Get to it."

In the water in front of the *John Hart*, Corporal Alan found the rope. He followed it to where it was tied to one of the two big trees, and he began to cut it there where it was tied. The knife was sharp, but the thick, wet rope was hard to cut, and Alan used the knife blade like a saw. Now and then he stopped sawing to look toward the north bank in case anyone there had spotted him.

Just at that moment, well back behind the trees on the north bank, Ranik, Rotison, Bangs, and the two Hunikers were in conference, huddled around a small fire. Ranik was trying to get his clothes dry.

"They said the water was rising," he told the others. "As soon as the sun's up, they'll be pulling out."

"That won't be long," said Bangs.

"We'll have to hit them before they get that tub moving," Rotison said. "Ranik, you take some of the men and go west a ways, so they don't hear you or see you. Swim your horses across. When you hear me shooting from this side, you attack from the south side."

"We'll get them from both sides," Ranik said with a grin.

"Watch out nobody shoots that gal," said Josiah Huniker. "She belongs to me and my brother."

"We're going to kill her personal," said Joshua Huniker, "but we're going to have a little fun with her first."

235

"You going to let the rest of us have any fun before you kill her?" Ranik asked with a whine.

"You just make sure she's safe," said Josiah Huniker. "Make sure we get our hands on her. We won't forget you."

Ranik grinned.

"You better get going," said Rotison. "The sun's going to be showing up any time now."

"Might as well," Ranik said. "Hell, I'm still wet from my last dipping."

The *John Hart* was too far out in the middle of the river for the planks to be laid out to the bank on the Texas side, so Krevs had to jump his mule into the water and lead it to land. Soldiers were ready on the larboard side watching the north bank in case the loud splash and braying drew the wrong kind of attention from over there. No one seemed to take note, and Krevs got the mule ashore. He led it to a nearby knoll that Donald had pointed out to him earlier. He gathered some twigs and small branches and built a fire.

As soon as he knew that Krevs and the mule had made it, Donald had two more soldiers slip over the edge and down into the water. Then two others, on deck, lowered the little field cannon down to them.

"Sarge," Alan whispered harshly from the water. Scot looked over the edge and saw Alan there below. He reached down and grasped Alan's right hand in his own and pulled. Soon Alan was crawling up on deck. He sat down in a spreading pool of river water, breathing deeply.

"It's done, Sarge," he said.

Scot slapped him on the shoulder.

"Good work, Alan," he said.

Smoke billowed from the stacks of the *John Hart* as the boilers were building up steam. Along the far eastern horizon, the sky was beginning to show red light, by the time Donald, now on the knoll with Krevs and the two soldiers, had finished his preparations. Krevs stood holding the reins of his mule. The small cannon, loaded and ready to fire, was strapped securely to the mule's back. Krevs squinted back over his shoulder at Donald.

"You think they'll attack, Captain?" he asked.

"If they think we're about to move out," Donald said, "yes, I think they will, and just any time now."

Krevs looked at his mule and shook his head.

"It's the damndest thing I ever seen," he said.

"You don't think it'll work?" Donald asked.

"I don't know," said Krevs. "For sure it'll be the biggest fart that mule ever let fly."

On board the boat, Sergeant Scot had all the soldiers lined up on the larboard side, waiting and watching for an attack from the north bank. In addition to the seventeen troopers, Tom Booker was there with a rifle. The morning was still and quiet. Ahead of the boat, in the water, the two large trees drifted aimlessly.

Then, through a slight clearing between the trees, Rotison burst on horseback, screaming. He was followed by others, all howling and firing rifles and pistols at the boat. A soldier cried out in pain and fell back on the deck. Sergeant Scot took aim with his rifle and dropped a renegade out of his saddle and into the water just at the river's edge.

At that moment, Ranik, having heard the shots and shouts, kicked his mount into a run to lead his own charge from the south, but as he rode toward the boat, he saw Donald and the others up on the knoll. Then he saw the cannon. He jerked back on the reins and howled at his men to turn tail and run.

"Fire, Mr. Krevs," Donald shouted, and Krevs touched a flame to the cannon's fuse. The fuse fizzed. The mule got nervous. "Hold her," said Donald.

A soldier got on either side of the mule and leaned into it as the fuse sputtered, spitting flame along the mule's neck. Suddenly the mule went wild, kicked, and whirled, knocking Krevs aside. Donald grabbed its halter as it turned in ever widening circles to the right, head turned and wide eyes focused on the sputtering fuse. One of the soldiers was sent flying. For a terrifying instant the cannon was aimed at the *John Hart*.

"Turn her," Donald shouted. Krevs got to his feet and ran for the mule's rear end. Careful to keep his own head out from in front of the business end of the cannon, he shoved on the mule's rear from the side. She bellowed and kicked and spun, and then she was aimed in the right direction again. "Hold her steady," Krevs said. She kicked up her heels.

There was a deafening roar and a cloud of smoke as flame belched from the cannon on the mule's back, and then there was no holding her. The shot went high because of her last kick, and the mule broke loose and ran, the cannon slipping to one side. Grapeshot rained terror down on Ranik's bunch, a piece almost tearing the ear off the left side of Ranik's head.

"Ow," he roared. "Get back across the river."

One man dropped from his horse and lay still. Another went over with his horse. Ranik and the rest plunged headlong into the red waters and fought their way back to the north side.

Donald, Krevs, and the two soldiers stood stunned atop the knoll. Krevs stared after his now lost mule. Donald stared after the escaping Ranik bunch. The two private soldiers, grateful to be alive, looked toward the *John Hart*, where firing seemed to have ceased.

"Sir," said one of the privates, at last breaking the silence, "it's got quiet."

"Yes," said Donald.

"Perhaps those on the other side is trying to figure out

238

where the cannon shot come from,'' said Krevs.

"Perhaps," said Donald. The cobwebs seemed to have at last cleared out of his head. "I don't think we'll be charged from this side again," he said. "Let's get back aboard."

They turned to head down the knoll to the bank, and Krevs stopped, looking across the river and beyond the tree-lined bank on the north side.

"Captain," he said. "Looky yonder. Osages coming."

Thirty-one

The mule and the cannon were long gone, so Donald, Krevs, and the two privates ran toward the river. There was nothing more to do. Running down the slope, Donald took a hard look at the approaching Osages on the far side. In the lead was Socrates Bangs's medicine wagon, Iron Head standing in front of the seat and handling the reins. The sunlight gleamed off the Spanish helmet on his head, and the wagon bounced up and down as Iron Head lashed at the two horses. Behind and on both sides of the wagon, armed Osage men on horseback raced.

"Goddamn," Donald said as he plunged into the red water. All four men splashed their way out to the boat and climbed aboard, dripping wet. Sergeant Scot hurried over to meet Donald.

"Are you all right, sir?" he asked.

"Yes," Donald said. "There was an attack from the south, but we managed to drive it off, and I saw them start to cross again."

"You drove them off with that cannon shot, sir?" Scot asked.

"Yes," Donald said, his face burning red, "but I don't want to talk about it. What's happening over here?"

"It got real quiet out there right after you fired that cannon, sir," said Scot. "I don't know what they're up to."

"Do we have enough steam to get started?" asked Donald.

"Yes sir," Scot said, "I think so."

"Then tell them to get us underway quick," Donald said. "There's more trouble on the way."

"Iron Head and his boys is coming," Krevs added. "And I imagine he's mad as hell."

Scot hurried away to get the boat crew hustling. Corporal Burns and the troops continued to watch the north bank closely.

"Stay alert, men," said Donald. "Things could get hot again just any minute."

Scot returned, and the boat's engine began to chug. Slowly, they began to move. Donald watched anxiously as the bow of the boat began to nudge its way between the two trees, and branches scraped the sides, making annoying, raking noises. Donald clenched his teeth and held his breath. He imagined a branch ripping right through the thin walls of the boat.

Suddenly from behind the trees on the north bank, Rotison emerged. "They're moving," he cried out. "Attack! Kill them!"

Then the outlaws came out in full force, some firing from behind bushes or trees, some charging on horseback, splashing into the water. The boat was still only creeping along in the low water.

"Fire," Scot shouted.

Soldiers opened fire on the attackers, and Tom Booker actually knocked a renegade out of his saddle with a rifle shot. The others who were rushing the boat on horseback

241

turned and headed back into the woods, seeking cover. Scot shot one of them in the back with his pistol, just before the man would have disappeared into the woods.

As the *John Hart* continued its slow and tedious way, the renegades scurried from bush to bush, trying to keep up with it, and continued to fire at anyone they could get a shot at on the boat. Another soldier was hit.

"Damn," said Scot. "Keep low, men. Protect yourselves."

The running fight kept moving east along the river, but again, it seemed as though both sides were only expending ammunition. No one else on the boat was hit, and if the soldiers hit any of the outlaws, they were totally unaware of the fact. Then the boat rounded a bend in the river, and suddenly the bank on the north opened up to reveal a vast prairie. Chief Iron Head in his wagon and the mounted men accompanying him came thundering into the opening, riding south, toward the river.

"Here they come," said Donald. "Get ready."

"We can't hold off all of them," said Scot. "There's too many."

"We can die trying," Donald said. "Get me a rifle."

Scot took a rifle away from a private and handed it to Donald. Donald laid it across the rail and zeroed in on Iron Head himself.

"Captain," said Krevs, "he's too far out yet."

"I know," said Donald. He held steady. The wagon seemed to be rushing straight toward him, and he had the figure of Iron Head straddling the front sight of the long rifle.

"Closer," said Krevs. "A little closer."

Then Donald saw that there were two people on the wagon seat behind Iron Head. He raised his head away from the rifle to look, squinting, and then he recognized them— Walker and Sings Loud. Iron Head clutched the reins in his left hand and raised a long lance up over his head in his right. He let out a long and shrill shriek.

The wagon hit a rock and bounced high up off the ground, and Iron Head fell backwards over the seat and disappeared. Both Walker and Sings Loud desperately reached for the loose lines.

"What the hell's going on?" Donald asked.

The Osage riders in the lead loosed their arrows just then, and it was only then that Donald realized what was actually happening out there.

"They're not after us," he said. "They're attacking Rotison and his gang."

The renegades made that same discovery at just about the same moment, and they turned to defend themselves against the terrible Osage onslaught. Bangs stood up from behind the bush there where he had been crouched. His eyes opened wide.

"My wagon," he shouted.

An Osage arrow whizzed close by him, and he ducked down quickly again. Rotison, Ranik, and the Hunikers all ran for the river and jumped in. The *John Hart* had already moved past them by then. And then the Osages were upon the outlaw gang. And they showed no mercy. From the deck of the *John Hart*, Donald watched. He thought about stopping the boat, but he did not.

"My God," said Krevs, "them Osages is wiping out that whole damn scummy bunch."

"Yes," Donald said. "It does look that way."

"I ain't seen a single Indian fall," Krevs said.

"Me neither," Donald said, "not since Iron Head fell over his wagon seat."

Walker and Sings Loud had been unable to get control of the team, but when the two horses saw that they were just about to race headlong into the river, they stopped themselves. Walker was thrown forward and would have fallen in between the horses, had not Sings Loud grabbed him by the tail of his jacket and held on tight.

With the wagon stopped, Iron Head crawled back over the seat. He stood up again and looked out, but all he could see in front of him was the river and to his left the steamboat chugging away. He could hear the fight raging around him though, so he took up his lance again and jumped down out of the wagon. He was followed by his two passengers.

One young Osage came running toward Iron Head, a wide grin on his face. He had a white man by the collar and was dragging him along. Close to the chief, he stopped and jerked the man's head up. And Iron Head recognized Socrates Bangs. He smiled at the sight and stepped forward. The fight was almost over. Back behind the wagon an Osage bashed in an outlaw's skull. One renegade popped up from behind a bush and ran toward the woods to the west. An arrow thudded into his back, and he fell forward. No renegades were left alive on the field of battle, save Bangs.

Iron Head held the point of his long lance aimed at Bangs's midsection, and he walked slowly and deliberately toward Bangs. Looking down horrified at the large, jagged, flint point, Bangs struggled, but the young man held him fast. Iron Head stepped in closer and gouged, and Bangs began to scream.

With the sun getting low in the western sky and the bloody battlefield well behind them, Donald had the boat tied up for the night. They would reach Jonesboro sometime the next day, pick up the senator and Eva Reddels, probably spend the night there, then head on toward Natchitoches the next morning.

Things had certainly not worked out the way Donald had wanted them to, but in spite of that, he found himself almost anxious to reach Army headquarters and put all of this behind him and onto the shoulders of someone else. He was tired, and for the first time in awhile, he felt as if he could really relax.

"Mr. Scot," he said.

"Yes sir."

"Post a light guard for the night," Donald said. "I'm turning in."

"Yes sir," said Scot. "Good night, sir."

Donald had just mounted the stairs to climb up to his room, when Rotison pulled himself up over the edge and stepped aboard. He was dripping wet from the river, and he was followed close behind by Ranik and both Hunikers. Then, with no warning, Rotison lifted a pistol and fired.

Donald felt the sharp, hot pain in his back as soon as he heard the shot. He clutched the rail, trying to keep himself from falling. Turning to face his unknown attacker, he fell back, landing in a sitting position on the stairs. Ranik raised a pistol, but Sergeant Scot saw him just in time. Jerking out his own pistol, he fired quickly, aiming for the chest. The shot went high, though, and the ball tore an ugly hole in Ranik's forehead. Ranik, dead already, flipped back over the rail and fell into the river.

Having heard the two shots, Bethie opened the door of her cabin, a pistol in her hand. She saw Rotison moving toward the stairs. There wasn't time to think. She fired. Rotison stopped. His pale face wore a puzzled expression. He looked down at his chest and saw a black spot there. Reaching up, curious, with his left hand, he felt the spot, and he found that it was a hole, and it was wet and warm and sticky. Then he knew that he had been shot.

He looked up again, trying to focus his eyes on Bethie there in the doorway, a smoking pistol in her hand. His vision was blurry. Then his knees suddenly weakened, and he dropped heavily to the deck. He did not move again.

Meantime, the two Hunikers had moved, one toward the bow, the other toward the rear of the boat. Joshua, forward, held a pistol in his hand. Corporal Burns suddenly was there confronting him, armed with a saber. Huniker raised the pistol and pulled the trigger, but nothing happened. His powder must have gotten wet in the river.

"Damn," he shouted. He drew back his arm to fling the pistol at Burns, but Burns stepped in quickly and took a swipe at Huniker with the sword. It sliced Huniker's belly open. The outlaw grabbed at his open wound with both hands and dropped to his knees.

Moving swiftly, like a cat, the other Huniker came up beside Bethie and pulled her out of the doorway. As she screamed, he put her in front of him, holding her around the neck with one arm. His other hand clutched a knife, and he pointed the tip of the blade at her throat. There were soldiers all around, moving toward him. He snarled and made a menacing gesture with his knife toward Bethie's throat.

"Get away from me," he said. "Get back or I'll slice her throat from ear to ear."

"Hold it, men," said Scot.

They all stood still.

"Now put down your weapons," said Huniker. There was no immediate response. "Do it now," he snapped, "or I'll cut her head off. I mean it."

"You harm her," said Scot, "and you're a dead man."

"And if I don't," Huniker said, "I'll be just as dead, so I might as well take her with me. Make up your mind."

"Put them down," said Scot, and the soldiers all laid down their weapons on the deck.

"Now," said Huniker, "all of you bastards get over there on the far side of the boat. Move."

Scot took the men to the starboard side, and Huniker, dragging Bethie along with him, jumped off on the port side. Scot heard the splash and rushed back, but it was dark, and all he could see below the side of the boat was water. He rushed to the stairs where Donald still sat.

"Captain," he said, "how bad is it?"

"I don't know," said Donald.

"Can you make it to your room?" Scot asked.

"I think so," said Donald.

"Here," said Scot. "Let me give you a hand."

Scot helped Donald to his feet, then put an arm around him to help hold him up. They started up the stairs. Calling back over his shoulder, Scot said, "Burns, take charge here."

"Mr. Scot," said Donald, "give me a casualty report."

"Only yourself, sir," said Scot. "But one of the outlaws got away, and he took Mrs. Booker with him."

Thirty-two

Donald woke up feverish. His sheets were wet with his sweat, sticking to his body. He flung back the top sheet, and a sharp pain stabbed through his upper body. He lay back sucking in a deep breath. And he remembered what had happened the night before.

Damn, he thought. *Well, at least I'm not dead. I know I'm not, because it hurts too much to be dead.*

He decided to try again, but he would be more careful this time. Slowly and easily he pulled the sticky top sheet to one side. Carefully he moved his legs to swing them over the edge so he could get out of bed. He grimaced, gritting his teeth with the pain, but he kept moving, and soon he was sitting up on the edge of the bed. Then the door to his cabin opened up and Sergeant Scot stepped inside.

"Sir," said Scot, "you shouldn't be trying to get up like that."

"Hand me my trousers, Scot," said Donald.

Scot handed Donald the trousers, but he kept talking all

the while. "You took a bad shot, sir," he said. "You really ought to stay in bed to let it heal. We're doing all right, sir. We've got the boiler going, and we'll be underway soon enough. There's no need for you to be getting up and about."

Donald stood up and bent to put a leg in his trousers. He cried out softly as a pain shot through his back and chest.

"You see, sir?" said Scot.

"Mr. Scot," said Donald, "shut up and help me get dressed."

"Yes sir," said Scot.

"Now tell me what happened last night," Donald said.

"Well, sir," said Scot, pulling Donald's trousers up to his waist, "after I got you up here to your bed, you passed out. And a good thing too. Mr. Krevs took the ball out of your back. He said he thinks you'll live, all right, but only if we get you to Capitan del Monte's surgeon in a hurry to make sure that no infection sets in. He said—"

"Did I hear you say last night that one of the outlaws got away with Mrs. Booker?" Donald said, interrupting Scot.

"Yes sir," said Scot. "That's right. There was four of them came aboard, sir. They were on deck before any of us knew it. It was Rotison, Ranik, and the two Hunikers, I think, sir. Well, sir, Rotison is the one that shot you, and that shot was the first inkling we had of their presence.

"Mrs. Booker came out of her room, and she shot Rotison. Killed him dead. Corporal Burns got one of the Hunikers, if that's who they were. I got Ranik, sir. But then the other Huniker had got ahold of Mrs. Booker. He had her in front of him, and he had a knife at her throat. He said he'd kill her if we didn't do what he said. I'm sorry, sir, but I didn't know what else I could do. I couldn't just stand there and watch him cut her pretty little throat."

"No," said Donald, "I'm sure you did the right thing, Mr. Scot."

"Well, sir," Scot continued, "he made me disarm the men, and then get all of us over to the far side of the boat. Then he took Mrs. Booker overboard with him. We took a count of the weapons after he was gone, and it looks like he picked up two pistols and a rifle on his way."

"We can't let him get away with Mrs. Booker, Scot," Donald said. "We've got to go after them."

"Sir," said Scot, "I'll do it. Let me have one good man, Corporal Burns, sir, and a couple of good horses, and we'll get on their trail. You're in no condition to ride, sir, and if you'll allow me, sir, I think the boat needs to get underway and get you to Jonesboro just as quickly as possible."

"All right, Scot," said Donald, "but take all four horses and take Krevs with you. The extra horse is for Mrs. Booker. If you manage to take Huniker alive, he can walk back."

"Yes sir," said Scot.

"Now help me downstairs," Donald said.

Donald was seated at the deck table with a cup of coffee waiting for his breakfast, while Scot went to find Krevs and Burns and get the horses saddled. Soldiers laid out the planks, and soon Donald saw them lead three saddled horses ashore. Krevs and Burns followed the horses off, and Scot came over to where Donald was seated.

"Where's the other horse, Mr. Scot?" Donald asked.

"Gone, sir," said Scot. "It seems that Mr. Booker saddled it up and rode off after his wife sometime during the night."

"Damn," said Donald. "He'll only get himself lost out there."

"It might be best if he does, sir," Scot said. "If he should stumble across Huniker and his wife, well, he's certainly no match for that Huniker."

"You're right about that," said Donald. "Well, you'd better get going, Scot. Good luck to you."

"Thank you, sir," said Scot, and he left the boat. The

planks were pulled back in and the engine revved up, and soon the *John Hart* was steaming its way back to Jonesboro.

Huniker knew that he was being followed, and he knew that he had left four good horses back on the steamboat. At the time, it had seemed that he had to get away fast, that it would take too much time and trouble to unload a couple of horses, even one horse, but running throughout the night and dragging that damn woman along with him, he wished that he had taken the time. He wished he had a horse.

He was worn out from running, and he needed some rest. It was almost daylight too. He thought he had gotten far enough away from the boat, but he was still afraid of pursuit. He dragged Bethie up a hill and into a clump of trees there. She fought him a little, but she was more worn out than he was. He slapped her once hard across the side of the face. Then she was easy to handle. He tied her wrists together and tied the other end of the short rawhide rope to a tree.

"That'll hold you," he said.

"Why don't you just go ahead and kill me?" she said.

"Don't you worry none about that," Huniker said, a leer on his ugly face. "I'll kill you, all right. But you're going to have to wait awhile. We're going to have a little fun together first. I just need to make sure those bastards are off my trail, and I need to get a little rest. Then we'll start to tend to business."

"You're the bastard," she said.

"Shut up," he said. He walked to the edge of the trees and looked back over his trail. He saw no one coming after him, but he still had an uneasy feeling. He wasn't quite sure. He decided that he'd just stretch out there on the ground, there at the edge of the trees, and get some rest. Just a little rest. If anyone should come riding that way, he'd hear them and wake up.

* * *

Tom Booker had no idea where he was going. He had no notion whatsoever about following a trail. He did feel a responsibility for Bethie, and he couldn't just sit around on the boat. He had to try. He was afraid of Huniker. He had always been afraid of the Hunikers, but now two of them were dead, and that showed him at least that they were not invincible. The main thing, though, was that this last remaining Huniker had Bethie, and there was no telling what he would do to her.

Booker figured that Huniker would not go toward Jonesboro, not after all that had happened. And he would want to steer clear of the Osages too. So where would he go? Which direction? If he went straight north, he would avoid the Osage town to the northwest and the Buffalo Crossing area to the west. Anywhere south or east he would be in danger of running into an Army patrol, either U.S. or Spanish. So Booker headed north.

After wiping out the renegade whites, Iron Head and his young men scattered in small groups, some remaining behind to pick over the bodies for anything of value they might find, some rounding up the dead men's horses. Some headed home, while others just wandered off to show that they could go their own way, that there was no one to tell them what they could or could not do.

Walker and Sings Loud, having climbed down out of Iron Head's wagon, stood together in silence for a few moments after the fight was over.

"I thought I was sent here to bring peace," said Walker. "It looks like I brought a big fight."

"This was just a little fight," Sings Loud said. "It's over, and we won. The big fight won't happen now. Not right away anyhow."

"I didn't know that I'd bring peace by causing a bunch of white men to be killed," Walker said.

"Oh, quit worrying about it," Sings Loud said. "These

were bad men. They were the ones causing all the trouble in the first place. Besides, no matter when they died, they were going to hell. They just went a little sooner than we expected. That's all. Where you going now?''

"I don't know," Walker said. "I guess my business here is done. Maybe I'll go find my people in Arkansas. I don't think I want to walk all the way home to Georgia. Not just yet anyway."

"I'm going to Jonesboro," she said. "Want to walk along?"

"Okay," he said.

They were about to walk away together, when Iron Head saw them going. He called out, speaking in Osage, and Sings Loud stopped walking to answer him. Walker waited. Then Iron Head called something out to one of the young men nearby. The young man answered him and started walking toward Walker and Sings Loud, leading a horse. Walker gave Sings Loud a curious look.

"Iron Head's giving us a horse," she said.

"Oh," said Walker. "Well then, would you tell him thank you for me?"

"Of course," she said. "For both of us." She said a few words to Iron Head and then to the young man who brought the horse. Then she mounted, sitting in the saddle, and offered Walker a hand. He clambered up onto the horse's back behind the saddle. Iron Head broke into good-natured laughter, and Walker gave him a sheepish grin and waved goodbye. Sings Loud kicked the horse into an easy lope, and they headed east.

Huniker roused himself from his fitful sleep, groaned, and looked out across the prairie. At first he saw nothing out there to cause any alarm, and he thought that he would get up and take his evil pleasure with Bethie, then kill her and get it over with. She was only slowing him down. He was

253

about to do that when he saw a movement out there. He watched and waited. It came closer.

Soon he could see that it was a horse and rider. No. Two riders. Riding double. He hunkered down behind a tree on the small hill to wait it out. He had to let them get close. If he shot one of them, the other would ride away before he could reload. If he let them get close enough, he thought, perhaps he could knock one of them out of the saddle with his rifle and then get the other with a pistol shot. But then the horse might run away. He did not like the thought of trying to chase it down on foot.

He decided to take a chance on being seen, for the hillside was covered with thick brush. He worked his way down to the bottom of the hill and found a good spot for hiding. Then he thought that his fondest wish was being granted, for it appeared that the riders were going to pass very close by the hill.

He would let them get real close to him, then step out and order them to dismount. That way he would get the horse before he had fired any shots. He checked his guns to make sure that they were primed and dry and ready to fire. Then the horse stopped. Something was wrong. He wondered if they had seen him after all. He panicked and stepped out into the open, raising the rifle to his shoulder.

"Watch out," Sings Loud shouted, and she swung her leg over the horse's back, at the same time using her arm to sweep Walker along with her. The two of them fell off the horse just as Huniker fired. Walker landed hard on the ground, but he knew why Sings Loud had done what she did. The horse nickered and stamped, then ran off a few yards and stopped again.

"Damn," said Huniker, and he ran toward the two people.

"He's coming after us," said Walker. "Let's run."

They scrambled to their feet and ran after the horse, but when they came close to him, he ran again. They continued after him, and behind them, Huniker was in pursuit. If they could get to the horse and get mounted again, they'd be all right, for they knew that he had fired his rifle. If he had anything else to shoot, it would be a pistol, and they were already out of range for that. They got close to the horse again, and again it ran. Walker looked back over his shoulder.

"He's gaining on us," he said.

Thirty-three

Tom Booker heard the shot, and it gave him a direction. He hoped that it was someone who had caught up with Huniker and shot him to rescue Bethie. He didn't want to think that it might have been Huniker shooting. Would Huniker shoot Bethie, or would he . . . He didn't like thinking about the alternatives. The main thing was to get over there and find out what was going on. He lashed at his already tired horse.

Iron Head stood up straight and alert when he heard the shot. It wasn't all that far away. He could tell. Who would be shooting, he wondered. The fight was supposed to be over. He called something out to the half dozen young men who were still with him there where the fight had taken place. He took his place standing in front of the wagon seat, picked up the lines, and gave them a flick. The team of horses started to run. The wagon rolled. The six young men all jumped on their horses and raced along behind.

* * *

Walker stumbled, and Sings Loud stopped running, to help him to his feet.

"Come on," she said.

"No," said Walker. "When we run at the horse, we only scare him. You walk up to him slow, and I bet you can get back on him."

"That man will catch us," she said.

"Go on," said Walker. "I'll stay here and slow him down. You go on."

"You old fool," she said. "He'll kill you."

"Better just me than both of us," Walker said. "Go on now. You'll get to pray for my soul."

Sings Loud walked toward the horse. She wanted to run, but she knew that Walker was right. That would only frighten the animal. She looked back over her shoulder. Walker was standing there between her and the white man. But the white man was getting close. She thought that he could probably run right over the frail little Cherokee and then get close enough to shoot her with his pistol. Still, she held back, walking slowly toward the standing horse.

Walker was braced for a hard hit. He told himself that it would be all right, just as long as the preacher woman could get to the horse and get away. After all, he had been dead before, and he knew what to expect. He wasn't afraid of dying.

Then the big ugly white man stopped running. He stood still, panting. He had run himself out. Good. That would give Sings Loud a little more time. He could see the white man's chest heaving, trying to catch its breath. Then, with one last great gasp, the man started walking toward him. He had a pistol in his hand, and he wouldn't have to get much closer now to be in range for a shot. Walker uttered a little prayer and waited for the shot.

Then he heard a strange racket, and then he saw, back behind the white man at a distance, the gaudy wagon that had once belonged to the white peddler of phony medicines.

It was racing toward them. And there were horseback riders alongside the wagon. It was Iron Head and some of his young men. Walker grinned. The big white man heard it too, for he stopped coming in Walker's direction and looked back. He saw the Osages coming.

"Damn," he shouted. He fired his pistol wildly at Walker, missing by several feet, and then he turned and started to run hard back toward the tree- and bush-covered hill. Iron Head turned the wagon. Walker could see that it was going to be a hell of a race. But Iron Head had no mercy on the team, and the big white man was already winded.

Sings Loud had forgotten about the horse and walked back to stand beside Walker and watch what was happening. The wagon was bearing down on the white man, and just at the last moment, the white man screamed and jumped headlong to one side. The wagon rolled past him as he rolled in the dirt.

As Iron Head struggled to get the wagon turned around for another run, the white man scrambled to his feet and headed once again for the relative safety of the bushes at the base of the hill, but one of the young men headed him off, yelping and riding straight at him. The horse bumped into the white man, sending him sprawling.

He got up again, only to be knocked down by yet another of the six riders. He was struggling to get back to his feet, when he looked up to see the wagon and team headed straight for him, the chief with the Spanish helmet on his head driving from a standing position and yelling as he lashed at the team. It was too late to do anything. He shielded his face with one arm and screamed, and then he bounced and tumbled and rolled, as the horses ran over him first, and then the wagon, and as it passed on, the wagon seemed to spit him out behind.

He managed to get up on one elbow. He knew he could do no more. He could tell that bones were broken, smashed, shattered. He was bruised and bloody all over, and his clothes were shredded from the sharp hooves of the horses. Looking down, he could see that his left leg was turned the wrong way at the knee. He knew he was done for, and he growled out his hatred as Iron Head aimed the wagon for one last run.

Bethie knew that something was going on down there, although she was tied too far back in the trees to be able to see anything. She waited until the noises died down before she started to yell. She heard the Indian voices, but she had no idea what they might be saying. She hoped they were the same Osages who had come to the rescue of the *John Hart*. If so, even if she could not talk to them, they might take her back. She yelled some more.

"I'm up here," she called out. "Somebody help me."

Then Tom Booker came riding in from the east over a swell in the prairie, his wretched horse all but done in. He saw Walker and Sings Loud, and he saw, a little farther away, Iron Head and the six young Osage men. He pulled up his horse there by Walker and Sings Loud.

"I'm looking for Bethie," he said. "One of the Hunikers took her."

"Huniker, huh," said Walker. "That must be him down there."

Booker looked and spotted the wretched mass on the ground in the distance. He quickly looked away again. "Well," he said, "then where's Bethie?"

"Somebody's yelling from up on that little hill there," said Sings Loud, pointing. "Maybe that's her."

"Come on," said Walker, "but get down off that poor horse. It's about to drop dead."

Booker dismounted, kept hold of the reins, and started moving along with Walker toward the wagon and the Osages and the hill. Sings Loud turned around and walked easily back to her own horse, which she got hold of with no problem. Leading the horse along, she caught up with

Walker and Booker. Ahead, two of the young men were running up the side of the hill. Booker started to move faster.

"Bethie," he said.

Walker restrained him with a hand on the shoulder.

"She'll be all right," he said. "Just keep walking."

Soon they were beside the wagon. Iron Head looked down on them with a fierce expression of pride. He spoke in his own language.

"He says he feels young again," Sings Loud reported.

Walker pointed to the mangled corpse just ahead of them. "Is that—what do you call him?" he asked.

"That's Huniker, all right," Booker said. "He's the last of that gang. His brother, Ranik, and Rotison were all killed last night when they boarded the steamboat. Rotison shot Captain Donald, though. The captain wasn't killed, but I have no idea how he's doing today."

"We'd better go see about that young white man," Walker said. "I like him."

The two young men who had gone up the hill were coming back down, one of them leading Bethie by the rope Huniker had tied her with. It still bound her wrists together. Walker again put a hand on Booker's shoulder. Sings Loud spoke to Iron Head in Osage, and he answered.

"I told him all the bad men are dead now," she said. "And I told him that this white woman belongs to this man. I told him about Captain Donald too. He says we'll all go to Jonesboro together."

Krevs was riding a little ahead of Scot and Burns, scouting along the way, looking for signs. He knew that he was on the trail of Huniker and Bethie. He also knew that Tom Booker was not always on that same trail. Booker didn't know what he was doing. Suddenly he hauled back on the reins. He squinted to see more clearly what was in the distance. Then he called over his shoulder to Sergeant Scot.

"Wagon coming," he said. "Some riders too." Scot and Burns rode up beside Krevs. "Looks like six, seven, eight horses," the scout said. "One of them ain't got a rider." They sat still watching, waiting for the small group to get closer. Then Krevs almost yelled. "That's old Iron Head and his boys," he said.

"Now what the hell is he doing way over this way?" Scot asked.

"Damned if I know," said Krevs, "but I don't think he's mad at us for any reason."

"Let's go meet him, Mr. Krevs," said Scot. "Maybe he knows something about Huniker and Mrs. Booker."

Riding at a gallop, Krevs recognized one of the riders.

"Hey, Sarge," he said, "there's Sings Loud riding with them."

"That's good," said Scot. "She can talk their language."

They waved a greeting and got waves in response, and a short while later the two groups met and halted their horses. Scot was about to speak when Walker poked his head out of the wagon.

"Mr. Walker," he said. "Sings Loud, what's going on here?"

"Iron Head just saved us all from that Huniker," said Walker. "Mr. and Mrs. Booker are in here too."

"Thank God," said Scot, and Sings Loud said, "Amen." Tom Booker and Bethie each came out of the wagon then and offered their greetings to Scot, Burns, and Krevs. "Are you both all right?" Scot asked.

"Just fine," said Booker.

"Thanks to these Indians," Bethie added.

"That's good," Scot said. "And what about Huniker?"

Walker said, "Well, uh, you won't get mad at Iron Head for killing another white man, will you?"

"Not if it was Huniker," Scot said.

"We might give him a medal for that," Krevs added.

"Then I'll tell you," Walker said. "Iron Head ran over him with this wagon . . . twice."

"He's dead?" Scot asked.

"He's already roasting in hell," said Sings Loud. "I can hear him howling right now."

Krevs looked at Scot. "You know," he said, "for once I hope the old gal's right about that."

"Well then," Scot said, "shall we continue on your way back to Jonesboro?"

Mat Donald still felt weak, and the wound in his back still hurt, but he was up and around. He refused to stay in bed. The *John Hart* had arrived safely back at Jonesboro, and del Monte and his Spanish troops had been there to meet it. Del Monte had immediately called his surgeon to see to Donald's wound, but Donald had insisted the doctor look first at the two wounded troopers. Neither was hurt badly, and they were quickly patched up. Only then was Donald's wound tended to.

The settlers he had forced to turn back were all gathered again in their tents and wagons off to one side of Jonesboro. They were surly, and when Donald passed by them, they all glared at him. Senator Reddels visited with them from time to time, commiserating.

Mat Donald was sitting in a chair at the table just outside the inn, sipping whiskey. Capitan Rey del Monte sat across from him with his wine. It was a comfortable and familiar setting for both young captains. Senator Reddels, his daughter Eva, and her maid Marie were nowhere to be seen. In fact, Donald had not seen anything of either of them since his arrival back at Jonesboro. Del Monte had informed him, though, that they were safely back in the settlement, sulking in good health.

"I think that you are in for some real trouble from this senator though, amigo," del Monte said.

"I'm sure I am," said Donald. "He thinks I should have left Bond and his settlers alone. Let them stay put, even though he was squatting illegally on the wrong land, and even though the Osages would have attacked them."

"You saved all of their lives, Mat," said del Monte, "but they can't see that. You're going to be the scapegoat. Just wait and see."

"I know that," said Donald, "and I'm prepared. My army career is over with. I've already written a letter resigning my commission."

"I'm glad of that, in a way," said del Monte, sipping his wine. "If our two countries ever get into a war with one another, I would hate to have to shoot at you."

Donald chuckled. "Thanks, Rey," he said. "Well, Reddels will have a great time telling them all about me back in Natchitoches."

"He's a fool," said del Monte. "You know, he even threatened me when I refused to escort him and his daughter and the maid all the way back to Natchitoches. I can't ride into your country, I told him, but he just puffed up and said, 'I am a U.S. senator, and I will guarantee you safe conduct, sir.' "

Donald and del Monte both laughed at that, and then Donald said, "That's Reddels, all right."

"Very nearly your papa-in-law," said del Monte.

"Don't remind me of that," said Donald. "Please."

He picked up his glass for another sip of whiskey, as del Monte straightened up in his chair for a better look at something in the distance.

"What is it?" Donald asked.

"Your sergeant is coming," said del Monte, "and he's got himself quite an escort."

Thirty-four

The arrival of Iron Head's wagon in the company of Sergeant Scot and the others created quite a stir in Jonesboro. Even some of the surly settlers gathered around to see what was going on and to hear the news. Scot reported to Donald, and Bethie made her way very soon to Capitan del Monte's side, as if seeking comfort after her ordeal.

She told del Monte how Tom Booker, after seeing that she was safe, had informed her that he meant to go back east as soon as possible to rejoin his wife and child, and she would be left out here all alone. Donald noticed that they had soon disappeared into the privacy of del Monte's tent, where he was sure Bethie would find all the comfort she needed.

Then even Reddels and Eva, overcome by curiosity, came out to join the crowd, and Krevs made an impassioned speech to all who were gathered there, on behalf of Chief Iron Head, without whom, he told them, they would all have been killed by the outlaws. He emphasized the importance to the settlers of maintaining friendly relations with the Osages. Donald smiled, hearing that. Perhaps, he thought, that would keep them away from Buffalo Crossing, at least for awhile.

Walker found his way quickly to Donald's side. "Are you all right, Captain?" he asked. "I heard you got shot by that albino."

"Yes, my friend," said Donald. "It will mend. By the way, I saw you out there with Chief Iron Head, and I can't help thinking that I probably owe you some thanks, though I'm not sure for just what."

Walker shrugged. "Well," he said, "the settlers are gone from around the Sacred Hill, and Iron Head's happy. He's going to go out there and burn what's left of their settlement when he leaves here. Things will probably be peaceful around these parts for awhile now. Anyhow, all the bad men are dead."

Donald's face suddenly took on a faraway look.

"All but one," he said. "But I fear I may be following that one for the rest of my life."

"Oh," said Walker, "are you talking about the one with the hair on the wrong end of his face?"

"Murkens," said Donald.

"Yes," said Walker. "That one. You know, it's a funny thing about that man. Last time I came down from the top of the Sacred Hill, you know, through that cave, there was something big and ugly there in my way. I didn't like to touch it, but I had to. I had to push it out, and then I saw what it was. That man had tried to come in. He thought there was gold up there. Can you imagine that? Gold. On top of the Sacred Hill. Anyway, he didn't get very far. The ones in that cave, they didn't like him trying to get through there. That's where they live, you know."

"It was Murkens?" said Donald.

"That one," said Walker. "Yeah."

"Dead?"

265

Walker nodded. "Real full of rattlesnake poison," he said.

Donald leaned back in his chair, stunned. He could scarcely believe what he had just heard. He had followed Murkens for so long, and now it was over. Just like that. Over. He hadn't caught the man, hadn't killed him, hadn't even seen the body. Yet it was over. He shook his head to clear it, to bring him back to present reality, and he reached over to touch Walker on the shoulder.

"Thank you, my friend," he said.

Walker shrugged. "What for?" he said. "I'm glad to see that you're healing up good anyway. Well, I don't know if I'll see you again. I've got to be on my way now. My business is over with here."

"Where will you go?" Donald asked.

"Maybe back to my own people," Walker said. "I haven't talked in Cherokee for a long time now. Maybe I forgot how."

"Well, wherever you go, friend Walker," Donald said, "I'll miss you. Take good care of yourself."

"You too, Captain," Walker said, and then he turned and walked away. Sings Loud had been standing there silent all this time, and she too watched him go. When Walker had turned a corner and was at last out of sight, Donald looked up at Sings Loud.

"Would you like to sit down?" he asked her.

She sat.

"I want to thank you too," he said, "for all your help."

"I didn't do nothing," she said. "Thank the Lord."

"Oh, I do," said Donald.

The crowd was beginning to thin, and Senator Reddels suddenly found himself standing alone with nothing and no one in between himself and Donald, there where he sat with Sings Loud. Reddels puffed himself up, put on a stern face, and walked over to the table.

"Captain Donald," he said, "Mat, we were friends once.

Good friends. I even thought for a time that you would marry my daughter. I had great plans for your future, but things are different now."

"Yes sir," said Donald. "Things are certainly different now."

"I think that it's only fair," the senator continued, "that I lay my cards out on the table before you. I have never been one to stab a man in the back."

"Are you planning to stab me in the chest, Senator?" Donald said.

"I wish you wouldn't take this so lightly, Mat," said Reddels. "I'm quite serious."

"I know you are," said Donald, "and believe it or not, so am I."

"Mat," said Reddels, "I mean to make a full report to your commanding officer, telling him about the disgraceful way in which you treated Mr. Zeno Bond, a great American patriot, and how you treated me, a United States senator. I mean to tell him the way in which you took the side of savage Indians against white American citizens. I mean to—"

"Did no one point out to you, Senator," said Donald, "that the men who were endangering the lives of us all, the men, in fact, who murdered Mr. Bond, were white outlaws? And that we were in fact saved from that same fate by those very Indians you're calling savage?"

"I'm aware of the details," said Reddels, "but that is all totally irrelevant to my complaint against you, as you had no way of knowing all that would happen at the time you first began harassing Mr. Bond and treating me so rudely. The fact that those events transpired after the fact means nothing."

"You mean to ruin my career, in short," said Donald. "Is that it?"

"No," said Reddels. "No, I do not. You, sir, have already done that for yourself."

Donald reached inside his military blouse and withdrew a folded sheet of paper. He held it out toward Reddels.

"What's this?" Reddels asked.

"Read it for yourself," said Donald. "It will make your unpleasant task all the easier. Now I don't believe we have anything more to say to one another."

Reddels huffed away.

"What was that paper you gave him?" Sings Loud asked.

"Oh," said Donald, "not much. It was my letter of resignation. That's all."

"What's that mean?" she asked.

"It means I quit the Army," said Donald. He poured himself another glass of whiskey. He started to put the bottle down. Then he looked across the table at Sings Loud. "I, uh, I guess you don't drink this stuff," he said, but it was like a question.

"You really quit the Army?" she said.

"Yes."

"Why?" she asked.

"I don't know," he said. "It's a long story."

"Because of all this stuff that happened just now?" she said. "Because of that hill out there and Iron Head?"

"Yeah," he said. "Because of all that."

"I'll have a drink with you," she said. "It's a special occasion. The Lord won't mind, I guess."

Donald smiled. He called for another glass, and soon he had poured her a drink.

"You know," he said, "this is very pleasant."

"This whiskey?" she said.

"Not just this whiskey," he said, "but sitting here like this, with you. It's very pleasant."

"Why with me?" she asked.

"I just this moment realized what a lovely lady you are," he said, "and I just this moment realized how free I am. Free from Eva. Free from the Army. Free from all the troubles with Bond and with Iron Head and all the rest. And

I'm just sitting here with nothing to do, no place to go, and in your very pleasant company. That's why.''

Sings Loud felt herself blush slightly, and she sipped her whiskey.

"Captain Donald," she said, "where you going to go?"

"I don't know," he said. "West, I think."

"You want some company?" she said.

"You?" he said.

"Yeah," she said casually. "It could be fun."

"Indeed it could be," said Donald, "but there's only one thing."

"What's that?"

"Would you call me Mat?"

"Okay, Mat," she said, "when do we leave?"

Uwas' Edoh' was walking east. He had a long walk ahead of him, he knew, but it wouldn't be nearly as long as the last one he had taken. He also had a better idea this time of his destination. He was going to go into the Arkansas Territory to find the homes of his countrymen who had moved west. The U.S. government wanted all the Cherokees to move west, and some of them had done it. They were calling themselves the Western Cherokee Nation, and for a long time they had been at war with the Osages.

Walker couldn't help but think that now that he had made friends with one Osage, now that he had been surrounded several times by Osages and come out alive each time, maybe now he could help bring that long war to an end. At least, it might be worth trying. That is, if he could live that long. He wasn't at all sure how long the spirits meant for him to hang around this time, now that they had brought him back from death once.

Maybe they would let him know, or maybe they wouldn't bother this time. Maybe he'd just fall over dead one of these days. Anyhow, he thought, until that time came, he had to do something. He thought he'd go visit that Western Cherokee Nation. At least for a little while.

AUTHOR'S NOTE

Incident at Buffalo Crossing is based on a story by my good friend Henry Lee Somerville of Paris, Texas. Old Henry Lee, a retired Air Force Colonel and a meticulous historical researcher, dug out of dusty archives the rather astonishing, though obscure details from early Texas history that inspired his original story. A U.S. Army patrol, scouting the Red River by steamboat in 1819, actually forced the removal of white settlers from Indian land. That in itself is unusual enough in the history of the United States.

But the really astonishing fact is that following the forced removal of the illegal settlers, the settlers, or a contingent thereof, attacked the Army, and the Indians came to the rescue. The experiment with mule artillery is an interesting "sidebar" in the middle of the whole fascinating episode. The career of the captain, by the way, did, in fact, come to an abrupt end, and he is thereafter lost to history.